THE
ARNIFOUR
AFFAIR

WITHDRAWN

WITHDRAWN

THE
ARNIFOUR
AFFAIR

A Colin Pendragon Mystery

GREGORY HARRIS

KENSINGTON BOOKS
www.kensingtonbooks.com

KENSINGTON BOOKS are published by

Kensington Publishing Corp.
119 West 40th Street
New York, NY 10018

Copyright © 2014 Gregory Harris

All rights reserved. No part of this book may be reproduced in any form or by any means without the prior written consent of the Publisher, excepting brief quotes used in reviews.

All Kensington titles, imprints, and distributed lines are available at special quantity discounts for bulk purchases for sales promotion, premiums, fund-raising, educational, or institutional use.

Special book excerpts or customized printings can also be created to fit specific needs. For details, write or phone the office of the Kensington Special Sales Manager: Kensington Publishing Corp., 119 West 40th Street, New York, NY 10018. Attn. Special Sales Department. Phone: 1-800-221-2647.

Kensington and the K logo Reg. U.S. Pat. & TM Off.

ISBN-13: 978-0-7582-9267-4
ISBN-10: 0-7582-9267-8
First Kensington Trade Paperback Printing: February 2014

eISBN-13: 978-0-7582-9268-1
eISBN-10: 0-7582-9268-6
First Kensington Electronic Edition: February 2014

10 9 8 7 6 5 4 3 2 1

Printed in the United States of America

For Russ,
who changed everything forever

CHAPTER 1

T he subject, as it so often is, was murder.

It was late in the afternoon, between the time when the sun has dropped sufficiently to be blocked from the city's streets, yet before it has gone low enough for the shadows cast by the buildings to have grown into one continuous black void. Colin and I were sitting by the fireplace in our study, me in the thrall of the American writer Stephen Crane's latest bit of fiction, while he was working up a sweat curling his dumbbells, when a great clattering of horses' hooves arose from the street below.

I laid my book down and went to the window, where I spied an elegant black carriage next to the curb pulled by two fine blue-black steeds. The carriage looked capable of seating a dozen people, yet revealed only a single family crest on its door: a vulture devouring a slain lamb under a thistle bush. It seemed its owner had either a fine sense of humor or extraordinary self-awareness.

"It appears we have company," I announced.

"Do we?" Colin muttered, still hoisting the weights back and forth.

"A coach has just pulled up. There's a crest on its door, but I don't recognize it."

"Oh?" He came over and took a brief glance out the window, dumbbells in tow, before bounding back to the fireplace. "That would be the crest of the once formidable Arnifour family."

"Arnifour?" A distant clanging was set off in my head. "Now why does that name sound familiar?"

"Because they've been a part of the gentry for generations," he said as he shoved the dumbbells onto an upper shelf in a nearby bookcase, "although their fortunes have contracted in diametrical opposition to our good Queen's waistline. Yet while Victoria remains the Queen, the Arnifours have become quite toothless and impotent in their waning years. Never a good combination." He snickered.

I chuckled as I watched a dainty ankle covered in swirls of burgundy fabric present itself from within the carriage, followed by a delicate hand held out to the driver. "It's a lady," I said.

"Mrs. Behmoth," Colin hollered down the stairs, "we've got company!"

"I 'eard. I ain't deaf," she called back. "Who the 'ell comes out at this 'our anyway? I ain't puttin' me shoes back on, I'll tell ya that. Me dogs are already snarlin' like beasts."

"Always so dainty." He chuckled, hastily mopping his face with a handkerchief.

The sound of Mrs. Behmoth thudding her way from the kitchen to the small foyer drifted up, and I was relieved to hear the clack of shoes back on her feet in spite of her protestations. The door creaked on its hinges before the muffled hum of sibilant voices too far away to decipher could be heard.

I went back to my chair as Colin picked up a small penknife and scrap of fine steel wool from the mantel, and started working at coaxing the antique blade back to its former luster. "Must you always be playing with weapons when someone comes to call?"

"I'm not playing." He frowned. "I'm preserving history."

"Still," I said as I heard the stairs begin to groan under the weight of Mrs. Behmoth and our guest, "it could be misconstrued as intimidating to our fairer clientele."

He waved me off. "You're worried about intimidating someone who has a slaughtered lamb being eaten by a vulture for a family crest?"

I conceded the point.

Mrs. Behmoth filled our doorway as she ushered in an elderly woman wearing a tightly curled brown wig intended for someone half her age atop of which sat a small curved bonnet cocked to one side and heavily laden with frilly lace. Her dress was as coquettish as a debutante's, with a flurry of bows and adornments across the bosom. There was heavy makeup smeared across the deep crevices of her face and a silver dollar–sized bit of cardinal rouge on each cheek. "The Lady Arnifour," Mrs. Behmoth announced, accepting the Lady's cloak and unceremoniously tossing it on the coatrack.

"Do come in," Colin said with the flash of a smile. "I only hope this inopportune hour does not portend too distressing a matter at hand."

"Oh, Mr. Pendragon," she said as she collapsed onto the settee. "It is a most dreadful situation that brings me to your door this night."

"I'm sorry to hear that." He cast a glance at Mrs. Behmoth still hovering in the doorway. "Then we'll need some tea, please."

"Yer supper's almost ready." She scowled.

"I don't mean to be a bother—"

"It ain't no bother, Yer Ladyship, but that roast is sure as Hades gonna turn ta leather if it ain't served on time."

"Nevertheless," Colin's voice tightened, "tea. Thank you."

"I really don't require anything more than a few minutes of your time, Mr. Pendragon." She turned toward Mrs. Behmoth. "Please don't trouble yourself."

Mrs. Behmoth shrugged agreeably before heading back downstairs.

Colin exhaled brusquely. "She basically raised me."

"She's refreshingly disarming." Lady Arnifour gave a brief smile as her eyes flicked over to me before darting back to Colin. "Mr. Pendragon?" She leaned toward him slightly, her voice as thin as a whisper. "Might it be possible for us to speak in private? The matter upon which I seek your assistance contains a degree of . . . delicacy—"

"You have nothing to worry about then. Mr. Pruitt is my most trusted companion and should be considered an extension of myself. Your confidence will be well kept by us both. Now do tell us what's brought you here."

Our guest stiffened as she continued to stare at him. It was clear she was not used to being countermanded. "Well . . ." Her eyes flew back and forth a moment. "It's my husband. . . ." She hesitated. "He was murdered nearly a fortnight ago and my young niece, who was with him at the time, was savagely attacked and remains in a coma even now."

"How dreadful." Colin arched an eyebrow at me as I suddenly recalled why her name had sounded familiar.

"Surely you read of his death in the papers?" she said.

"Newspapers are a dreary business," he scoffed. "And have you ever read an accurate accounting of anything? No, I leave the perusal of those to Mr. Pruitt," his eyes slid to me, "who usually keeps me informed of such goings-on." I could only shrug. "But it's always better if you tell me of it yourself anyway. From the beginning, if you please."

"Oh my." She sagged back onto the settee, looking increasingly fragile. "It's such a nasty business."

"Murder tends to be."

Her brow furrowed and I took that moment to speak up lest she think he was trifling with her. "Hearing the event in your own words is far more likely to allow us to gain insight into the crime than reading some sensationalized account in the paper."

To my relief, Lady Arnifour's face softened as she heaved a heavy sigh. "I suppose you're right. As it is, Scotland Yard has withheld several details from the papers; they claim it's for the sake of their investigation, but they've seemed so muddled by it all," she groused before drawing in a deep breath and appearing to gird herself to begin. "Ten nights ago my husband took his customary walk after supper. Unless he was ill, he never missed his excursions.

"On this particular night he somehow managed to make it all the way down to the northwest corner of our property. We have a barn there in which we store hay and other feed for our horses and cattle. It's a considerable distance, Mr. Pendragon, and I am not exaggerating. And while I freely admit that my husband was several years younger than I, neither was he a young man." Her eyelids ticked slightly as though she had just confided something we would not otherwise have presumed. "How he got as far as he did, and why he would choose to do so, I cannot say."

"How far are we talking?" Colin snatched up his penknife and absently started buffing it again.

"Half a dozen kilometers at the least."

"And you don't believe him to have been in the habit of going such a distance?"

"It would've been impossible. He was seldom gone more than an hour and I can assure you, Samuel couldn't have walked a fourth of that distance in that amount of time."

"I see," Colin muttered. "Do go on."

Lady Arnifour watched his hands flutter assiduously over the blade for a minute before she finally resolved to continue. "That night, for whatever reason, Samuel got himself all the way down to that barn, and when he did, he apparently came upon our niece, Elsbeth. Elsbeth is my late sister's only child. Samuel and I have raised her from infancy. My sister did not survive the birth and there was no one else," she said deliberately. When she dropped her eyes I knew better than to inquire about the father. "It was not uncommon for Elsbeth and our daughter, Kaylin, to go riding together." She stopped and clutched at her throat. "Thank heavens Kaylin stayed in that night."

"Indeed," Colin said. "And your niece remains in a coma?"

Lady Arnifour's hand continued to hover at her throat in evident distress. "Yes, Mr. Pendragon. My niece received a horrible blow to her face during the attack. She was found near my husband's body and has yet to regain consciousness. The doctor . . ." She shook her head as she yanked a handkerchief from her sleeve. "I'm afraid he's been unable to offer much in the way of comfort regarding her recovery."

Colin laid the penknife down and peered at Lady Arnifour. "This is indeed a double tragedy then."

She dabbed the handkerchief to her nose in an oddly self-conscious manner and it suddenly made me wonder if perhaps she'd done it more for our benefit than hers. "Yes," was all she said.

"You must forgive me," Colin pressed on with uncharacteristic restraint, "but I must ask you precisely how your husband was killed?"

"A terrible blow to the back of his head," she fairly whispered.

"Supper's almost ready!" Mrs. Behmoth took that moment to holler up from downstairs.

I bolted from my seat and rushed across the room to the landing. "We'll be down as soon as we've finished with our guest," I hissed. "You will kindly refrain from shrieking up the stairs again." She scowled at me before huffing back to her kitchen. "I'm so sorry," I said as I came back to the study, not at all surprised to find that Colin had not even moved.

"She has a good heart." Colin flashed a quick grin as I sat down again. "Please go on, Lady Arnifour. Tell me what our esteemed Scotland Yard has made of all this. Have they formed any theories yet? Or are they still trying to decide who should ask the questions and who should write them down?"

I shot a hasty glance at Lady Arnifour and found her seemingly oblivious to his contempt of the Yarders.

"The inspector assigned to my husband's murder informed me this afternoon that my groundskeeper, Victor Heffernan, and his son, Nathaniel, have become his primary suspects." Her voice had become quite overwrought. I watched as her gaze slid about the room as though she was unable to comfortably settle it anywhere, and thought it yet another curious gesture on her part. Colin leaned forward in a way that suggested he had caught it as well.

"But the inspector is wrong?" he asked.

"I would stake my very reputation on it."

"And would you be referring to Inspector Emmett Varcoe?" Lady Arnifour started. "How could you know that?"

"Your estate is under his jurisdiction."

I could see she was impressed, though in truth that was exactly the sort of thing he should be expected to know.

"It's hardly a surprise you believe him wrong." Colin sat down and leaned back in his chair. "The man's ineptitude is matched only by his ignorance of his own shortcomings—

proving that failing upward is neither an art nor a science. But we needn't concern ourselves with him just yet. Why don't you tell me how it is you're so certain he's mistaken?"

Lady Arnifour fixed her eyes on Colin before sliding delicately forward on the settee and throwing a discreet glance backwards, as though Mrs. Behmoth might actually have roused herself to creep up the stairs and eavesdrop. "This is difficult . . . ," she mumbled.

"It usually is." He flashed a mischievous grin. "So tell me, were you having it off with your groundskeeper?"

"*Mr. Pendragon!*" She bolted to her feet with remarkable speed, both hands streaking to her décolletage as though to physically shield her honor.

"You misunderstand . . . ," I blurted out as I too hopped up. He'd fooled me, as I hadn't seen that coming. "Let me get us all a brandy," I barreled on. "A touch of brandy will settle everyone's nerves." God knew it would mine. I hurried to the liquor cabinet and flipped over three snifters, pouring little more than a finger into two of the glasses, but adding a healthy shot more to the third. I noticed that Mrs. Behmoth had been into the sherry again, for cooking purposes she would insist, and then steeled myself as I turned back to our guest.

Lady Arnifour had moved to the fireplace and stood staring into the flames as though her dignity might be regained somewhere in among them. I scowled at Colin, but he seemed wholly unconcerned as he fished out a silver crown and began absently spinning it around between the fingers of his right hand. Only then did it occur to me that as Lady Arnifour had failed to storm out of the room with righteous indignation, there was likely some kernel of truth to his question.

"Lady Arnifour . . ." I handed her a snifter, taking care to avert my gaze so as not to discomfort her further.

"You're very kind," she muttered, and I caught a bit of a flush beneath her heavily powdered cheeks.

"You mentioned . . . ," I chose my words carefully, ". . . that you disagree with Inspector Varcoe's assessment. Might you tell us why?" I shot Colin another warning glance as I pressed a snifter into his free hand, his other continuing to swirl the coin effortlessly, and was rewarded with a comparable rolling of his eyes.

"Victor Heffernan is a good man," she began slowly, keeping her gaze on the fire. "His family has worked for my family for three generations and that doesn't even include his son Nathaniel. I've known Victor since we were children. I was present at Nathaniel's birth. My husband and I have always been fond of the Heffernans. There's simply no reason why Victor or Nathaniel would want to hurt Samuel or Elsbeth. It's inconceivable. As I told you before, I would stake my reputation on it." She turned and glared at us as though daring us to disagree. "I can see that you've earned every facet of your reputation, Mr. Pendragon, but I would still like you to take this case. So will you prove that Mr. Heffernan and his son are innocent of this terrible crime?"

"And if the perpetrator *does* turn out to be your Mr. Heffernan or his son?"

She blanched slightly, her face drawing rigid as though she'd been struck. "I do not fear the truth," she said, but there was little conviction in her words.

"Then I am your man." He gave her a quick tilt of his head as he snatched the coin into the palm of his hand. "But you do understand, Lady Arnifour, that the truth is seldom what we want it to be."

"I only ask that you live up to the *best* of your reputation."

He smirked, but gave no other quarter to her having chastised him. "I think I've already proven that I shall not disappoint you." He flashed her a rakish smile that showed off his dimples. "We will be out tomorrow to have a look around."

Lady Arnifour nodded earnestly before downing her

brandy in a single ferocious gulp. "I shall look forward to it," she said as she set her glass on the mantel and glided past us.

"There are two things you must do, however." Colin spoke up before she reached the landing. "If you've not already done so, you must hire a guard to sit with your niece twenty-four hours a day. We cannot risk the chance that whoever committed this crime might wish to correct their unfinished business. Your niece could solve this case quite handily."

"A guard has been in place from the first night."

"Then there is only the matter of my fee," he gestured toward me, "and I shall leave that to the two of you."

I escorted our new client to the front door as we discussed an agreement, quickly coming to terms on a figure she had not hesitated to accept. Colin's repute does preclude most clients from balking at his fee.

"What did you make of that?" Colin asked, carefully pouring the contents of his untouched snifter back into the decanter, as I reentered the room.

"It's a horrible crime. The poor niece."

"Indeed." He finished with his glass and did the same with mine. "Yet Her Ladyship hardly seems the grieving widow."

"I'm sure their marriage was arranged and you know those things just never seem to turn out well."

"Tell that to dear Victoria. She seems unwilling to ever let off mourning Albert. If it weren't for my father and his scheming with her stable man, John Brown—"

"That's nothing but rumor."

"Ah, Ethan, ever naïve." He chuckled. "As to Lady Arnifour . . ." He moved to the fireplace. "She not only lies to herself every time she looks in a mirror, but she was most certainly lying to us tonight. There is much more to this crime than she's letting on. It's preposterous to think that she would place her reputation on the line for a groundskeeper."

"I thought I could hear her forefathers spinning when she said that." I laughed.

"It will be most interesting to meet this Victor Heffernan. And we shall see if I am not right about him and the Lady."

I chuckled. "And what if you are right about the two of them?"

He looked at me with a mischievous grin. "Then we shall have our first motive."

CHAPTER 2

We set off for the Arnifour estate on the outskirts of London only after the new day had eased past one o'clock, jouncing along the cobbled roadways in the cab Colin had procured. We had chosen this specific time of day as there are few things as indulgent as teatime in the finer homes. Finger-sized sandwiches of cucumber and butter, petit crown-shaped biscuits, thinly sliced hard-cooked eggs, cream cheese with minced olives atop water wafers: all the delicacies Mrs. Behmoth has had no patience for. We came through the massive stone archway that marked the edge of the Arnifour property, catching our first glimpse of the family home: a rambling Greco-Roman structure in the shape of an elongated U rising from the green hillsides around it like a white monolith. A double row of Ionic columns adorned its façade and there were well over a dozen chimneys crowning its rooftop. As our carriage rose and dipped over the uneven hills, the house was never lost completely from view, but rather stretched out like an imposing anomaly, reminding all that it did not dwell *within* its surroundings, it *ruled* them.

It was only after we gained the final hill that we could see how this seemingly regal building showed its age every bit as much as its overly lacquered mistress. Its wooden columns were chipped and flaking while the stone block façade covering its lower half was in need of both cleaning and repair. Both wings of the house had boards fastened across their windows, leaving only the long central section showing signs of habitation. And even there the large French doors fronting the portico revealed that many of those outlying rooms were devoid of furniture.

"It would seem . . . ," Colin mused as our cab rounded the driveway at the main entrance, ". . . that this tea will likely be less than we were hoping for."

"Now don't start," I scolded. "These people are dealing with a terrible tragedy."

"This entire estate is something of a tragedy."

"It is a wonder she didn't blink at your fee."

"She'd have been stuck with the inspector if she had," he said as he climbed out of the cab.

While I made quick arrangements for the driver to wait for us by paying only half his fee, Colin availed himself of one of the door's large, scripted-*A* iron knockers. As I joined him on the porch I noticed that the massive doors were warped and weather-beaten as they abruptly yawned open to reveal a thin, pinch-faced woman dressed entirely in black. Her salt-and-pepper hair was pulled taut into a bun. She offered nary a smile nor a nod of welcome.

"Mr. Pendragon and Mr. Pruitt?" she asked with obvious disdain.

"Well done," Colin answered. "You've saved me a card."

Her brow furrowed as she glared at him. "I will remind you this is a house in mourning."

"Indeed. . . ." He arched an eyebrow.

Whether she understood his inference or not I cannot say,

but she did finally feint to the side and allow us entry. Colin gave a tight smile and passed so close to her that she was forced to take an awkward step back while I, on the other hand, gave her as much room as I could.

We were ushered into the study and directed to a pair of brocade armchairs. Dutifully obeying the housekeeper's silent bidding, we settled into the chairs and watched as she turned with the rigidity of a Queen's guard and left through a rear door.

"That woman has disapproval refined to an art."

"Whatever could she be so sour at us for?"

"An excellent question." Colin stood up and began to inspect an oil painting of a grim family hanging above the mantel. "This must be the Arnifour family in happier times." The portrait showed a stilted, balding man with a sour face seated next to a woman obviously older than him, with three stoic children shy of their teens—one boy and two girls—standing behind them. The woman at the portrait's center was clearly a twenty-some-years-younger version of our client. "It is extraordinary how unhappy some people look when being immortalized."

"I don't remember you looking much better in that portrait your father had done when you were living in Bombay," I needled, recalling the equally stuffy rendition of Colin and his father.

He scowled at me a moment, but his expression quickly slid into a warm, generous smile, his dimples flashing and his eyes sparkling like sapphires as he said, "It's a pleasure to see you again."

I turned as Lady Arnifour ambled into the room, appearing even more haggard in the harsh daylight. "I regret I cannot say the same. How I wish this were a social call." She sat on the edge of a sofa across from me.

"I appreciate how difficult this is for you," he said as he came and sat down next to her.

"Do you, Mr. Pendragon? Have *you* suffered the loss of a loved one to murder?"

Colin flicked his eyes at me and I knew what he was asking. I returned a slight nod and he said, "Mr. Pruitt has, but I have not. Yet I would suspect there are few who do not understand what it means to lose someone they love."

"How perfectly maudlin." A disheveled, rail-thin man in his early thirties stood in the doorway the housekeeper had exited through, clenching the doorjamb so tightly that I wondered if he had an infirmity that left him unsteady on his feet. "Comparing war wounds, are we?"

Lady Arnifour glowered at her son, yet he seemed either unaware or unconcerned as he stalked into the room with a gait that was at once as unstable as it was cocksure. I guessed his infirmity to be intoxication.

"Mr. Pendragon." He stuck out a hand and gave a protracted bow that seemed more mocking than deferential.

"*Eldon!*" Lady Arnifour snapped.

Colin stood up and pumped the younger man's hand, flashing him a rogue's grin. "Such a formal greeting. I assume you are doing your best to adapt to your new role as lord of the manor?"

Eldon's eyebrows shot up as he pulled himself to his full height, several inches taller than Colin, a slow smile spreading across his face. "Yes." He smirked at his mother. "That would be me. Lord of the manor."

"You will excuse my son's insolence," Lady Arnifour scoffed as she snatched up a small bell from the table beside her. "His manners tend to wither with the advancing day."

"Now, Mother . . ." Eldon dropped into a chair near me. "Let's not be priggish. I'd much prefer to hear what Mr. Pendragon has to say about Father's murder." He settled his gaze on Colin, in whose furrowed brow I noticed the seeds of distaste. There was clearly no love lost between this son and his father. "Tell me, do you agree with Mother's contention regarding the innocence of the sainted Mr. Heffernan?"

"Do you disagree?" Colin shot back.

"I would sooner stake my bits to a fence post, Mr. Pendragon. It's not prudent to disagree with Mother." He forced a laugh that did not cover the unsettling rage that momentarily shifted behind his eyes.

Before either Colin or Lady Arnifour could respond, however, the mirthless housekeeper returned with a silver tray piled high with sandwiches and a tea set.

"Perfect timing, Mrs. O'Keefe," Lady Arnifour said as she began fussing over the tray, slowly regaining her composure.

"Yes, ma'am." Mrs. O'Keefe exited as hastily as she had come. The only warmth she'd shown, and that only rudimentary, was when she'd addressed her mistress. She'd not even given Eldon the slightest look. He seemed ever the misfit, or perhaps something more.

"Mr. Pendragon . . ." Lady Arnifour held out a cup of tea. She was about to do the same for me when Eldon popped out of his chair.

"Perhaps our guests would like something to invigorate their tea?"

"Really, Eldon," Lady Arnifour rebuked. "It's not even a proper hour."

"That's never stopped the Arnifours," he sneered.

"Tell me . . . ," I interrupted to keep things from denigrating further, "do you still cultivate your land?"

"Not anymore. Mrs. O'Keefe tends a small garden out back, but it's been generations since these lands were properly worked. It's too much, I suppose . . . the staff, the upkeep, the toil—"

"The expense . . ." Eldon chuckled. "That's why this old pile looks as tired as it does. The family gentry forgot how to earn its keep a long time ago."

"*That's enough!*" Lady Arnifour banged her cup back onto its saucer. "I will *not* have you talk about your heritage that way."

He waved her off. "We can hardly sully the Arnifours or your Langhems any more than they've already done to themselves."

"I've had all I'm going to tolerate!" she snapped. "You may take your leave."

Eldon shrugged and stood up. "And there you have it, gentlemen. The lord of the manor can still be dismissed by his doting mother." A smile thick with resentment spread across his face. "It's been a pleasure."

"I should very much like to speak with you later," Colin called to him.

"You'll have to get dispensation from the dowager empress!" he growled as he stalked out.

"You must forgive my son. My husband and I married later in life and my children were born to me at a time when most women are finished with such duties. I remember thinking them little miracles," she grimaced, "but Eldon's never been well and I cannot help but wonder if my choice to bear him at such an age had an impact."

"I'm sure you did everything you could," I said.

Colin smirked. "I'd say it has more to do with your son's passion for drink than your age at conception. Either way, it serves no purpose to blame yourself."

"That's . . . ," Lady Arnifour paused before giving an awkward grin, ". . . very kind of you, Mr. Pendragon," she finally said. "Now tell me," she shifted in her seat, "how can I assist your investigation?"

"I should like to ask a few questions, after which we shall need to go out and see where the attack occurred," he said.

"Of course." She nodded, a hand nervously fluttering up to her face. "I'll have someone take you."

"Excellent. Now you mentioned that your husband and niece met at the barn that night. What makes you think they didn't meet along the way? That perhaps she gave him a ride? Wouldn't that explain his covering such a distance in so short a time?"

"I think not, Mr. Pendragon. My husband was not a small man. There'd never have been room for him to get onto her horse. Samuel was of average height, but he was quite stout."

"I see. And has Inspector Varcoe shared with you his theory on how your husband covered that distance?"

"He brought up precisely what you've suggested. An inauspicious beginning to your investigation, it would seem." She gave a flinty smile.

Colin arched an eyebrow but held his tongue as he sipped his tea and snatched up a petit four. "And what alerted the household that something was wrong that night?"

"Nathaniel saw smoke on the horizon. The barn where my husband and niece were found had been set on fire."

"On fire?" Colin leaned forward. "You didn't mention that yesterday."

"It hardly seems relevant."

"How a thing seems is seldom how it is."

"Of course," she said, but there was little resolve in her words.

"And what of Mr. Heffernan and his son, Nathaniel? Has the inspector rounded them up yet?"

"He's allowing them to stay here at my behest. But I fear he's only biding his time. It would be a tragedy if they were arrested, Mr. Pendragon, and this family has suffered enough already."

Colin offered a quick smile, one that left me wondering what notions were racing about in his mind. "Permit me one last question. Has the inspector found the weapon used in the attack?"

"No."

"I didn't suppose he would." He drained his tea and stood up. "That would require actual detection. May I trouble you to have someone escort us down to what's left of the barn then?"

"I shall have Mr. Heffernan take you. It will give you an opportunity to speak with him."

"Outstanding." Colin leaned forward and grabbed two more petit fours, palming them into a napkin and sliding them into his pocket. "I should also like to speak with your daughter—Kaylin, isn't it?"

"Yes. But I'm afraid she's not here just now. All of this business has put her quite on edge, so I've sent her to stay with a friend in town. If you'd like, I'll arrange to have her meet you at your flat one afternoon?"

"That would be ideal. The sooner the better."

We followed Lady Arnifour through the rear door Mrs. O'-Keefe had used and found ourselves in a sparse hallway that opened onto a large, immaculate kitchen. It was the most pristine space I had ever seen. Not a speck, not a smudge anywhere save for the harsh, black-clad personage of Mrs. O'Keefe peeling carrots into a rubbish can at a well-worn table.

"Have you seen Mr. Heffernan?" Lady Arnifour asked.

"Out back, ma'am. Trimming roses last I saw."

"Very well."

We filed through the kitchen and out back, and I was aware of being under the watchful gaze of Mrs. O'Keefe the entire time.

A compact vegetable garden ran along the back of the house just off the kitchen, displaying an assortment of lettuce, tomatoes, cabbage, carrots, broccoli, cucumber, spinach, and a few other bits of greenery I did not recognize. Just beyond was a hedge of boxwoods clipped to precision, but it wasn't until I looked out among the array of rosebushes beyond that I noticed the thick man attending them. He had a plaid cap slipped down on one side of his head and the plain gray-green jumper of a groundsman. I knew at once it had to be Victor Heffernan.

"Here you are," Lady Arnifour fairly purred.

"Ma'am." He stood up and I saw that he was barely taller than our hostess.

"You must be Mr. Heffernan." Colin stuck out his hand.

"If you aren't here to arrest me, you can call me Victor. Everyone does."

"I assure you, Victor," Colin smiled amiably, "I have no interest in arresting anyone."

Victor Heffernan stared at Colin, a dark curling mustache an accent mark above his lips, and appeared to be trying to determine whether we meant trouble. Colin kept smiling, revealing nothing, his dimpled grin as natural as the rose petals Victor had been fussing among. He appeared to be about twice as old as Colin's thirty-eight years, but even so, I could tell he had no idea what to make of us.

"This is Colin Pendragon." Lady Arnifour came forward in a peculiarly maternal way. "I've hired him to prove you and Nathaniel innocent of this tragedy." She let her voice drift off as though she was overcome by the very thought.

"Now, now . . ." Victor reached out and patted his mistress's hand with marked intimacy. "Don't get yourself worked up again."

Lady Arnifour gave a tight smile and took a slight step back, effectively moving out of his reach. Victor seemed to realize his indiscretion and suddenly stumbled backwards, carelessly slicing off the top of an errant rose. I was beginning to believe that Colin's initial assessment of the alibi Lady Arnifour could provide this man might be true.

"Would you take them down to see what's left of the barn?" she said. "I simply cannot bear to go."

"Of course. I'll go hitch up the buckboard."

"Thank you." Lady Arnifour gave him a gentle nod as he headed off. "I'll wait for you in the study."

"When we come back I'd like to check on your niece." Colin tipped his chin toward me. "Mr. Pruitt knows something of wounds and healing and such."

"But I'm not a doctor," I pointed out.

He clapped my shoulder. "That he's not, but he can be a fount of medical bric-a-brac just the same."

I fought to keep from scowling at him as I caught Lady Arnifour glancing my way. What little knowledge I possess was learned by necessity during a regrettable tenure spent in the coarser areas of the city during my youth. It is not something I prefer to advertise, so I was relieved when Victor and his buckboard came rounding the corner of the house. Two minutes later the three of us were trundled onto the open seat of the wagon heading for the farthest reaches of the Arnifour estate.

CHAPTER 3

Our journey began in relative silence with only the occasional snort of the horse to interrupt the steady drone of our wheels as we rocked along the dirt ruts of the driveway, me watching the breadth of their property unfold while Colin appeared to be studying nothing in particular as he smoothly coaxed another crown between the fingers of his hand. The moment we turned off the path and started out across an open field, however, Colin turned to Victor and began peppering him with questions about the family history.

"Barnaby Langhem was given this property and the title of Baron by King George the Third, himself," he said with evident pride. "Lord Langhem was Lady Arnifour's great-grandfather and was one of the men responsible for keepin' that poor man on the throne until long after he shoulda been removed." He snickered. "Not six months later the King had a violent fit and accidentally throttled Lord Langhem, which meant that the land, but not the title, was passed on to his eldest son, Jacob. That's when the great house was built—paid for by a royal decree under the circumstances. That's when the whole Langhem family moved in and my family first began workin' for them.

"Everybody prospered under Jacob, but his life also came to a sudden end not more than ten years later. He either slipped in the mud stirred up by a downpour and was run over by a funeral carriage making haste to a plot before it was turned into a quagmire, or the carriage cut a corner too close and ran him down. Whichever the case, the outcome was the same.

"That left the estate and all its lands to Jacob's eldest son, Alanon." He heaved a weary sigh and I knew the story was becoming personal. "Alanon liked women and drink, and spent more time going through the Langhem fortune than addin' to it. He and his wife only had one child—a daughter, the future Lady Arnifour herself."

"What about bastards?" Colin muttered.

Victor shrugged. "None that I ever heard about."

"And what happened to him?" I asked before Colin could toss out another indelicacy.

"Unfortunately, he lived into his eightieth year before he finally took a tumble out an upper-story window into the garden below. Destroyed the family's prize roses, not to mention the damage he'd done to the Langhem name and fortune. A real pity."

"And as his only surviving heir," Colin interrupted, "Lady Arnifour inherited the estate, such as it is."

"That's right."

"Must have been a shock to the Earl to discover he'd married into a family almost as penniless as his own."

Victor glanced at Colin and shrugged self-consciously. "I wouldn't know about that," he said, but his manner suggested otherwise.

A moment later we skirted around a stand of trees and caught our first glimpse of the charred remains of a small building a short distance off. "The barn . . . ," Colin muttered as he flipped the coin into his vest pocket and stared at the approaching destruction. It was impossible to notice anything else beyond the hulking blackened wreck, its remains baking in the sun like some great sea creature's carcass that had managed to wash up on this waterless terrain. Only the stinging residue of charred wood lingered to assault the nostrils.

Victor pulled the horse up short and Colin hopped out, walking in a sideways arc around the ruined barn. "Did the Earl and Lady Arnifour raise their family here then?"

"They did. Lady Arnifour has spent her whole life here. Born and reared in that very house."

"And the niece too?" he asked as he continued to take slow, careful steps toward the wreckage, studying the ground meticulously as he drew nearer as though the earth itself might reveal some clue.

"Yes," Victor muttered as he stared out at the horizon, an odd look of discomfort clouding his gaze.

We both watched Colin kick at something with the toe of his boot and then crouch down to inspect it. Only after he stood up and brushed his hands against his slacks, having lost interest in whatever he'd been pawing at, did I turn back to Victor and ask, "How long ago did Alanon Langhem die?"

"Eldon was just a tot. Must be almost thirty years ago."

"He must've been pretty angry when he learned she'd married a title without the means to pluck him out of debt." Colin chuckled. "That's so often the way: antiquated titles without a farthing for a piss pot."

Victor shrugged.

"Tell me something," Colin called out from within the remains of the barn. "Who came out here the night of the attack?"

"Lord Eldon, Nathaniel, and me."

"Did you take any notice as to how the blaze was started?"

I watched as Victor's face registered an obvious level of confused disbelief. "Kerosene," he said. "The whole place smelled of kerosene just like it does now."

Colin smiled without even bothering to throw a glance at us. "Quite so." He wandered around a minute, glancing at what was left, toeing a few fallen timbers and running his fingers down the black framework. All the while his eyes flicked from place to place and I knew he was trying to take everything in, to remember it. "Why don't you tell me about that night," he said as he sauntered out the far side.

"There's not much to tell," Victor said, his gaze still locked on the horizon. "It was after supper. Nathaniel and I eat in the kitchen with Mrs. O'Keefe. I was done first, same as always, and had gone out to the stable by the house to check on the horses, and that's when I noticed Miss Elsbeth's horse was gone. Don't get me wrong; there's nothing unusual in that. She and Lady Kaylin often go out for a ride in the evening."

"But was it unusual for Elsbeth to go alone?"

"Not really." Victor lifted his cap and scratched his scalp, glancing down at his feet. "She goes off by herself as often as not. She's an independent sort." He smiled, and for a moment I thought I detected a note of pride. "She always takes care of herself . . . ," he started to say, and then winced as he registered the irony of his words. " 'Til that night."

"Of course," Colin replied absently, drawn more to the scorched earth than anything Victor was saying. "Go on."

"I was putting the tack up and tending a mare when Nathaniel came running in shouting about seein' smoke on the horizon. We didn't know it was the barn. From the house it looked like part of the woods was on fire."

"How long had you been in the stable before Nathaniel came in?"

"About an hour, maybe less."

More than enough time for Nathaniel to have come down

here, perpetrated the attack, and returned to the stable to report the smoke, I realized. His father certainly wasn't providing much of an alibi.

"And what happened then?" Colin prodded.

"I grabbed two horses straightaway. Didn't even bother with saddles. But before we could get the bridles in place Lord Eldon came out hollering about the smoke and insisting on goin' with us. Mind you, he can't ride bareback, so I had to take the time to get a third mount ready before we could get under way. As soon as his horse was sorted Lord Eldon took off. Didn't wait for us."

I could tell he was still aggrieved by Eldon's behavior; the extra time he had cost them, and his determination to get under way first, but he did not dare utter the words.

"Do continue," Colin said without seeming to have taken note.

"Nathaniel and I followed Lord Eldon and we all ended up here."

I thought his story came to a decidedly abrupt conclusion.

"So . . ." Colin put his hands on his hips and turned toward us, having apparently finished investigating the ground. "Eldon got here first—"

"By a deer's breath. It was past supper, Mr. Pendragon, and you can be sure Lord Eldon had consumed his share of drink by then. Nathaniel and I were able to catch up to him by the time we got here."

"But you didn't overtake him."

"Lord Eldon was riding like Death himself was chasing him. I'd say his condition kept him from realizing just how reckless he was being."

"Of course. And what did you find when you got here?"

"The barn was in flames. Most of it had already collapsed." He gestured with his chin. "Just like you see now. Nathaniel spotted the Earl. He was laid out just about where you're standing," he said, his brow slowly furrowing.

Colin gave a quick smile and I knew he'd already figured that out. "And Elsbeth?" he asked. "Where was she found?"

"On the other side. Closer to the woods. We never would've even looked for her if I hadn't seen her horse stamping at the tree line." He gestured to the woods just beyond.

"The horse hadn't run off?"

"No, sir," Victor said proudly. "The Arnifours have fine animals. Trained never to abandon their riders. Nathaniel and I seen to that."

"Impressive."

"It was Nathaniel who found Miss Elsbeth too." He dropped his gaze again. "It was terrible."

"Was she unconscious when you found her?" Colin asked as he headed off in the direction Victor had gestured.

"Yes, sir. It was her face. . . ." He sucked in a deep breath and shook his head again. "I didn't think she was alive."

"And the Earl? Had he been beaten the same way?"

"No, sir. He was the opposite of Miss Elsbeth. He was face-down with the back of his head stove in. Whoever hit him meant to kill him. An awful sight." He kept his gaze lowered and I couldn't tell if he was swamped by the memory or if it was something else.

"Did you find any sort of weapon nearby?"

"No, sir."

"Elsbeth was about here then?" Colin called as he reached a position a dozen or so yards beyond the ruined barn.

Victor barely glanced up. "About that."

Colin knelt to the ground and fingered several spots before standing up and finally coming back around to where Victor and I were. "It was clearly a most unfortunate scene," he said as he reached us.

"Yes, it was."

"I only need trouble you with two more questions."

Victor nodded.

"Did you notice if the Earl had been robbed?"

"No, sir. But the inspector found a roll of bills in his pocket and said he still had his gold watch on him."

"It's always important to rule out the obvious," Colin murmured. "Which brings me to my last question. Did it appear that Elsbeth had been violated in any way?"

"No . . . no . . ." He shook his head rapidly and looked almost ready to swoon.

"She was fully clothed?"

"Yes, sir."

"Her dress was not torn or mussed about in any way?"

"No, sir. There was nothing of the kind like that. Nothing at all."

"Thank you. I'm sorry if I've made you uncomfortable, but I trust you understand the need for such questions."

Victor Heffernan nodded but did not reply. It made me wonder if he thought he'd said too much, too little, or simply feared that he sounded guilty in spite of himself.

CHAPTER 4

"There's definitely a familial resemblance," Colin said as he gazed down at Elsbeth. "I'd say the Langhems have the dominant gene pool."

"I don't know how you can see any such thing with all the damage that's been done to her," I answered. Her face was a rainbow of mottled blues, yellows, greens, and purples, and it was obvious that she had suffered multiple fractures to her nose and cheeks given the distortion of the bones beneath. However she had once looked, she would never be the same again, assuming she survived at all.

"Well . . . ," he allowed. "Try using a bit of imagination."

"Imagination, is it?" I said, glad we were alone with her.

"I'd say she was attractive—before the attack."

"Does that matter?"

His gaze shot over to me. "Everything matters. And that includes both the way a person looks and how they are perceived. Physical beauty can be a motivator, a crutch, a distraction, or a curse. And the lack of it every bit the same."

"I suppose you have a point."

"Other than her injuries," he pressed, "what are the first things you notice about her?"

I looked down at her battered face and knew that these were indeed the only things I had made note of thus far. "Well . . ." I cleared my throat as I studied her and tried to decipher what he meant for me to see. "I'd say she's about twenty and has long brown hair. She's very slight, really just a slip of a thing, and she's breathing so shallowly that I can hardly see her moving at all."

"There . . . ," he said with finality. "All things physical."

"Well, I can't very well say she's a compelling conversationalist."

"No, but you could have pointed out the meticulousness of her room, or the color of her bedding, or even the high-necked and positively unremarkable dressing gown she's wearing, all of which speak volumes about who she is."

"I don't think I like this game."

"Just keeping you honest."

"What have you learned so far?"

"Several things. I know that the Earl was knocked to the ground by a blow that most certainly came from someone atop a horse. I know that he was running when he was struck down, and that he persisted in pulling himself along the ground by his elbows for another fifteen feet before the killer finally dismounted and came right up beside him, and then beat him with the absolute intent to kill.

"As for this poor girl . . . ," he turned his gaze back to Elsbeth, ". . . she was running for the woods when she was struck, the assailant having once again mounted his horse. She collapsed on the spot and was left in the condition we find her now, though I would presume her attacker thought her to be dead."

"You figured all that out by pawing at the ground around that barn?!"

"It was very telling, especially since much of the grass had been burned away. If we'd been able to get a look at it before the whole of Inspector Varcoe's buffoons descended upon it, I'm sure I'd be a damn sight closer to telling just who did this." He shook his head and let out a sigh. "But the one thing I can't profess to have the slightest notion about yet is *why*."

"Well, we know it wasn't robbery."

"That's true. Yet even so, can we be sure there wasn't something in that barn worth stealing? That perhaps all of this is about covering the theft of something from there?"

"I hadn't thought of that."

"Doubtful, though." He shrugged.

"Come now, we are only collecting information," I teased.

"Always a quick learner."

"I'd hardly call twelve years quick."

"Well, you're doing better than the inspector and he's been at it the whole of our lifetimes and then some. Did you recognize the man he has posted outside the door?"

"Yes, I remember him from the Rathburn case. Seems agreeable enough."

"Perhaps, but he *is* a Yarder."

"You can't blame them all for the inspector's ineptitude."

"They've accomplished nothing in a fortnight," his eyes were alight with fire, "and I'm already certain that Victor Heffernan is innocent."

CHAPTER 5

Victor's son, Nathaniel, was a lanky, painfully thin boy of twenty-one whose pasty complexion belied the work he did outside. While he shared his father's hawkish nose he did not so much as bear a whisper of the older man's compact frame. His mother had died before Nathaniel learned to walk, the victim of a frail constitution, Lady Arnifour had informed us, right before she instructed us to go easy on the boy, as she termed him delicate in both mind and constitution like his mother.

Lady Arnifour had relayed the story of the late Mrs. Heffernan in a voice both wistful and content. It was clear she was moved at the loss suffered by the two Heffernan men, yet losing his wife had left Victor available for the attentions of the Lady herself. I was reminded again about Colin's initial suspicion of the nature of Lady Arnifour's relationship with her groundskeeper and was all but convinced that he was correct. I was beginning to believe that the only person who actually harbored any real emotion for the late Earl was the dour housekeeper, Mrs. O'Keefe. Other than her, I didn't see anyone who was truly lamenting his death.

We were seated in the kitchen with Nathaniel, Victor having already disappeared out back after making the introductions. Nathaniel was still standing by the back door, all gangly limbs and awkwardness, as he self-consciously dragged the cap from his head.

"Please . . . ," Colin pointed to a chair across from us, "sit down. Make yourself comfortable. We are not the enemy."

Nathaniel did not embrace Colin's gesture of camaraderie, as he remained standing a good minute longer before finally making the decision to stay, skulking over to the table, and slipping into one of the chairs without even having to pull it out.

"I shall only trouble you with a few questions," Colin said in a voice I knew he meant to sound placating. "I'm sure you'll have discussed it all with the Yarders anyway."

Nathaniel gave a slight nod even as he kept his gaze riveted on the table. I was thinking he looked guilty and would be likely to grunt his answers when he suddenly blurted out, "I didn't kill that rotten bastard. It wasn't me and it sure as bloody hell wasn't my father. And if you think it was you can go straight ta hell with that old piss pot inspector!"

Colin leaned back in his chair with an easy smile and casually folded his arms across his broad chest. "Piss pot. I rather like that." Nathaniel's eyes raked across Colin's face, searching for some sign of sarcasm, but he found no such thing there. "We're not so unalike, you and me. At least not where Scotland Yard is concerned." The young man blinked repeatedly, his outburst drained with the rapidity of a flash flood. "Now why don't you tell us what you remember about the night of the Earl's murder."

Nathaniel snapped his eyes back to the tabletop, but not before I spotted something dark and angry trying to hide there. "It was after supper . . . ," he began with marked reticence. "The Earl had gone off on his walk and I was watering the garden by the stables when Elsbeth came out and said she wanted ta go riding." He shifted in his chair but did not lift his gaze. "I told her it was too late, but she wouldn't listen. She never listens ta me."

"Was your father in the stable?" Colin asked.

"If that's what he said," he shot back.

"Convincing."

"What difference does it make?" He finally looked up, glaring at Colin again. "You already think we're guilty. I can see it in yer face."

"The only thing you see on my face is that I'm beginning to find you an ungrateful little tosser. I'd suggest you knock off the ruddy attitude or I'll return Lady Arnifour's money and leave you to hang. What do you prefer?"

Nathaniel sagged and dropped his chin to his sternum so that all I could see was the sharp cut of his nose protruding from beneath his brow. This interview seemed to be yielding about as much information as we'd gotten from Elsbeth.

"All I'm asking, Nathaniel, is for you to tell us the truth of what you remember that night. And I give you my word that I'll not come to any conclusions until the solution is irrefutable. Are we agreed?" We watched the boy until he vaguely shrugged his shoulders. It would do. "Good. So Elsbeth wanted to go for a ride and you were warning her off. . . ."

Nathaniel sighed heavily. "That's right."

"I presume it was dark and you were worried about her?"

"No . . ."

I figured Nathaniel would explain what he meant, but seconds quickly turned into minutes without so much as a hint of clarification. He sat there, morose and slouching, his gaze tucked in on himself and his arms folded like two crossed swords. He looked like a man with a great deal to hide.

"Then why, Nathaniel?" I could hear the strains of impatience seeping into Colin's voice.

"Because I knew what she was up to." He raised his eyes

just enough to meet Colin's, and behind his inky black irises I saw a flash of something unsettling I could not place. "I'm done talking," he suddenly announced, pushing himself up from the table and stalking back outside before either Colin or I could say a word.

Colin shook his head and stabbed a crown out of his pocket, quickly running it between his fingers. "Curious."

"Curious?! It's more than curious. It's disturbing. No wonder Varcoe's convinced he's guilty."

He glanced at me. "Well, that should tell you something, because Varcoe's seldom right. Though I will say that I've never seen so many angry people in one house hiding so very many secrets. This place was like a tinderbox just waiting to be set off. Even Elsbeth seems to have been up to something."

"You think that based on the word of that infuriating boy?"

"So quick to judge," he clucked. "I'm sure that's precisely why our uninspired inspector is so eager to throw the blame on the Heffernans. Varcoe must have been ecstatic with such easy targets." He tossed me a tight look. "But I'm not so sure."

I nodded, mortified to discover myself aligned with the inspector.

"A crime like this is seldom so easy. The blows to the Earl's head were delivered with malice and forethought. The same is obviously true for Elsbeth. This was not some spontaneous act of vengeance; it was a purposeful and calculated crime. I will be astonished if this level of cleverness was wielded by that agitated boy."

"But you don't know that. He could be exactly what he seems. Guilt can be an extraordinary burden to carry, especially for a boy like that."

"A boy like that? . . . ," Colin echoed, furiously rotating the coin.

Before I could tell him what I'd seen lurking behind the young man's eyes Victor came scurrying back inside. "Is everything okay?" he asked, a note of dread in his voice. "Nathaniel *is* a moody lad, but you mustn't hold that against him. It's my fault. I did the best I could to raise him without a mother."

"I know he means well," Colin answered as he slid the crown back into his pocket.

"He does!"

But I couldn't help thinking Victor was pushing too hard.

"Might you be able to answer a few more questions for me?" Colin said as he rubbed his chin.

"Of course."

"Do you know where Nathaniel was that night while you were tending to the horses?"

Victor shifted uneasily, wringing his hands without appearing to have any awareness that he was doing so. "He was working in the garden until Miss Elsbeth asked him to saddle a horse for her, which he did. All very proper," he added, and I wondered why he'd said that.

"And then what did he do?"

"What did he do?"

"Yes."

He hesitated and I knew his answer before he gave it. "I don't know."

"I see. And the first you heard of the smoke at the far end of the property was when Nathaniel ran into the stable to tell you about it, is that right?" Victor nodded. "So if I estimate that it took about thirty minutes for Elsbeth to ride down there and the attack to happen, does that sound conceivable to you? Thirty minutes?"

"Thirty?"

"Yes. You know, the number after twenty-nine."

Victor took a step back and shrugged. "I don't know. I suppose so."

"Right. So after you heard Elsbeth ride off, do you have any idea where Nathaniel was for any part of the next thirty minutes?"

"Where?"

"Come now, Victor, these are the easy questions."

I suddenly found myself feeling oddly defensive of Victor and could not keep from speaking up. "We're here because Lady Arnifour believes you and Nathaniel to be innocent," I reminded him. "Just tell us the truth."

Victor's body sagged as his chin dipped toward the floor.

"Sit down, Victor." I gestured to the chair his son had vacated. "You mustn't stand on formality."

Victor slumped into it and ran a hand across his brow. His hesitation was palpable. "I don't know where Nathaniel went after Miss Elsbeth left," he muttered. "He was upset. I thought he would come back to help me in the stable, but he didn't."

"And *why* was he upset?" Colin cut in irritably.

"It's not what you think," Victor answered at once. "It was Miss Elsbeth. He was upset about Miss Elsbeth."

"I'm not thinking anything particular at this moment. So please just tell me what his quarrel with Elsbeth was about?"

"No quarrel." Again he spoke quickly. "He wasn't *angry,* he was *upset.* You see?" His eyes sought mine and I gave a confirming nod.

"Just the same," Colin pressed, "you've made it clear that Nathaniel was in a mood and I should very much like to know what it concerned."

"You have to understand—"

"*Mr. Heffernan!*" Colin slammed a fist on the table. "I cannot understand *anything* unless you start talking to me. I am not your judge. In fact, I am trying to be your ally. But I'll be quite useless if you insist on continuing to hinder me." He leaned forward as though doing so might make his point clearer. "Between your son's contrarian behavior and your dissembling, I'm about ruddy well worn-out. I'm thinking the best thing you and your boy can do is throw yourselves on the mercy of the Yarders."

"Victor," I spoke up while Colin plastered a brooding gaze out the window, "Mr. Pendragon and I understand how determined you are to protect your son. Any parent would be." The words caught in my throat a moment as the years I'd spent in the shadow of my mother's illness ridiculed my sentiment. Years in which the voices—the hysteria—so pernicious and invasive, had deftly peeled back the layers of her mind until the perfect family, *my* family, was forever rendered in the most brutal way. "But your employer," I pressed ahead, determined not to be undone by the coiled remnants of my own memories, "has been murdered and his niece savagely beaten. We can only pray that she will recover. You and your boy are Scotland Yard's only suspects. You've got to help us, Victor. You must tell us everything you know. Mr. Pendragon will ferret out the truth one way or the other, I promise you that, but what you tell us may lead us to the proper resolution more quickly. And that would allow you and your son to put all of this behind you. You have to trust us, Victor."

He turned a sorrowful gaze on me and I suddenly understood what he'd been afraid to say.

"Nathaniel cared very much for Miss Elsbeth," he muttered under his breath. "He concerned himself with her when he shouldn't have. It was wrong. I told him so, but a boy's heart . . ." He let his words drift away.

"Did Elsbeth know?" Colin asked.

"She was a bright girl—*is* a bright girl," he quickly corrected.

"When Nathaniel told her he didn't want her riding off by herself, what did she say?"

He grimaced and folded his hands in his lap. "She laughed. I couldn't hear much of what they said, but I did hear her tell him that he had no say over her, and she was right. It made him mad. He said foolish things."

"Did he threaten her?"

"Absolutely not." Victor looked straight at Colin. "He would *never* do such a thing. I raised him better than that. And he cared for her. That's what I'm trying to tell you."

"After you heard Elsbeth ride off did you look for Nathaniel?"

He shook his head and dropped his gaze again.

"Didn't you wonder if they'd ridden off together?"

"Not after the row they'd had."

"And you didn't see him again until he came rushing in to tell you he could see smoke at the edge of the property."

Victor nodded sullenly.

"So he was missing," Colin mused.

"He would *never* hurt Miss Elsbeth," Victor said again, this time with fierce determination.

Colin's face was unreadable as he stood up. I gripped Victor's shoulder and thanked him as I walked past, telling him not to worry though I knew he would. And in truth, I thought he should.

CHAPTER 6

"Show them to the parlor when you've finished," Lady Arnifour instructed her housekeeper, Mrs. O'Keefe, from the doorway of the late Earl's study, where we'd been ushered. "I shall wait there."

"Of course, mum," came the answer in a tone more perfunctory than dutiful.

"Mind what they ask," Lady Arnifour added as she seized the double doors. "We've no secrets here." And with that she heaved the doors shut, leaving her declaration to hang in the air like soot.

Mrs. O'Keefe remained just inside the door where Lady Arnifour had deposited her. Between her gangly frame, all angles and knobs, pursed face, and perpetually pink complexion she looked somehow quite formidable. Even given the exacting proportions of Colin's powerful frame, it still looked like Mrs. O'Keefe could chuck him out the door if she desired. I wondered if therein lay the answer to the fate of *Mr.* O'Keefe.

"Please make yourself comfortable," Colin said expansively as though it were his home to do so.

"I'm fine right here."

"As you wish. I'll try not to take up much of your time."

"See that you don't. I've a household to maintain."

One of Colin's eyebrows arched up and I knew that wouldn't portend well for this woman. "All right then," he tossed her a smile that glittered with frost, "after supper on the night of the Earl's murder, Nathaniel Heffernan was told by Elsbeth to saddle a horse. Did you hear their exchange?"

"I've a great many things to do after supper. Listening in on the conversations of others is not one of them."

"So you heard nothing?"

"I heard the sound of water in the sink and the rattling of dishes and pans as I cleaned them."

"Do you have help in the kitchen?"

"I don't need help."

"Did you look out the window? Did you *see* Nathaniel and Elsbeth?"

"I don't spy on people and I don't listen to their conversations. I'm finding your implications offensive."

"And I'm finding you—"

"Not very cooperative." I leaned forward and cut him off, certain he was about to say something that would only hurt our cause. "Come now, Mrs. O'Keefe, I'm sure Lady Arnifour means you to be helpful in our investigation of her husband's murder."

She only glared at me, but I hoped it had given Colin enough time to collect himself again. "Tell me," he started slowly, though his voice was still tight, "how would you describe your relationship with Nathaniel and his father?"

"Professional."

"I'm surprised given how little you're offering in the way of help."

She scowled, pursing her lips into an almost invisible line. "Is it my help you want? Or the truth?"

"Mutually exclusive, are they? Most people make an effort to combine the two." He stood up and glowered at her and I knew he was well finished with this woman. "You seem to display sorrow for the death of your employer and yet remain deceptive, unhelpful, and unaccountably rude. You cannot have it all ways, madam. I would suggest you choose your side with care."

"Choosing sides, is it?!" She held her ground. "You come into this house like a rooster and think you can judge the lot of us. Well, you don't know me. I won't stand here and be accused by the likes of you." She turned on her heels and made for the doors, but not before Colin managed to sprint past her and plant himself directly in her path.

"I've accused you of nothing more than an ill temperament," he scoffed. "So if you're blustering about in an effort to cover some guilt, you've nothing but your own conscience to mollify." And with a decisive flourish he swung the doors wide and stepped aside.

For a moment I thought Mrs. O'Keefe might actually step on his shoes, but she kept her deportment impeccable as she swept past him and headed back to the sanctuary of her kitchen.

Colin stared after her, his expression moody and dark, and I too felt the better part of our journey had been for naught. All we'd done was alienate the people whose cooperation we most needed. Lady Arnifour was the only person who wanted us here and her motives were questionable at best. She wasn't even bothering to play the grieving widow our sovereign had single-handedly elevated to an art form, which left only Victor Heffernan to be counted as an ally—and I wasn't entirely convinced about him.

"What an insufferable cow," Colin groused as he abruptly dropped to the floor and quickly knocked off twenty push-ups.

"Well, you didn't exactly win her over with your charm. We might need her help, you know."

He stood up again and cast me a frown. "She has no intention of providing any help, so I'll not be bothered with the likes of
her. Come on, I've had enough of this place. Let's be on our way."

"Ever patient." I snickered. "I'll let Lady Arnifour know."

"Tell her we won't likely be back for several days. I've had
quite enough of this brood for right now," he grumbled.

I sighed. "She won't like that—"

He scowled as he headed for the door. "I'll solve this case,
but at the moment I don't really give a bloody bollocks what
she likes."

CHAPTER 7

Two days passed without Colin giving the slightest inclination of returning to the Arnifour estate. He had just gone off to seek his solace in a tub of hot water again when a sudden pounding drifted up from the front door. I strained to hear if it was Lady Arnifour come to rail at us for going missing for so long, but quickly caught the rapidly escalating tones of Mrs. Behmoth and either a young woman or boy. Whoever it was, they were fast matching Mrs. Behmoth's shrillness as their exchange rose up between the floorboards beneath my feet. "Is everything all right?" I called out.

"Does it sound like it is?" Mrs. Behmoth hollered back.

"I 'ave ta speak ta ya. Ya *gotta* lemme up." It was a boy—an East End boy.

"You'll be speaking to the back a me ruddy 'and if ya don't get yer blasted arse outta 'ere!"

"It's all right, Mrs. Behmoth. Let him up."

The sound of footfalls racing up the stairs told me that the youth wasn't about to wait for a second invitation. He rounded the landing in a flurry of scrawny limbs and as soon as he saw me stopped and snatched the cap from his head, releasing a pile of stringy black hair that fell to his shoulders.

"Don't send me out 'til I say me piece," he pleaded.

I waved him into the room and caught a sour whiff of him as he rushed over to shake my hand. This boy, somewhere between thirteen and fifteen, was at home on the streets, his ready manners notwithstanding. He was under someone's tutelage and I knew I would be wise to keep an eye on his hands while he was here. I signaled him to a settee at the same moment Mrs. Behmoth hollered up the stairs, "Don't let the little shite sit on any a the furniture!"

"If you *please*, Mrs. Behmoth!" I growled back at her, offering an apology to the young man as he wandered over to the fireplace, twirling his cap in his hands. "She means well," I bothered to say.

He shrugged. "It ain't nothin'."

I offered a smile as I gestured toward the settee again, taking my customary seat across from it, but the boy only shook his head. "The lady's right, me clothes is dirty."

I nearly choked on his use of the word "lady" to describe Mrs. Behmoth; this lad was well trained indeed. "Furniture, like people, can be cleaned. Please make yourself comfortable."

He smiled, smudge marks on his cheeks separating like clouds before the sun. He headed for Colin's chair and I flung an arm out and said, "There," like some monosyllabic cretin as I gestured to the settee again. "If you don't mind," I added.

Offering an easy smile, the disheveled youngster happily settled himself onto the couch Lady Arnifour had occupied only a few days prior, making me wonder what she would make of that. "Me name's Michael," he said, jutting his chin out with pride.

"Michael . . ."

"Jest Michael."

"Well, Just Michael, I'm Mr. Pruitt. I'm Mr. Pendragon's partner."

"Is 'e 'ere then?"

"I'm afraid he's indisposed. Is there something I can help you with?"

His face crinkled with confusion. " 'E's wot?"

"Unavailable. Busy. He won't be able to see you right now." The boy had finesse even if he lacked education.

" 'Oo er you again?"

"Ethan Pruitt," I shot back. "I'm Mr. Pendragon's partner. I've been working with him for the better part of a dozen years. Speaking with me is like speaking with him."

" 'Cept you ain't 'im," he pointed out.

"Ah," I smiled even though my patience was quickly thinning, "you are a keen one. So go on, tell me why you've come."

He started twisting his cap again as he looked at me from beneath his lowered brow. "It's me little sister," he said. "She's gone missin'."

"Missing? For how long?"

"Since Sunday."

"Six days?!" Anything less than three wouldn't have warranted a second thought among those of the East End, but six days meant something, especially for a young girl. "Did you notify Scotland Yard?"

"They don't care nothin' 'bout us that lives in Whitechapel. One less ta trouble themselves with."

Of course he was right. "Has she ever disappeared before?"

His eyes flitted about the room and I knew what the answer was. "A day or two. Nothin' like this."

I heaved a sigh, certain that she was either a pickpocket, prostitute, addict, or most likely all three. "How old is she?"

"Twelve."

I cringed. "Do you have a room in a boardinghouse some-where?"

"Yeah. Up near Stepney Green. We got a corner of the base-ment 'bout the size a yer entry run by an old slag wot thinks it were a palace. She don't treat nobody good 'cept them she calls 'er gentlemen callers. A bunch a drunken sots she gets upstairs and rolls. She's wicked clever though. Keeps a mess of 'em on a string."

How well I understood the woman he was describing, for I had spent years under the thumb of someone like that myself. "Tell me about your sister."

"Angelyne." He smiled. "Named after the angels." He de-scribed her as a freckle-faced girl with raven black hair who was not quite five feet tall. He said she was slight and hadn't even begun to reveal the shape of the woman she was on the verge of becoming. I only wished that might make a difference. "Last Sunday I 'ad ta go out for a while. I 'ad things ta take care of. I told her not ta go anywhere, but when I got back . . ." He dropped his eyes and rubbed the heels of his hands across them.

"Does she disobey you often?"

"Naw. She's a good girl. Never causes no trouble."

"Did you ask the woman who runs your boardinghouse if she saw or heard anything?"

He screwed his face up. "That one don't 'ear nuthin' but 'er-self mewlin' at all the men she drags 'ome."

"Do you remember Angelyne complaining about anyone bothering her lately?"

"I'd a killed 'em if she 'ad. You can bet yer arse on that," he blasted back, and I didn't doubt him. "So will you 'elp? You and Mr. Pendragon?"

"I'll have to speak with him."

"Ya want I should wait?"

"There's no need for that." I stood up. "Just tell me how we can get in contact with you. What's the address of your boarding-house?"

Michael got up and stabbed his cap back onto his head. "It'll be easier if I come by tamorrow evenin'. That okay?"

I eyed him a moment, wondering whether his reticence was directed toward me or his own bit of subterfuge. "That'll be fine."

I showed him out with a promise to receive him in twenty-four hours' time, all the while thinking how young he was to be dealing with such matters. It was a disgrace that this was the best our city had to offer these children, but then I was reminded that sometimes we create our own worst times.

"When ya go back up . . . ," Mrs. Behmoth poked her head out the kitchen as I relatched the door, ". . . tell 'is Majesty not ta use up all the 'ot water. I wanna take a bath meself tonight." She punched her fists onto her hips. "And 'urry up. 'E's 'ad it runnin' awhile."

I tossed her a frown as I padded up the stairs and went to the bathroom. "It's me," I said as I poked my head inside.

"Don't let the cold air in." He was reclining in his liquid cocoon, a dozen candles scattered about, flickering a warm embrace.

"I've been commanded to tell you not to use all the hot water."

"Ah. Dear Mrs. Behmoth. I would hate to begrudge her the occasional bath." He rotated the spigot with his foot. "I think I'll require your warm body to keep the water heated up then. Climb in and tell me who was just here?"

"There's hardly room for two," I protested halfheartedly.

"Don't I always make room?" He sat up and patted the water as though it were the cushion of a chair. "Come on."

I did as bade, pleased to note the change in his mood and hoping that it might signify progress around the Arnifour case.

"Much better," he said as he rested his chin atop my head with his arms hanging about my shoulders. "Now tell me who was here and I shall pay close attention." But he didn't pay attention, and after a few minutes I stopped trying to tell him anything at all.

CHAPTER 8

"Who let you out of your hole, Pendragon? I'd like to know to whom I owe the displeasure of your company."

"Oh, come now, Inspector." Colin sidled up to the man's badly beaten desk piled high with its array of papers and binders, and plopped himself into the creaky chair beside it. "I've just come from a bit of sparring at the gymnasium. Worked my aggressions out. You should try it."

He snorted. "We'll see if that even lasts the length of this conversation. What are you here for?" He glowered, his naturally opaque complexion deepening. Given his dazzlingly white hair he looked positively monochromatic except when moved to a mood. Tall and thin, Emmett Varcoe was the complete opposite of Colin in both form and function in spite of their shared passion for detection. "You'd best make it quick because I haven't time for you," he added, rotating his chair so that we were left staring at his profile.

"Really now...," Colin replied with a snarky smile. "We've only come to share some information."

"Oh, I'll just bet you have." He swung around just as I sat

down. "Don't get comfortable, Pruitt. The two of you are *not* staying."

"Not to worry." Colin leaned forward mischievously. "We're only here to let you know that we've been hired by the bereaved Lady Arnifour to solve the murder of her husband. I thought it only fair to—"

"*Bloody hell!*" Inspector Varcoe bellowed, slamming a fist onto his desk. "That case is practically solved. Why is that ridiculous woman wasting her money on you?"

"Well, I should hardly consider it wasting—"

"Piss off, Pendragon. We're about to make an arrest. Nobody needs you slinking around stirring up a bunch of bollocks."

"About to make an arrest, are you? That's not always worked out so well for you in the past—"

"How dare you!" he blasted, his voice elevating with the color of his face. "You pompous little twat. What do you know about working a crime? You're just a coddled diplomat's boy who attended independent schools and probably never even let his sacred little feet touch the streets of Bombay. How dare you come in here and look down on me."

I could see that Colin's posture had become rigid as he said, "A bit jumpy about this case, are you?"

The inspector turned a steely glare on Colin. "If you're here to share, then what have you got so far?"

"Not that much, really." He gave a tight smile. "Though I did notice a rather pointed lack of emotion regarding the Earl's death on the part of everyone in the household—with the possible exception of the housekeeper, Mrs. O'Keefe."

"That old toad."

"Ah . . . ," and now he chuckled, "I must agree with you there."

The inspector did not share his amusement. "What else?" he growled.

"Well . . ." I watched Colin pretend to ruminate a moment and fought to keep from rolling my eyes. "I believe Victor Heffernan is innocent."

The inspector's left eye ticked almost imperceptibly as he managed to maintain his composure with a shrug before allowing, "Perhaps."

"And I've a suspicion that Lady Arnifour has some notion about who may be involved."

"That's absurd." He waved Colin off.

Colin shrugged lightly as he dug a crown out of his pocket and effortlessly began rotating it between his fingers. "I'm betting you're circling Nathaniel Heffernan."

"Damn right," the inspector sneered with pride. "That Heffernan boy did this and his father ruddy well knows it too. That's called collusion."

"But what of his motive?"

"Motive?! Bugger off about his motive. I'm not telling you anything, Pendragon. It'll be my pleasure to see you looking the fool on this one. Now piss off." And with a flourish of rattling papers Emmett Varcoe let it be known that our time with him was done.

"Very well." Colin palmed the coin as he stood up and gave a nod that Inspector Varcoe took no note of. "Perhaps you're right."

"Oh, I'm right." He spun back on us. "You watch and you'll see him deliver his son right into my hands."

"Victor Heffernan? Deliver Nathaniel to you? Why would he do that?"

"Because in a few days when I arrest them both, he'll give the boy up like a rotten apple. That type would eat their young if they thought it would help."

"That type?" Colin's voice sank precipitously.

Varcoe sneered at us. "You know exactly what I mean, Pendragon. Street rubbish like Pruitt here. They never lose the stink."

"You know bloody well Ethan was raised in Holland Park!" Colin snapped back. I reached over and clutched his sleeve, not wanting him to do this, but he only shrugged me off. What nettled me was wondering whether he felt compelled to do it for my benefit or in defense of his own honor. "His father was the Deputy Minister of Education. Which makes Ethan a damn sight better bred than you, Emmett."

"All the same." Varcoe's face lit up with a satisfied smile, clearly well pleased to have riled Colin so. "My ruddy mum didn't go bleedin' starkers and off everyone. What kind of man lets his wife do that? Is it any wonder your Pruitt ended up a sniveling addict in the East End?" His grin widened. "He comes from rubbish all right." He burst into harsh laughter as my heart seized and my stomach dropped below my feet. I opened my mouth to say something, to defend myself—my father—when I caught sight of Colin balling his fist out of the corner of my eye, so instead grabbed him and yanked him out of there.

CHAPTER 9

W‍ithin the hour we were back in our flat, dinner behind us, Colin fussing over tea while Mrs. Behmoth tried to coerce a fire back to life by poking at its cinders and kindling, her annoyance evident in her every muttered curse. Colin handed my tea to me with a sigh. "You must do me a favor in the future," he said as he settled back into his overstuffed chair. "If I ever tell you I want to visit that old bastard again, please remind me how I despise him."

"That may be so, but you can still be quite charming when you choose." I peered at him over the rim of my cup. "At least until he starts taking out after me. I'm sorry I embarrass you."

He stopped and glared at me a moment before quickly downing his tea as he stood up and snatched at his dumbbells. "It's not me," he mumbled with seeming preoccupation. "I'm angry for you."

"Then you're wasting your energy. I cannot change the regrettable choices I made as a lad. After what happened I was afraid I might be the same. I was bloody well terrified. You know that. I went and hid in the only place that allowed me to truly dispel my fears: the opium dens."

"Don't say that. It makes you sound weak."

"I was!" I shook my head, not embarrassed, but ashamed. "I was not quite ten years old when it happened. My grandparents were thick with guilt and about as afraid of me as I was of myself. I wasn't in their house much more than a year before they couldn't stand having me around anymore."

"That's ridiculous," he chided, waving the weights around madly.

"It isn't. That's why they sent me to Easling and Temple. To get me out of their house." I heaved a sigh. "I'm sure it also helped them assuage some of that guilt by affording me such a fine education, despite my squandering of it. And it did allow me to meet you." A small smile easily crossed my lips. "I thought you so self-assured and handsome." I chuckled. "Of course that only terrified me more. And you didn't even know I existed."

"I knew who you were," he protested without conviction before suddenly turning on Mrs. Behmoth, still cursing at the flagging embers. *"Do you need a ruddy hand with that?"* he barked.

"Don't get cheeky with me!" she growled back.

I shook my head. "Well, no matter. Though I do wish it hadn't taken you nine years to rescue me from Maw Heikens."

He screwed up his face, halting the weights in midair. "That regrettable old harridan," he snarled. "I won't have that name in this flat."

There was no surprise in his reaction. He always hated Maw. I suppose it was easier to blame her for what had happened to me than to blame me. "What I really want to know," I said, content to let that topic be, "is why we went to see Varcoe in the first place?"

"For the information," he muttered blithely as he settled back into his chair and began curling the dumbbells behind his head.

"Information? What information?"

He glanced over at me as though I were daft. "We now know that his suspicions toward Nathaniel are wholly rudimentary, without the slightest whiff of a motive. You saw how he acted when I pressed him. I'll bet his entire case rests on nothing more than his own speculations. Once again he has proven that he owes his endless tenure at the Yard to his inability to intimidate the lesser minds who have risen above him."

"Brutal." I chuckled. "But what do you mean about his suspicions against Nathaniel?"

"The boy is gruff, uncommunicative, and so clearly hiding something that he couldn't possibly appear more culpable if he had been found beating the Earl. And then there's that bit about how he fancies Elsbeth. I can't stop wondering about the argument they had that night. Jealousy is a potent motivator for the worst in a man."

"But it doesn't make sense. He works for the Arnifours, for heaven's sake; how could he ever think that he might have a chance with her? It's too preposterous."

He tipped one of his dumbbells toward me. "Then what do you suppose happened that night?"

"I'm sure I haven't the slightest idea, but there's a lot more rotten out there than just that old house."

"Ach," Mrs. Behmoth groused. "It's always that way with them that has too much money." She abruptly reached up, seized my Jules Verne novel off the mantel, and flung it into the still-sputtering fire.

"*My book!*" I leapt up, spilling much of my tea onto myself. "What the hell are you doing?!"

"I'm tryin' to get this bloody fire goin'!" she barked. "That book's twaddle. It'll do a lot more good in there."

"You'll buy me a new copy," I shot back as I tried to blot the stains from my clothes.

"Like 'ell," she answered, pointing to the quickly escalating flames. "It served a fine purpose. I don't owe no one nuthin'." A knock at the door was the only thing that kept me from responding in kind. "Don't trouble yerselves," she said as she headed for the staircase. "Allow an old lady the pleasure of fetchin' that."

"Absolutely." Colin chuckled.

Mrs. Behmoth shot him a withering glare, which he took no notice of as he shoved the dumbbells under his chair, and then she disappeared down the steps.

"Are we expecting anyone?" he asked.

"I'd guess it's that scruffy East End lad with the missing sister I was telling you about yesterday. He said he'd come back this evening."

"Oh yes. What are their names?"

"Michael and Angelyne."

"That's right. Very Church of England."

The thunderous footfalls of Mrs. Behmoth's ascension brought a halt to our conversation. "Yer alley cat is back," she announced, glaring at me.

"Well, let him up!" I snapped, only to be surprised when he suddenly poked his head out from behind her. I was appalled that he'd heard her disparage him.

"Do come in." Colin swept past me and ushered him into our study. "We've been expecting you."

"Thank you, sir," he said as he doffed his cap and nodded at me. The smudges on his face had been scrubbed away to reveal a fragile complexion, which also exposed the hollowness in his cheeks. He went back to the settee and balanced himself on the edge of it just as he'd done the evening before. "Tell me, Michael," Colin settled into his chair as Mrs. Behmoth trudged back downstairs, "when exactly did you last see your sister?"

"Ye'll take the case then?"

"We are at your behest."

"Wot?"

I leaned forward. "He's taking the case."

"Oh, ruddy excellent," he said, his face lighting up for just an instant. "Ya know I ain't gonna be able ta pay ya much."

"You needn't pay us at all. You shall have us for free."

"Ya mean that? I don't gotta pay?"

"You can't very well spend what you haven't got."

"I'd get somethin'."

Colin held up a hand. "That won't be necessary. On occasion I do a service for someone in need, and today you are that someone. Perhaps you will return the favor one day for someone else."

"I will." He smiled broadly. "You bet I will."

"Now, tell me about your sister," Colin said, surreptitiously extracting a crown from his pocket and smoothly flicking it through his fingers.

"Angelyne. Like the angels. And she is one too. A reg'lar angel. The last time I saw 'er were a week ago. I'd left 'er in our room and told 'er ta stay there, but when I got back she were gone. I ain't seen or heard nothin' from 'er since and that ain't like 'er."

"I see. Did anyone at your boardinghouse hear or see anything?"

"No one saw nothin'. Least not wot they tell me."

"What time was it when you left her alone?"

"Middle a the afternoon. Round two or three, I suppose."

"And when did you return?"

"Suppertime. I brought food with me. I knew she'd be 'ungry."

"So you went up to your room . . . ," he prodded, his coin continuing to make its silent rotations.

". . . And she weren't there. Just like I said. Our room ain't big. I knew right away she were gone. I knew it soon 's I opened the door."

"And what did you do?"

"I went to see me landlady."

"And did she know anything?"

"Nah." He swatted his cap on his knee. "She's a cur, that one. She don't 'ear nothin' but the sound a men with a pocketful a change."

"I see. And did you talk to anyone else in your building?"

"Me and Angelyne keep ta ourselves. I don't know nobody else. I knew she 'adn't gone ta see none a them. She 'ad no business with any of 'em."

"One last question then." He held the coin up in front of his face and seemed to be admiring its luster. "Did she mention anyone bothering her lately? Following her around?"

"I'd a killed anyone was messin' with 'er."

"I trust you mean that figuratively."

"Wot?"

"We'll need to come over and have a look around. And I'll want to speak with your landlady."

"You kin try speakin' to 'er, but she'll only wanna take ya fer a grinder."

"Then she'll be sorely disappointed." He stood up. "What's her name?"

"Rendell."

"Fine. Leave us directions and expect to see us tomorrow. We shan't waste time given how long it's been."

Michael stabbed his cap back on as he bounced up and started for the door. "I've got a bit a business ta run in the mornin', but I'll be round. Specially if I know yer comin'."

"We shall be there."

"Thank ya, sir." He bowed regally, his studied polish commendable if suspect.

Colin smiled and nodded his head. "Until tomorrow then."

The lad bounded off down the stairs, a lightness in his step that had not been there before.

"Is that ragamuffin gone?" Mrs. Behmoth hollered up as soon as the front door slammed.

"That's our new client you're disparaging," Colin called back.

"Ya must be starkers," came the muffled reply.

He chuckled as he settled back in his chair and began flipping the crown through his fingers again. "What do you make of that?"

"Are you kidding? I know that boy. I used to be that boy. He's too practiced. Too slick. I'd wager he's up to something." While I knew Michael couldn't be driven by the same demons I had been, any boy scraping by on the streets of the East End knew how to get what he needed. You either learned it or became a statistic. I had certainly done it, for a while anyway, and it seemed obvious to me that this lad was very much more savvy than I had ever been.

Colin stuffed the coin back into his pocket and rolled the dumbbells out from under his chair again, seizing them and curling them along his sides. "When you say you know that boy . . ."

"Well, I don't mean literally."

"Of course. But don't you think what he said sounds plausible?"

"Certainly it sounds plausible. It *needs* to sound plausible. The question is, how much of what he's saying is true?"

"You don't think his sister is missing?"

"I don't doubt she's missing, but I'm not so convinced it was on a Sunday afternoon when she was supposed to be waiting at home like a good little waif."

"What difference do the details make?"

"Well, it won't be very easy to find her if we don't know the truth of her disappearance. He could've prostituted her to the wrong man, or lost her in an opium club, or had some scam go sour only to see her carted off by an infuriated mark determined to get his revenge. I know that life."

The weights buzzed back and forth as a smile slowly snaked across his face. "You're making this personal. Just because *you* were always up to something doesn't mean every urchin is."

"I was *never* an urchin," I sniffed. "Highborn and -bred, and you know it."

"That's not what I meant," he dismissed. "And anyway, that only makes it worse." He stood up and rotated the weights so that they surged against the broadness of his chest. "But I don't disagree with you. I also suspect that something is missing from the story. A young girl doesn't simply disappear in the middle of the afternoon without somebody seeing or hearing *some*thing. Indeed, that viral-sounding landlady would seem a prime suspect for both access and opportunity."

"I think he makes too much of a fuss about her. After all, she lets them live there. If it weren't for her they'd both be in one of those Dickensian orphanages."

He paused and stared at me, the weights held out perpendicular to the floor. "You're just saying that because of the old slag who took you in. What was her name?"

"Maw. Maw Heikens."

"God, I hate that name."

"Will you be wantin' more tea?" Mrs. Behmoth shouted from the bottom of the stairs, and for once I was glad she did so. Our conversation was headed for an unfortunate place, making her interruption divinely inspired.

"Please," I called back, thankful to hear the jostling of china as she immediately began her ascent. I met her at the top of the stairs and took the tray from her as she followed me back into the room.

"Must ya get yerself all worked up in 'ere?" She scowled at Colin. "Ya sweat all over the carpet and it leaves stains. Yer like a bloody drudge."

"I am a fine specimen of health and vitality," he answered, nevertheless setting the dumbbells aside.

"Ya need more fat on ya. Ya oughta 'ave a bit a roundness by now like any good man."

Colin screwed up his face as he went back to his chair and grabbed a fresh cup of tea. "Perish the thought. But what I'd really like to know is why you agreed with my earlier assessment of rotten things at the Arnifours'?"

She leaned over and carefully brushed off the settee where Michael had been before she sat down and slid her well-worn slippers from her swollen feet. "I 'ear things. Everybody says the son's a drunk, the daughter's a harpy, and the ol' lady's been flauntin' about with 'er stable man fer years. She got no use fer that 'usband a 'ers." She shook her head. "But who can blame 'er? I 'eard that Earl was 'avin' it off with some chippy. A woman never cheats first, ya know. It ain't in our nature."

"I'm sure we could disprove that without much effort," Colin said. "The most perfunctory peek into just about any titled family would garner us a host of women every bit as lascivious as their male counterparts."

She waved him off. "Ya don't know shite about women." She stood up and wriggled her toes a moment before stooping to pick up her slippers. "There's a difference between lyin' and cheatin'. Women are better liars than men—which is why we don't think a cheatin' first. It's nature's way a creatin' balance." She padded across the room, her slippers swinging at her side. "Now I'm gonna go soak me feet. Some of us don't spend 'alf the day on our arses." And with that final bit of truth she trundled out the door and down the stairs.

"Sometimes it's hard for me to believe she raised you from boyhood. What *was* your father thinking?"

"I'm afraid I didn't give him much choice. I suppose I was a bit hardheaded back then." He laughed.

"Back then?!" I laughed.

"Well, you must admit, given the amount of gossip she picks up we almost could've stayed home the other day and learned as much about the Arnifours as we did going all the way out there. Though I did learn a great deal poking about their barn."

"Did you? And is that what makes you so sure Victor is innocent?"

"I think Victor is innocent because he believes his son is guilty. And perhaps he is. I don't know yet. But the only thing Inspector Varcoe is going to succeed in doing is forcing Victor to confess to a crime he didn't commit in some misguided effort to save his boy. Which is precisely why Lady Arnifour hired us. She means for us to keep her dear Victor out of the hangman's noose."

"But if she suspects who did it, why wouldn't she just tell us and be done with it?"

"Why indeed?!" He toasted the air with his teacup, grinning at me from over its rim.

"So just what did you learn at that barn?"

"I gathered a few details of the attack by poking through its remnants. As Victor pointed out and I'm sure your nose assured by virtue of the residue of kerosene, that fire was deliberately set. I should think the only reason someone would purposefully burn down an old, seldom-used barn would be to hide something."

"Or perhaps to throw off the authorities. It could've been set for no other reason than as a diversion."

"That's true." He stroked his chin and snatched up his hunting knife and kerchief. "The only problem with that idea is that someone went to an extreme amount of trouble to make sure the barn burned all the way down to its barest bones. Think of it, our killer follows Elsbeth that night on his own horse. I'm certain of that given the second set of hooves left at the precise locations where both the Earl and Elsbeth were set upon. Which means this second person watched as Elsbeth met up with the Earl somewhere along the way, helped him up onto her horse, despite Lady Arnifour's insistence that he couldn't have done so, and then followed the two of them down to that barn."

"How can you be so sure the Earl was able to get up on her horse?"

"The same tracks." He stood up and went to the fireplace, his brow furrowed and his hands working madly on the sheen of the knife blade. "There were only *two* sets of horse prints evident near the barn. One set deeply imbedded in the earth—a horse bearing the weight of two riders—the other very much lighter. It was the second set, the lighter tracks, that I followed in order to discern the short distance the Earl was able to run before being struck down. The first blow came from atop that second horse. Once he'd fallen, the rider dismounted and delivered the mortal wound."

I swallowed hard, chilled in spite of the firelight dancing off the sides of my face. "And Elsbeth?"

"Also struck from above." He set the knife onto the mantel and gazed into the fire, his eyes gradually unfocusing as he stared at the gently licking tongues of flame. "But she'd gotten quite a bit farther by the time the killer turned his attentions on her. She was heading in a forty-five-degree angle away from the barn, back toward the woods. The killer remounted his horse, chased her down, and struck her full in the face."

"Good god . . ."

"Indeed. And then . . . ," a scowl crossed his face, twisting it with confusion, ". . . after all that, the killer went back to the barn, saturated it with kerosene, and set it ablaze. If he meant only to confuse the boorish inspector and his sycophants he could have tossed in a match and fled. It was old; it would have burned just fine. But that's *not* what he did. He took the time to deliberately soak that decrepit pile of timbers, so much so that nearly two weeks later it still *reeks* of kerosene. Why? It *has* to be more than sleight of hand. There has to be something we aren't supposed to find."

"But what? What if it *is* just a deception?"

He slid his eyes back to me. "That *is* the question then, isn't it?"

CHAPTER 10

We disembarked from a cab the next morning earlier than the sun could be expected to properly infiltrate the streets and alley-ways edging the tall, grimy brick buildings of Stepney Green. We'd set out from our flat at just after six thirty, which meant it couldn't be more than half past seven by the time we stepped onto the filthy cobbled street.

"Where do we go from here?" Colin asked, sidestepping some filth. "Wouldn't you think they could clean these streets once in a while," he added irritably.

"Spoken like a man who never comes to the East End." I chuckled. "It's over there." I pointed toward an alley distinguished by a soot-covered arch. "But we'll be lucky to find anyone willing to answer the door at this hour."

"The whole point . . . ," he explained, delicately picking his way, ". . . is to catch these fine citizens unprepared. Lying is so much more difficult when one is still suffering the scourges of the previous night."

"Certain we'll be confronted by lies then?"

"Absolutely."

"Then it's good to see you've learned something from my tenure here," I chided.

"Learned something?!" He scowled at me. "I saved your ass from this scourge."

"Yes," I said with all seriousness as I pulled up short. "You did." And so he had. At the moment when I was more bone than flesh. When opium's numbing embrace soothed me more utterly than air or water, relentlessly driving every moment of my day and night, he had quite suddenly been there. That fierce, striking boy from the Easling and Temple Senior Academy who I was sure had not known my name had indeed, inexplicably, saved my life.

I gestured to the dingy brick tenement building in front of us enshrouded in soot from its belching chimneys. "This is it." The entrance door was constructed of warped slabs of wood that appeared to have begun cracking long before Victoria took the throne, and was fouled with unimaginable matter. Distorted, yellowed windows dotted the face of the five-story structure, none without a spider's web of cracks.

"I don't believe for one minute," Colin said as we stared at the building, "that no one in this hovel saw or heard anything. The business of others is the prime entertainment here."

"Only until the sun has ambled off. Shall we?"

"After you." He waved me on. "But let us start with the landlady. I'm most eager to disrupt her day."

"You don't think we should see Michael first?"

"I'd much prefer to meet the proprietress of this fleapit. Call it a whim . . . call it morbid curiosity . . . but let's call on her first."

I pushed through the fouled remnants of the door with the cuff of my sleeve and stepped into a musty hallway that was redolent with the scent of stale opium. It struck me like a blow to the face, beguiling my senses with a promise I had long thought relegated to a distant past. I must have faltered, because I felt Colin's hand grip my arm and heard him whisper, "You all right?"

"I'm fine."

"You don't have to do this," he said as I plodded forward. "I can speak to her myself."

"I'm fine," I said with greater determination as much to convince myself as him. I would not let that fiend manipulate me again. It could have no effect. I'd come too far, been through too much, to be lured by that beast anymore. So I turned my attention to the two dimly lit lamps and the thread-bare carpet worn through to the under-planking in places as I kept moving forward. I banished the fact that the walls were stained yellow with age and opium smoke from my mind as I stepped to the first door I came to, noticing that it was standing the slightest bit ajar due to the bow along its spine that left it gaping at its outermost corners, and announced, "This has to be it," though, in truth, I was only guessing.

"Good," he said, staring at me a hair's breadth too long before adding, "Then let's have at it." He stepped forward and pounded on the door with a bellowed, "*Hellooooo!...*" like some busybody neighbor come to call.

An instantaneous response blasted back in a shrill tone that sounded like a cat who'd just had its tail crushed under a boot. " 'Oo in *'ell?!*... Oo in the *bloody* 'ell... ?!"

I slid my eyes to Colin and found him wearing a dazzling smile of great joy. This, I realized, was exactly what he'd been hoping for.

The door jerked open as far as its accompanying chain would allow and a bloodshot eye presented itself in the space. "Oh!... A minute, love...." The door clicked shut as best it could and the chain was hurriedly released before it was

thrown wide to reveal a thin woman of indeterminate age—
though I guessed her to be somewhere in her mid-thirties like
me. She was tightly wrapped in a thin yellow robe that revealed
more of her anatomy than was proper. "Didn't know I 'ad such
a 'andsome gentleman calling." She leered, batting her eyes a
moment before spotting me. "This with you?" she asked half-
heartedly.

"Quite."

"Well, ya can both come in," she stepped aside, "but I ain't
one a those that plays it like that. I can take right care a you,"
she winked at Colin as he moved past her, "but yer friend is
gonna 'ave ta go upstairs."

"Particular, are you?" I snorted as I crossed her threshold,
glad to find the air inside her flat freer of the cloying scent of
opium. "You don't see that often around here."

"What would you know about what goes on around 'ere?"
she sneered as she yanked her precarious robe closed. Her
pockmarked face spoke of years of disease and poor health,
which instantly made me regret that I'd been so cavalier.

Colin gave her a warm smile, but there was little real mirth
behind his eyes. "What we're *really* here for . . . ," he began, casually perching on the arm of one of the proffered seats as he
dug out his usual crown and started rotating it between his fingers, ". . . is some information about two of your tenants:
young Michael and his little sister, Angelyne."

" 'Oo?" Her face curled up as she poured two fingers of
whiskey and downed it like a gulp of air.

"A boy of about fourteen and his sister . . ." He flicked his
eyes to me.

"Twelve," I said.

"Right. Twelve. They rent a room from you. Live in your
basement. . . ."

"Oh. Them two," she said with about as much enthusiasm

as she'd shown me. "They're always late with me rent." She downed another shot and actually looked a little better for it. "You 'ere ta make good for 'em?"

"Well . . . ," he tossed me a quick glance, "we might be able to offer a little help. They owe you, do they?"

"Damn right they do. One pound fifty."

Colin urged me with the look in his eyes and I begrudgingly handed over the money, all but certain that they didn't owe her a thing. She snatched the bills and stuffed them down the front of her robe. "What do you wanna know about 'em?" she said as she threw herself onto a well-worn chaise, sending a stream of undergarments and periodicals to the floor. "That Michael can be a stand-up lad when 'e ain't scammin' the rent."

"And Angelyne?" Colin pressed.

" 'Oo?"

"His sister . . ."

"Oh . . . 'er . . . She's about the size a me arm and as bright as me left tit."

"Is she comely?" he pressed on.

"Oh!" She abruptly pushed herself up, allowing her robe to peek open again. "You like the young ones then, eh? The little girls?"

Colin froze, the crown stilled on the back of his hand. "The only thing I would like is to know whether you consider Angelyne pretty."

"Pretty . . . not pretty . . . 'oo can really say?" She giggled. "There's somethin' fer everyone in this world. There are men 'oo will shag anythin', breathin' or not."

"Have any of your clients asked about her recently?"

"I don't know." She shrugged. "I can't 'member everythin' goes on round 'ere."

"But you remember who pays and who doesn't," I pointed out.

" 'Ell yeah."

"And I'll bet you remember when someone asks for something unusual. Something you can't satisfy . . ."

"There's a lot a nutters." She looked right at me.

"And is the request for a twelve-year-old not something out of the ordinary?" Colin pressed.

She shrugged noncommittally.

"Miss Rendell—"

"Mademoiselle!" she snapped back. "It's French."

"My apologies. I didn't realize that Rendell was a French name."

She scowled at him and then abruptly bolted off the chaise and stormed across the room, pushing past me to yank open the door. "I've 'ad enough a this. I don't get paid fer sittin' round talkin'. Now get yer arses outta 'ere."

Colin tossed the crown into the air and easily caught it, Mademoiselle Rendell's eyes locked on it the entire time. "As you wish," he said tightly as we made our retreat back to the hallway. He turned at the threshold, eager to have the last word, but he had no such chance, as she immediately slammed the door in our faces. "What a deplorable woman," he muttered to the battered wooden door. "Though thankfully an atrocious liar."

"That's the truth." I nodded. "It's a wonder she can be convincing with the blokes she entertains."

"Well, they can't be a discerning lot." He gave me a lopsided grin as he glanced at the dilapidated stairs that led down and let out a sigh. "You still okay?"

"I'm fine," I said for the third time since our arrival even as I was struck anew by that ubiquitous scent. "Don't ask me again." But as I followed him down to the basement, I became increasingly aware of the familiar lure at the back of my brain, whispering . . . beckoning me . . . promising to distill every concern . . . and suddenly I wasn't so certain anymore.

CHAPTER 11

Just as we were sitting down to a lunch of Mrs. Behmoth's lamb stew there was a knock on our door that proved to be a messenger dispatched by Lady Arnifour, enquiring whether we would be available to meet with her daughter, Kaylin, in an hour's time. The timing was ideal, as we had decided that I would go back to Stepney Green in the late afternoon while Colin participated in his final elimination match of the current wrestling championships—a title he was determined to maintain for the third straight year. It suited me fine since I knew I could move about that area of the city more expeditiously without him in tow and, beyond that, I'm not much of a fan of his brawling, even if he does insist it's all good sport.

We indulged in our stew and the accompanying biscuits with due haste before setting ourselves to preparations for the arrival of our guest. I tidied up the study, which consisted of straightening up my clutter of writing papers and dispatching the wayward pieces of Colin's pistol and knife collection back to their display cabinet, while Mrs. Behmoth put on a kettle and mixed up a batch of currant scones. For his part, Colin was tasked with stoking the fire back to life, which he dispatched forthwith before seizing his dumbbells and hoisting them about in myriad ways. In no time at all we were awaiting the arrival of Kaylin Arnifour to the rich, buttery smell of Mrs. Behmoth's scones baking beneath our feet.

I found myself brought back to thoughts of Mademoiselle Rendell, who was about as French as blood pudding, and her insistence that she knew nothing about Angelyne's disappearance when it was clear she was far craftier than she was letting on. Which was the very reason I was to return there in a few hours' time. What she would not tell could be discerned in other ways.

Michael had told us nothing new and it had been disturbing to see the way in which he and his sister were forced to live. Their single room was less than half the size of our study and contained neither a fireplace nor radiator with which to heat it in even the most perfunctory way. The plaster on the walls teemed with hairline cracks and great chunks of it were missing altogether. Two pallets lay on the floor for the children to sleep on and there was a single battered chair and equally sorrowful table upon which sat the room's only candle. It made for a depressing tableau in the sunlight and I only hoped it might somehow look better by the flickering glow of that one fatty taper. The sight of it all had left Colin quite maudlin while I had found myself grateful for ever having escaped, though the verity that I had come to be there of my own regrettable volition left me ashamed all over again. I was gratified that Colin had not raised that spectre again on our way home.

A sudden knock at our door shook me from my prickly contemplation.

"I'll get it!" Mrs. Behmoth hollered as her slippers slapped against the wood foyer.

"Outstanding." He chuckled as he set the dumbbells aside and pulled his jacket on. "She does have everything to do with the man I am today, you know."

"Yes, but I do try to forgive her."

He laughed as the sound of her plodding up the stairs brought us to our feet. A moment later she appeared on the landing with a slight young woman at her side. "Kaylin Arnifour," she announced with her usual lack of enthusiasm.

"Lady Kaylin . . ." Colin smiled broadly as he moved to the landing and took the young woman's hand, ushering her inside. "We do so appreciate your thoughtfulness in indulging us this meeting in the midst of such a difficult time. We would certainly not have requested it if we didn't feel it to be of the utmost importance. Please"—he beckoned her to the settee—"we were just about to have some tea. I insist you join Mr. Pruitt and me."

I stepped forward to greet her and got my first good look at her. She instantly put me in mind of how her mother must have appeared as a young woman. Delicate and trim with a jumble of light brown curls cascading down her back, she was quite striking. She also displayed a hint of color in her crystalline complexion, and given her lithe, muscular arms revealed just below the puffy sleeves of her dress, I determined they spoke of her fondness for riding. They also gave her a more substantive air than her slender build initially suggested. While she and Eldon were clearly crafted from the same physical mold, he had none of his sister's gravitas.

Mrs. Behmoth gave a disapproving sniff as she turned to leave the room, though what she was objecting to I had no idea. "I'll fetch the tea," she said as she thundered back down the stairs, giving me momentary pause as to how she managed to maintain her girth given the number of times she assaulted those steps each day.

"I must apologize for being so difficult to reach," Lady

Kaylin said, thankfully setting my mind back to the task at hand. She settled onto the settee across from us. "I really haven't felt much like talking."

"Understandable, and we shall not press you any further than we must."

"You mustn't worry about me," she said, folding her hands across her lap as though girding herself.

Mrs. Behmoth plodded back up with the tea service in hand but got no farther than the doorway before Colin relieved her of it, sending her on her way. He meticulously served us and did not speak again until we had all settled in. "I must ask you to tell me what you remember about the night your father and cousin were attacked."

"Of course." She delicately placed her cup on its saucer and set them back on the table between us. "I'm sure you've heard this all before," she said, giving a disquieted smile. "We were having dinner: my parents, Eldon, Elsbeth, and I, and I had to excuse myself partway through the meal as I was not feeling well. I suffer from headaches that can be quite disabling. After a while Elsbeth came up to check on me and see if I might be able to go for a ride while there was still some sun left, but I was no better and could not." She fell silent for a moment, staring down at her hands. "I've wondered every day since if things might have been different if I had been able to go with her."

"You mustn't," I said.

"It is not for us to change what is," Colin added.

"Of course . . . ," she muttered, but did not sound the least convinced. "I fell asleep as soon as she left my room and did not wake again until I heard Eldon hollering about smoke at the edge of the property. It was terrifying. I hurried downstairs and saw him and the Heffernans riding out, and waited with Mother for their return. Victor was the first to come back. He was the one who told us. . . ." Her voice trailed off.

"Had there been any visitors to the house that day?"

"Father's business partner, Warren Vandemier, had spent part of the afternoon going over books or ledgers or some such thing with him, and a neighbor, Abigail Roynton, had stopped by and had tea with Mother."

I could tell at once by the way she said Abigail Roynton's name that there had to be a bit of bad blood there. I was certain Colin caught it as well, but he did not prod her, choosing instead to shift the conversation to the nature of the business her father had with Mr. Vandemier.

"I'm sorry . . . ," she twisted her hands in her lap, "but I wasn't really privy to my father's business dealings. I'm sure you're acquainted with those who say business matters are best left to men."

"Ahhh . . ." Colin grinned. "Are you one of Emmeline Pankhurst's followers?"

She smiled. "Well, I would hardly cuff myself to the gates of Buckingham, but I do think she has some wonderful ideas."

"She has certainly caught people's attention. Does your mother share your views?"

"Oh heavens no."

"What about your neighbor, Abigail something, I don't recollect what you said her name was."

"Abigail Roynton," she scoffed without apology. "She's a widow who saw fit to have an affair with my father some time ago, and if my mother had any sense she wouldn't let that wretched woman in her house."

Colin peered at Kaylin, his expression in check, while I fought to keep the surprise from my face. "Are you certain your mother knew?"

Kaylin nodded. "At the very *least* she suspected. But she would never admit such a thing. It wouldn't be proper. So instead, she and Mrs. Roynton maintain this reprehensible charade."

"Civility," Colin tsked. "If nothing else you have to admire our higher class for their civility. Is there no chance you could be mistaken?"

She shook her head. "I found them in the barn once, the two of them disheveled and full of bluster. It was a disgrace. I knew what they were up to."

"How long ago did that happen?" Colin forged on.

"About a year ago, I suppose. I really don't remember. But he ended it after that. He swore to me that he ended it."

"Of course." Colin flashed a tight smile.

"I believed him, Mr. Pendragon. My father was many things, but he was not a liar."

"I'm afraid that by its very definition an adulterer *is* a liar. You cannot be one and not the other."

"I'm sure your father meant what he told you," I interrupted, shooting Colin a look that I hoped would divert him.

"Yes . . . well . . . I must ask you to indulge me one last question," he said as he tossed a scowl back at me.

"Of course."

"Do you agree with your mother's assertion that the Heffernans are innocent?"

She paled and gave a small shrug. "I really don't know."

"Then you believe it is possible that one or both of them could be involved?"

She shifted on the settee and brushed a quick hand through the curls on one side of her face. " 'Possible' is a word without limitation," she finally answered.

CHAPTER 12

The afternoon was ebbing toward twilight as I tucked myself into an entranceway across the alley from where Michael and Angelyne lived, fixing my gaze on the flat where Mademoiselle Rendell plied her trade. Standing in the waning light with an old, black cloak wrapped around my shoulders, I felt like a fourteen-year-old boy again, once more in the questionable employ of Maw Heikens. This time sent out to lure another clutch of imprudent sots with more cash than cares, or to fetch another batch of opium from the old Chinese man at the wharf from which I always cleaved a nip off the top for myself, or perhaps to troll the local taverns to earn my keep with whatever I could pilfer. The memory of it all made my stomach sour as though I had licked the very cobbles in the street. For it was too easy to blame Maw for the things I had done, what I had become. But the truth was darker than that. She had merely provided what I sought without judgment or question. Colin was wrong about her, not entirely, of course, but wrong. There was much that remained solely on me.

A cold wind teased my face and ruffled my hair as it brushed past me. The wind had picked up slightly and the chill along with it as I began to ask myself how long I was going to stand here like this. I knew Colin would expect me to wait all night if need be, but then he was in a warm gymnasium proving his bravado against any number of comers.

Another great sigh escaped my lips just as the light from Mademoiselle Rendell's room abruptly snuffed out, ratcheting up my heartbeat in the same instant. Something, at last, was going to happen. I sank back into the alcove as far as I could and waited for the appearance of my quarry. It did not take long. The main door quickly opened, revealing my target in a billowy cream-colored dress that had likely been white the day it came out of the dressmaker's shop, adorned with a ragged strip of gray lace around its bottom. A dark brown shawl covered her mass of dyed-blond hair. She was, I decided from the look of her, attempting to travel incognito. It was a hopeful sign.

The ersatz mademoiselle glanced in one direction and then the other before venturing down the handful of steps to the cobbled alley. She did not cast an eye in my direction and I knew the moment she made it to the street there would be little chance of her realizing she was being followed. There were too many people, horses, and carts about for her to notice me trundling along behind her, and besides that, I am not without some skill.

The mass of activity on the street made it easy for me to keep Mademoiselle Rendell in sight as I dallied along behind her. She kept to the center of the roadway, dodging the streams of burbling waste flowing through the gutters with assurance and a fair amount of speed. She held her gaze down as much for defense against the filth as to dissuade anyone she passed from trying to engage her. There was no doubt in my mind now that she was doing her best to get somewhere quickly and without distraction.

She rounded the corner and snatched a look in my direction, bringing me up short as I pretended to engage a woman who was passing beside me. I let the distance between us widen as I pulled a cap from my pocket and plopped it on my head before turning the collar of my cloak up. If need be, I could turn my cloak inside out to reveal a light gray color as opposed to the black I was now swaddled in, but it was not yet necessary, as she once again hurried down the street. Innumerable blocks slid by before I began to notice how vastly improved the neighborhood was becoming. We'd left behind the effluvium of Stepney Green for a far more gentrified area. Even the throngs of scurrying people had noticeably thinned, with fewer of them walking and more being trundled about in carriages and cabs, notable of gentility.

It wasn't until I noticed the divergent flags above the porticos of one building after another that I realized we had entered Embassy Row. That explained the lack of foot traffic that had forced me to gradually drop farther back from my prey. This area of the city was well patrolled and offered almost nothing in the way of diversion, neither shops, cafés, nor any but the most occasional pub. It meant to be uninviting, this domain of diplomats.

Mademoiselle Rendell continued hurrying along the street, paying me little mind as I forced myself to fall back yet again. I couldn't imagine what we were doing here, as it was too early for her evening's work to have begun. I began to fear she was on to me, that she'd spotted me some time ago and was taking me on a circuitous route to nowhere, when she abruptly grabbed an old, unmarked door and ducked inside.

With trepidation I approached the door I thought she'd used, willing my heart to stay steady. There were no markings to allow me to determine just what sort of establishment it was, which left my options few. Either I had to forge ahead and stumble into this unknown or I could slink back home and admit to Colin that I had failed. Neither option appealed to me, but I certainly wasn't about to let Colin down.

I girded my breath and leaned forward, gently nudging the door a sliver to give me a chance to try peering inside before making the final commitment. It took several moments for my eyes to finally be able to discern that I was staring into one of the more distinctive pubs I'd ever seen. The floor and booths were carved from great planks of dark oak, with the bar itself rent from a slab of honey-colored burl set off by etched-glass cabinets running along the wall behind. It was a small establishment with only a handful of booths and an equal number of freestanding tables, leaving most of the seating to wind around that spectacular bar.

I flipped my cloak inside out and threw it over my arm before stepping inside and coaxing the door closed. The only light emanated from a few gas lamps dangling from the ceiling. A picture of Nicholas Romanov hung over the bar, though he had yet to be coronated, and two small flags with the double-headed eagle hung from the ceiling, making it evident to whom this pub intended to cater.

I spotted Mademoiselle Rendell at once curled up in a booth near the back with a dark, bearded man. She seemed well in the throes of a rampant flirtation and it made me fear that all my efforts had been for naught. The nearer of her hands was already settled on the man's leg and her other was flitting about like a hummingbird in search of nectar.

Once again I sucked in a quick breath and steeled myself before moving to a barstool just beyond Mademoiselle and her mark. I ordered a stout and laid my cloak across my lap, turning sideways so I could better listen in on the conversation happening between the two of them. What I expected to hear I cannot say, but between the throaty giggles, playful slaps, and whispered innuendos I heard nothing less than the most blatant form of seduction.

"Yer makin' me 'eart pound like a race 'orse," she purred at one point. "Care ta feel?"

"I fear ze cost of such an act," her companion snorted, his accent thick and guttural, definitely a Slavic tongue but certainly not Russian, which surprised me given the bar's obvious allegiance.

"This one's on me," she parried back.

"Ve are done here," he answered, obviously not tempted by the course of her prodding. "I leaf this veekend. You know vhere to find me if you have reason; udderwise I vill consider our vork finished until I return."

"And when will that be?" she whined, all pretense of seduction dropped with the haste of a flicked ember.

"Zix months . . . eight months . . . I dun't know." I watched him reach out and take her arm, carefully removing her hand from his leg. "You vill hear from me." He pushed himself out of the booth and gave a curt nod.

"I ain't 'appy 'bout this," she called, but it was too late, as the man had already made his way out the door.

For a minute I considered following her companion rather than staying here to watch what she might do next, but then another man approached her table and quickly slid in beside her. Given that it was she whom I was here to shadow I decided to stay put, though I committed the hairy Slavic man to memory, as I was certain their business dealings were nefarious at best. At least then, if I did return to our flat with little more than tales of her flirtations I would do so having been successful in the intent of my purpose.

I casually nursed my stout and feigned a look of boredom

and inapproachability so as not to be sidetracked by someone who might want to spill his every thought onto the first fool who looked like he was alone. My frustration quickly mounted, however, as I could hear little of the conversation with Mademoiselle and her new companion. If I had any hope of learning anything further I was going to have to find a way to twist around to see what the two of them were up to. I only hoped I would not turn to find them glaring at me.

Shoving my cloak onto the seat beside me, I slumped against the bar and peered around with what I thought was extraordinary restraint, only to find Mademoiselle Rendell slowly sinking beneath her table. A table that held no cloth atop it. Instantly it became apparent to anyone who cared just exactly what she was up to, so it was hardly surprising when I felt a great rush of air barrel past me as the establishment's owner brusquely moved in to save the reputation of his pub.

"Get out from under there!" he growled. "I'll not have such goings-on in me pub!"

"For a quid ya can be part a the goin's-on," the unperturbed mademoiselle snorted from below.

"Piss off!" her companion snapped. "You're ruinin' me stiffy."

"*I will not have this!*" the man thundered, pounding a meaty fist onto the table's top.

"*Bugger!*" Mademoiselle Rendell bellowed as she came scuttling out. "Ya 'bout broke me bleedin' eardrums, ya shite."

"*Get out!*" he bellowed. And although the proprietor was no taller than the diminutive mademoiselle herself, he shook with such rage that neither she nor her burlier companion seemed willing to press him any further.

The two of them made their way out, the rest of the patrons holding their collective breath until the door swung shut behind them. Only then did the general murmuring start again, although this time with a renewed sense of vigor. I cursed myself for not having followed the Slavic man out. Surely her business with him had been more apropos than what I'd stayed here to witness. We were making scant headway on either of our cases and each day their trails were becoming fainter.

CHAPTER 13

$\Longrightarrow\!\!\circ\!\!\Longleftarrow$

My failure to gain much information about Mademoiselle Rendell was tempered by the fact that Colin had won not only the wrestling tournament for his age group, but also the exhibition round against a man nearly fifteen years his junior. He gave me the glowing details before finally settling in and agreeing that the Slavic man was likely to prove a man of interest. Thereafter he left me on my own for the remainder of the evening while he retreated to the bath.

We had little interaction the next day as well and I knew he had withdrawn into his thoughts in an effort to ferret out the next best step. I'd suggested that perhaps I should try to find the Slavic man, but he'd dismissed the idea for the moment, and so it was that we were in our study late that afternoon; me reading while Colin paced relentlessly, incessantly disassembling and reassembling his new Nagant revolver, when there came a sudden and frantic pounding at our door. Colin spun away from the fireplace so quickly that the cylinder of the Nagant he'd been fussing over was launched from his hand in great cartwheels before coming to land across the room.

"Damn . . . ," he cursed as he hurried after it. "If that got bent . . . ," he threatened rhetorically. I watched him give it a quick inspection as he went to the window and peered outside. "It's the Arnifours' buckboard," he announced. "Has to be one of the Heffernans. Nathaniel most likely. Victor would never have the audacity to pound on anyone's door like that."

"I wonder why he's here?"

"We shall know soon enough," he said as he wrapped the pieces of the revolver into his handkerchief and laid them on the mantel.

The sound of two sets of shoes mounting the stairs drifted up as Colin took his seat next to me. A moment later he was proven correct when Mrs. Behmoth ushered Nathaniel Heffernan into the room.

"Nathaniel 'efferead ta see ya."

"*Nan . . . ,*" he corrected sourly. "Heffer*nan.*"

"If ya like." She shrugged and made her exit.

"I take it," Colin stood up, "that you bring news?"

"I do." He stared at Colin blandly and said, "It's Miss Elsbeth." And at once I feared the worst. "They're saying she's begun ta come round." There was little inflection in his voice.

"Extraordinary!" Colin popped out of his chair. "You must be anxious to get back and see how she's doing."

Nathaniel did not answer at once, and I wondered if he was trying to gauge whether there was any accusation in Colin's words. "Is there any message ya want me ta take back?" he finally said.

"No message . . ." Colin slid a glance to me and then looked back at Nathaniel. "What I'd really like you to take back is us." He didn't even wait for a response before he bolted down the hallway toward our bedroom.

"What?"

"We're going with you, boy," he called back. "Make yourself comfortable while we put a few things together, because this time we'll be staying. We shan't be but a minute or two."

"You will excuse me." I stood up and gave what I feared was a pained smile, as surprised as our guest by this unexpected turn of events.

I hurried to the bedroom and found Colin rooting through the top drawer of the dresser. "Prepare to spend a night or two," he said as he flung undergarments onto the bed. "If she's coming around I'll not come back until we've had the chance to speak with her. I don't trust that house of rogues."

"House of rogues?!" I chuckled as I pulled a valise from under the bed. "Now you sound like Mrs. Behmoth."

"You're forgetting that someone there would almost certainly prefer to see her dead, and at this point it's rather impossible to tell who might be her friend and who her foe." He tossed me an arch look as he withdrew a small double-barreled derringer from the dresser.

"You're bringing a gun?"

"I'd bring three if I could get you to carry one."

I screwed up my face, the memory of once having had a derringer prodded against my ribs during a soured opium transaction causing me to shiver. Even that had not led me to forsake the drug, which is why I suppose the memory retains its ability to provoke such a reaction from me. "Don't you think you're overreacting?" I tried my best to sound glib. "It's the estate of nobles. They're not all beyond redemption."

"And are you prepared to decide who is and who is not?" He eyed me as he stuffed the little gun into his boot. "Who is it you find trustworthy?"

"What about Lady Arnifour? She hired us after all."

He waved a dismissive hand as he went over to the holster hanging from the headboard on his side of the bed. "I'd bet she hasn't given a whit about her husband since she conceived their daughter, and they were both probably well plied with alcohol at the time. The only person our dear patroness seems to even remotely care about is Victor Heffernan, and even that impression is probably hysterically generous."

"Well, you have to admit that he seems kind and loyal."

"A dog is kind and loyal," he grunted. He pulled a Colt revolver from the holster and stuffed it into his waistband, yanking his overcoat closed atop it. "Of course her husband was clearly a scurrilous man who had more dalliances with other women than his own wife. But then that is what those chaps do."

"Your father didn't."

He leveled a frown on me. "The Pendragons are a cut above. Besides, my mother died too young. He didn't have the chance. Are you ready?" He headed for the door.

"Ready?! I've hardly begun. And all you've done is throw a few things on the bed and litter yourself with guns. I'd say you're not ready, either."

He shrugged. "I've got what I want. Throw in whatever else you think I might need."

"Fine."

I heard him beckon from the front of the flat as I stuffed the last few things into the valise and tucked it under my arm. "On my way!"

It would be nice to come back to this room and have the worst of this case behind us or even solved. My eyes raked over Colin's empty holster and I felt that familiar knot clutch at my stomach. How I hoped we would return with his guns unneeded. I turned down the lamp on the dresser and headed out.

CHAPTER 14

The evening was cold enough to make the ride in the open buckboard uncomfortable. Even so, Colin appeared oblivious to the wind's chilling fingers as they sliced across the exposed flesh of his face. The fire in his eyes seemed to be heating the whole of his body so that he wasn't even bothering with the scarf Mrs. Behmoth had pressed on him on our way out. In contrast, I was well wrapped in mine and noticed Nathaniel repeatedly yanking his collar closed. Given the potential turn in this case there was little wonder Colin felt so impervious.

As we pulled through the gates, catching a glimpse of the house on the ridge ahead, I was struck by how different everything looked under the cloak of night. The trees appeared menacing as they bent overhead like a sepulchral army of skeletal soldiers, their great withered arms only fleetingly allowing a sliver of moon to peek through. Then, quite suddenly, they gave way to a field of tall grass. Yet even that otherwise sanguine field stretched far off into a forbidding, black oblivion on either side of the driveway even as it seemed to threaten to press in on the house at any moment. I forced my attentions to the house and found that even *it* could not manage to suffuse any aura of warmth or invitation. With its darkened wings like atrophied limbs it looked like life had long ago vacated its vast corridors. Only its center section glowed with any light at all, and that sporadically, leaving the impression that those who remained here were slowly losing their battle against the shadows closing in around them.

Nathaniel guided the buckboard to a halt at the center of the crescent drive and Colin immediately leapt out and attacked the stone steps two at a time, seizing the door knocker with his usual relish. He was clearly not suffering any trepidation.

"Well, bless our unholy rolling empire." Eldon Arnifour stood at the threshold with a dopey grin and a tumbler. "Just look at what the night creatures have heaved onto our doorstep."

"Mr. Pendragon!" Lady Arnifour's voice cut in from somewhere behind her well-oiled son. "I've been praying you would come soon. Go on, Eldon, make room for our guests, for pity's sake."

Eldon stiffened at the sound of her voice, his grin transforming into something closer to a grimace. Nevertheless, he followed his mother's command and stepped aside, bowing and sweeping an arm across his body with all the formality one might use to usher a revered guest into an otherwise humble dwelling.

"I'm sorry it took us as long as it did," Colin said, entering without so much as the flick of an eyebrow toward Eldon. "It is a miracle indeed that your niece is showing signs of recuperation. We may soon have a quick end to this most horrendous crime."

"I'll drink to that." Eldon smirked. "Care to join me?"

"*That will be all!*" Lady Arnifour snapped as she descended the stairs in the foyer.

He tossed her a withering glare. "Just trying to be charitable."

"You've been charitable enough with yourself all afternoon. I would say you've had enough for one night."

"Is the thought of your cousin awakening driving you to drink?" Colin asked with a feinted grin.

"Oh, Mr. Pendragon, your inference cuts me to the bone."

"I meant to infer nothing."

"I'm afraid my son needs no particular reason to overindulge."

"Spoken like the driving force she is."

"That's quite enough." She turned on her son. "I would suggest you retire for the night."

Eldon's face pinched into a contemptuous scowl. "Fine." He turned and headed for the study. "I'll do that just as soon as I've had a nightcap . . . or two. . . ." He paused in the doorway and glanced back. "Assuming such a repast does not make me a suspect for murder." And with that he slammed the study's door so fiercely that Lady Arnifour winced as though her body had absorbed the injustice accorded the doorjamb.

"Some people really shouldn't drink," Colin muttered.

I stopped myself from chuckling and, when I noticed Lady Arnifour's shoulders gently rise and fall with a wearied sigh, knew it was time to focus on the business at hand. "How long ago did you notice Elsbeth beginning to come round?" I asked her.

"A couple of hours." She turned abruptly and headed back to the marble staircase. "The man on duty heard groaning and ran to get Mrs. O'Keefe. She was the first one to check on her."

"Has she opened her eyes?"

"No." She led us up the sweeping stairway. "The poor dear must be in terrible pain. I sent Mr. Heffernan to notify the doctor and he sent him back with an elixir of Belladonna to ensure she sleeps through the night. He's promised to come first thing in the morning."

"Have you given her any?" Colin asked.

"We haven't needed to."

"Good. There's little chance she'll gain consciousness with a bellyful of *that* in her. I'm anxious to speak with her before your doctor sends her into any sort of medicated slumber."

"But she mustn't be allowed to suffer," I reminded.

"Of course not." He shot me a sideways glance that encouraged me to contain myself. "Her well-being is paramount, which is why we mustn't forget that she alone holds the key to what happened at that barn, so until she's able to speak with us, her life remains in grave danger."

"It's all too horrible." Lady Arnifour sagged. "How someone could want to cause that poor girl harm."

"Not just harm," Colin corrected. "It's about self-preservation now, which can be a most powerful inducement."

"Well, there's no one in this household who would wish such a thing."

"No? . . ." Colin said that single word in such a pointed way that Lady Arnifour missed the top step and lurched precariously forward before he stabbed an arm out and steadied her. She took a moment to collect herself, but none of us made any further comment.

The man posted outside Elsbeth's door barely glanced at us from his tipped-back chair, head thrown back, legs akimbo, arms folded neatly across his chest. He wasn't asleep—yet—but it was easy to see it would only be a matter of time. As soon as everyone in the house settled in for the night, he could almost certainly be counted on to join the ranks of the dreaming. Another fine example of Inspector Varcoe's crack staff.

Lady Arnifour swept past him as dismissively as he deserved, most likely having arrived at the same conclusion. Yet he could still be counted a deterrent just by virtue of being there, for it was less likely anyone would try to strike against Elsbeth with him planted outside her door, whether fully awake or not.

The three of us crept into the room as though we might disturb her slumber. Mrs. O'Keefe was seated by the bed crocheting what looked to be a large coverlet. It billowed across her lap and cascaded to the floor in a tumult that surrounded her for three feet around. She looked as if she were on the verge of cocooning herself inside its very profusion and I wondered if that might not be part of what she meant to do.

"Anything?" Lady Arnifour whispered as we pressed near the bed.

"No, ma'am." She immediately began gathering the blanket in great folds, tossing it over one arm with the practiced hand of someone who has done it many times before. "She moans and flinches every now and then, but that's all."

"Thank you."

"You needn't thank me, ma'am. You know how I feel about Miss Elsbeth." She aimed her sentence at Colin and me, and I thought her sentiment heavy-handed. Just who was she trying to convince? She moved across the room, drawing the train of knitting as she went, and gently pulled the door shut behind her. It was the only delicate thing I would ever see her do.

"How do you think she looks?" Lady Arnifour cast an anxious glance at me, remembering, I was sure, Colin's reference about my passing knowledge of medicine. I thought it a good thing she didn't know it was actually nothing more than survival skills garnered while in the East End. Nevertheless, I leaned in close to Elsbeth to get a better look. There seemed little change in the few days since we'd last seen her. The swelling of her face had only marginally receded and the bruises around her eyes and cheeks had deepened to the blue-black of thunderheads from an impending storm. There was some improvement in her breathing, however. It was less labored and no longer contained the rattle that so often signals the last struggles of a soul to tear itself free of its body.

"I do believe she is a bit better," I announced, though I did not dare go further. I reached out and touched her forehead, and was stunned to find her exceedingly hot. I knew it to be the sign of a battle against infection raging within, but before I could reach for the basin of water at her bedside she flinched slightly and muttered something as thin as her breath. It was all Colin needed. He wrenched me aside and bent so far over her that his ear nearly grazed her lips.

"What . . ." It was Lady Arnifour's turn to plow through me. "Can you make out what she's saying?"

Colin's brow furrowed as he patiently hovered a hair's breadth above her, but there was nothing else. I suspected her sudden outburst had been due more to the feeling of my cool hand on her burning face than any desire to reveal information, but decided to keep my peace.

"No," he lamented as he stood up. "But I can assure you that we shall be spending the night here tonight and the next one after that if need be. We will protect this young woman as if she were our own, and should she truly awaken at any time, you will be the first person we send for." His brow furrowed as he turned to look at Lady Arnifour. "I trust my determination to stay at her bedside will not in any way impugn your finer sensibilities."

Lady Arnifour's hand fluttered up to her neck. "Of course not . . . whatever you think best, Mr. Pendragon. The room next door is empty and I shall have Mrs. O'Keefe prepare it at once in case either of you should require some rest. I'm sure you will find it suitable."

"You are most thoughtful." He smiled. "And let us hope we will have the answers we seek by morning."

"For the sake of your niece," I hastily added.

"That would be such a blessing." She sighed heavily and I knew she held little hope. "Very well then," she said after a moment. "I shall leave you be."

As soon as she closed the door again I turned to Colin. "I really don't think she's going to be waking up and telling us any stories tonight."

He yawned as he pulled Mrs. O'Keefe's chair closer to the bed. "I'm sure you're right, but I don't mind if the rest of the household thinks it possible."

"One thing we have to do is get her fever down. Dunk your handkerchief in the basin of water and apply it to her forehead. As soon as it becomes warm rinse it out and do it again. That alone should help her to feel better."

"Then perhaps she will be able to surprise us tonight."

"I hope so." I stifled a yawn. "Do you really think Lady Arnifour knows who did this?"

He glanced at me. "She may not have proof," he said, his sapphire eyes crackling with the surety of his words, "but I'm certain she's suspicious of someone. It's the only reason she's hired us with such conviction to prove the innocence of her dear Victor. If she had any doubts, if she wondered at all, we wouldn't be here now."

"It's all very disturbing, made ever more so by the fact that we're here to protect Elsbeth."

He nodded. "We are here to protect her as we tighten the noose. With a little bit of well-placed pressure we shall see who cracks about the seams first."

"You mean to incite the perpetrator to action again, don't you?"

He patted his waistband where his revolver was hidden. "I'm prepared for whatever may come."

"I hope so. We both know that desperation can be a tragic motivator."

"That it can," he said as he unbuttoned his jacket. "Now go get some sleep so you can spell me in a few hours."

I yawned again and went back to the hallway to find the room we'd been promised, and as I passed Inspector Varcoe's nameless sentry I was incensed to find him with his head lolled fully back, a tiny thread of drool spinning down from one corner of his slackened jaw. He looked as comatose as Elsbeth, so I nicked the side of his chair as I strode past. His head snapped forward and he bolted up with a snort, batting his eyes furiously to chase the tendrils of sleep away. He glanced at me as he dragged a sleeve across his wet chin.

"Sorry," I muttered without a shred of regret.

He shrugged me off with a scowl, but at least Colin's first line of defense was back in operation.

I headed down the hall and nearly collided with Mrs. O'Keefe as she came barreling out of the next room. She was cradling a wad of linens under one arm and nursing an expression of marked exasperation. "Oh," she grumbled as she pulled up short. "That room is ready for the two of you."

"Thank you."

She stared at me but said nothing more before turning and moving down the hall in the opposite direction.

"She's a bloody sow, that one," a male voice piped up behind me, and for a moment I thought it was the sentry outside Elsbeth's door. As I turned, Eldon stepped out from the shadows, a sneer alight on his face. "Can I tempt you with a nightcap?"

My instincts demanded I give a polite refusal, yet curiosity overruled my brain as I considered that I just might be able to learn something useful. Eldon was the only one in the household whom we hadn't had a chance to speak with alone. I was tempted by the prospect of being able to coax some information from him. I held my tongue and allowed him to lead me back down to the library.

"What will you have?" he asked as he circled the wood-paneled bar in the far corner of the room.

"Whatever you're having," I replied flippantly, as I had no intention of drinking anyway. I'd already eyed a plant near my chair to surreptitiously "water."

"I'm drinking scotch with a whisper of soda."

"That'll be fine, though I will ask you to lean my drink in the opposite direction. A bit of a lightweight, I'm afraid." I chuckled.

"Oh I could give you some lessons." He winked at me as he came around the bar and handed me my drink. "It's really all about tolerance. The more you drink the more you can tolerate." He clinked our glasses with a laugh. "So tell me . . . ," he said as he settled into a chair across from me. "How long have you and the prestigious Mr. Pendragon been saving the world from itself?"

"About twelve years." I took the thinnest sip of my drink and wondered if the smarmy expression on Eldon's face ever gave way to anything even remotely resembling warmth.

"Twelve years?!" He shook his head with that same smirk. "Then you must know all the secrets."

"Know them, and have written them down."

"Intoxicating . . . ," he sneered with a laugh. "Perhaps we'll all get a read one day. . . ."

"Perhaps," I gave him a coy smile, "but what about you? What secrets might you be hiding?"

He held up his glass. "I'm afraid my secret is poorly kept."

"Well, I would hardly call a preference for spirits to be the stuff of secrets. Now murder . . ."

"Oh!" He wagged a finger at me as he snickered, "Aren't you the wily one."

"Has your sister returned yet?"

"Kaylin?"

"You have others?"

He snorted delightedly. "My darling sister is due home by week's end. Have you met her yet?"

"We have."

"I'm sure you found her charming." He stood up and meandered back behind the bar. "But let me assure you that she can be a right tyrannical little bitch when she wants."

"I'll try to remember that."

"I'm sure she was on her best behavior," he scoffed, foregoing the subterfuge of soda as he refilled his glass. "The Arnifour progeny can be such a mixed bag. But I'll bet you've noticed that."

"Is this about secrets again?"

He came back around with his glass and pulled his chair so close to mine that our knees were nearly touching when he sat down again. The stale smell of scotch radiated from him like putrefaction from a corpse. "You're a clever one, aren't you? I will tell you this: You get my sister started on that women's suffrage bollocks and you'll find her every bit the rabid dog the rest of us are. She and that ridiculous pack of man-eaters she insists on idolizing have the temerity to advocate that women are the equal of men. Can you imagine?" He bellowed a great, sloppy laugh. "If you ask me, that Pankhurst twat should be hauled home by her disgraceful husband and chained to her washbasin."

"You do know our sovereign is a woman—"

"How very puckish, Mr. Pruitt. No wonder your Mr. Pendragon likes having you around." He lifted his glass and took a drink, all the while keeping his eyes leveled on me. "I do find you intriguing," he said as he lowered his tumbler. "Do I intrigue you?"

"Everyone in this household fascinates me."

His grin widened. "Outstanding. I love being a suspect."

"Then why are you always so well oiled when we're around? Seems like you might be finding it all a bit too much."

"Now you're just being boorish." He stood up and wandered over to the fireplace with a pout, allowing me to finally tip part of my drink into the nearby plant. "Do you want to know what I think about my father's murder?" He turned around and glared at me and I could see that I had finally pressed through his artifice.

"More than anything else." I toasted him with my half-empty glass.

"And I thought it was my company," he sneered before laughing and toasting me back. "Here's the thing, Mr. Pruitt: My father didn't have any enemies. Underachievers seldom have enemies." He tossed back part of his drink. "Don't misunderstand—my father was a good man in his own way: reliable, knew his place, that sort of rot, but I'm convinced his life goal was no greater than to marry into money. After he did that there really wasn't much else for him to do but sire a few offspring and twaddle about in a bit of business here and there."

"What sorts of businesses?"

"He ran a stud farm for a while, but couldn't make a go of it. My mother made him divest it when he hadn't turned a profit in eighteen months." He shook his head and chuckled. "She's a bloody corker, that one. But who can blame her? It was her money. My father would've been better off if he'd just rented out his own services," he snorted lecherously. "That became evident when he put some money into a West End production. Turned out he was giving more to the leading lady and most of the chorus than financial backing. Such prowess is a curse of the Arnifour men." He leveled his eyes on me and smirked as he tipped his glass back again. "You can just imagine my dear mother's dismay . . . or perhaps relief. Needless to say she put an end to that business as well."

"What about your father's last business partner, Warren Vandemier?"

"Warren Vandemier?" He leaned against the fireplace mantel as though giving it some real thought before abruptly snapping his eyes back to mine and growling, "Warren Vandemier is a weasel!"

"A weasel?! And what sort of business were they engaged in?"

"Opium."

"Opium . . . ," I repeated like a fool, sucking in a quick

breath even as my stomach curdled. "No one's mentioned that before."

Eldon laughed out loud, too long and too hard. "My parents spent the greater part of their marriage staying out of one another's way." He came back around and stopped right in front of me, staring down at me. "Tell me the truth, Mr. Pruitt: My mother didn't hire you to find my father's killer, did she? She only hired you to prove that Victor's innocent, isn't that right?" And to my amazement the look on his face was every bit as lucid as my own.

"I'm sure I don't remember the exact details of what she said at our first meeting," I replied, unwilling to give him that win.

"A selective memory." He snickered. "I'm sure many of your clients have appreciated that quality."

"I'm sure they have." I returned a terse smile. "But tell me, how did your father get himself caught up in the opium trade?"

"Caught up?!" He laughed. "You make it sound like my father was an innocent, and I can assure you he was not. My father went through a great deal of my mother's money on countless schemes over the years, which is why this place and its pathetic staff look the way they do. That was my father's contribution. You should've heard the rows my parents had over the years. Is it any wonder my sister and I remain unattached?"

"And the opium?" I pushed again, trying to keep this feckless man in a singular direction even as I grappled with the spectre of my old nemesis.

"A pretty shrewd opportunity for the old bastard to earn some of the fortune back, I suppose." He sauntered back over to the bar. "It was the money. That's what drove my father. He'd hand over a pile of it if he thought he could get a bigger one in return. Refill?"

"No. What about his latest business? Was it widely known?"

"He had little to do with the details. It was all very neat, very upper-class. Would you expect anything less of the Arni-fours?"

"And your mother?"

"That old sack of bones knows exactly what she wants to know. Don't let her bluster fool you. She certainly knew about Abigail Roynton."

"You're referring to the rumor of an affair?"

"Rumor?! That's priceless." He came back over to me and sat down, his voice thick with sarcasm. "Father was a bore at discretion."

To my surprise Eldon did not seem to see the irony in his statement. "So what *are* your thoughts on this case then? You say your father had no enemies and yet he was involved in the opium trade. That is most certainly a dangerous business. In which direction do *you* think the perpetrator lies?"

He stared at his tumbler as though peering into a fortune-teller's ball, his mood darkening as his eyebrows slowly knit to-gether. "My mother," he finally muttered. "She hired some cretin to bludgeon my father's skull. My cousin . . ." He gave a dismissive shrug. ". . . An unfortunate casualty, I suppose. The price of war." His lips curled down and then he suddenly turned and threw his glass into the fireplace, sending the flames roaring back to life. "God help that vile bitch."

CHAPTER 15

Night had permeated every living thing by the time I found myself inexplicably standing by the blackened bones of the barn at the far end of the Arnifour estate. I was tired, exhausted really, and couldn't even remember why I'd dragged myself all the way down to this miserable spot at such an hour. The wind had picked up and was whistling around with such force that it stung my face. I tried to recall what lunacy had compelled me down here even as I gradually became aware of the lathered snorting of a horse being ridden hard from somewhere over my left shoulder—from the woods.

I realized at once that Colin must have discovered me missing and sent one of the Heffernans to fetch me back, and yet, as the thundering sound drew ever closer, I began to feel, though I cannot say how, that the unseen presence bearing down upon me was not an ally. I looked around just as the rider cleared the dense underbrush from atop a great midnight stallion, his face hidden within the dark recesses of a hooded cloak that billowed behind him like the snapping tongue of Satan himself.

The stallion reared up and bolted toward me, its powerful

haunches gleaming in the moonlight with the sweat of its effort as it carried its spectral rider relentlessly forward. I turned to run, straining to suck in gulps of air as I tried to reach the relative sanctuary of a nearby stand of bushes. Even so, I could smell the horse's hot grassy breath quickly closing the gap. *This is it!* my mind screeched.

I opened my mouth to holler into the vast night before I could be struck by the blow I knew was coming even though no one would hear me.

And then it came.

Not to my head as I'd been so sure that it would, but to my shoulder. And as I struggled to twist around I jarred myself so abruptly that my eyelids flew open and I lurched up from the bed I'd been lying on to find myself staring into the blasé face of the sentry who'd been posted outside Elsbeth's door.

"Mr. Pendragon sent me ta fetch you," the guard mumbled. "It's past midnight. I think he means ta switch."

"Of course." I pushed myself fully up and mopped my brow with my sleeve, grateful to see the man heading out of the room without further comment. It would be good to stay awake for a while.

I went to the basin and splashed water on my face and quickly ran my wet fingers through my hair. As I passed the guard, already well situated in his chair with his legs akimbo and his head threatening to bob back, I grunted a hasty thank-you.

"The cavalry's here," I announced with much false bravado as I let myself into Elsbeth's room to find Colin alert at her bedside, a shiny crown spinning effortlessly between the fingers of his right hand.

"So it is." He stood up and stretched. "And none too soon. This is dreadfully dull duty."

"Has she stirred at all?"

"Not even a whimper since I got her fever down. Did you have a good rest?" I told him about my conversation with

Eldon, how the Earl was invested in the opium trade, and the young man's thoughts about his parents and sister. "Well done." He grinned. "Though this case grows more complicated by the day. The opium trade . . ." He let his voice trail off.

"We've time to talk about that later. Get some rest."

"Yes . . . ," he yawned as he shuffled toward the door. "Be vigilant, my love."

"You needn't worry," I said. "I shall be fine."

The door clicked gently as he left, making me suddenly feel very much alone in spite of poor Elsbeth. I settled into the overstuffed chair and reached across to feel her forehead, and was relieved to find it cool to the touch. A sigh escaped my lips as I folded my arms across my chest and leaned my head back, preparing for the hours that lay ahead. My eyes were drawn to the sweep hand of the bedside clock as it bounced off the demarcated hash marks by the light of the flickering oil lamp. In no time at all I could feel my eyelids beginning to droop. Before I could push myself back upright to mount the good fight, I had already lost. The night's seductive caresses crept in upon my mind, releasing my alertness with the vague shadings of mirage, only this time the illusions were even more cunning, for I found myself sitting in Elsbeth's room staring at a shadowy vision. There was a man on the opposite side of the bed leaning far over Elsbeth. All I could tell was that he was tall and slender and had dark hair, which was plainly evident since I was staring at the crown of his head.

I wanted to cry out, to find my voice and startle this apparition, but as so often happens in dreams, try as I might, nothing would come. I seemed destined to sit there in my delusory slumber while this faceless man finished the horrific job he had started. But as I sat there in my panicked catatonia, the most remarkable thing happened; for the first time that I can recall I was able to bear down to the bottom of my being and produce a stifled sort of yelp. It came out rather otherworldly, like the final strangled squeal of some fallen mythical beast. Which led to the second most remarkable thing; the man abruptly jerked his head up and in the wavering light of the single oil lamp I could see the spectral face of Nathaniel Heffernan.

He looked stricken; clearly as stunned as I was to hear my garbled cry, and quickly rose and rushed for the door. I leapt to my feet before my head could register what was happening and had to seize the back of the chair to keep from toppling over. In that moment I realized that I had *not* been dreaming. I *had* seen Nathaniel.

I lunged after him, my mind swimming nonsensically, but was forced to come to a quick halt when I reached the darkened hallway. He was nowhere. Because of my carelessness, he was already gone. I glared at Inspector Varcoe's guard; the man was snoring as peacefully as a contented mutt. Infuriated with him and myself I kicked at the side of his wooden chair and sent him, and it, rattling to the floor.

"Nathaniel Heffernan was just here!" I bellowed, ignoring the fact that he might realize I'd also been dozing. "A ruddy fat lot of good you were."

"I'm . . . I'm sorry. . . ." He scrambled up and righted his chair, sliding back into it sheepishly. "Is she all right?"

She . . . Elsbeth . . . I hadn't even looked at her.

I flushed with renewed fury as I hurried back to her bedside. I don't know if I noticed the stillness of the covers pulled across her chest first, or the fact that the rhythm of her breathing was no longer evident. Whichever the case, the outcome was the same.

"Get Colin!" I howled. *"Get Mr. Pendragon now!"*

CHAPTER 16

Time, although admittedly rigid, sometimes feels as though it has a multiplicity of variances depending upon a given situation. For instance, when a moment is joyous and filled with laughter it seems to dash by like a dizzying streak of wind. Conversely, when an event is stout with boredom it appears to pass with the lumbering grace of a beached walrus. Worst of all, however, are the occasions of dread when time insists on dragging its unwilling participant irrevocably closer to the consequence against which nothing can be done. This last scenario is precisely where I found myself as I waited in the study for Colin to gather the household. I felt at turns adrift, condemned, and tortured, and always with that same insidious sense of regret and failure.

Eldon was pacing in front of the fire he'd prodded to life in a blue-and-white-striped nightshirt, his hair askew, but for once without an attendant drink in his hand. Lady Arnifour was seated across from me, her full-length robe pulled tight at the collar and a mask of white cream glued to her face with a cap yanked fully down over her hair. Mrs. O'Keefe, as always, had come no farther than the door, having taken a seat just inside the room while clutching her old flannel robe tightly about herself. She wore no facial unguent like her mistress, so there was nothing to soften the sour expression that seemed to be her constant companion regardless of the time.

Victor Heffernan was the last to arrive and was slumped on a stool on the far side of the fireplace wearing a look that made me think he suspected that something unique to him was terribly wrong.

Colin had banished us all here but had yet to join us himself, although I couldn't figure out why. He'd said little to me after I'd confessed the truth other than to vanquish me to the study to wait for the others. As I glanced around at the others I wondered what they thought of being awakened and pulled from their beds at such an hour. If any of them feared that Elsbeth had awoken to name her attacker, I couldn't see it on their faces.

When it began to feel like Colin might never come back, time playing its nasty tricks again, he finally strode into the room with the ease and serenity of a man arriving at a midday luncheon. "I do apologize for this unfortunate timing," he said, "but I've some bad news and I thought it best for you all to hear it at once."

"Where's Nathaniel?" Victor bolted up. "Why isn't he here?"

"Nathaniel is missing," he answered. "And I'm afraid Elsbeth has died."

Lady Arnifour gasped and let out a sob.

"It wasn't Nathaniel," Victor stammered, casting his eyes about the room with desperation. "You can't tell me you think Nathaniel had anything to do with it."

"Of course he thinks it," Eldon sneered. "Don't be an ass."

"My boy's innocent!" Victor shouted even as he sagged against the fireplace mantel.

"I haven't accused your son of anything." Colin spoke calmly. "It's too soon to make any presumptions. We will have to wait until the inspector's man returns with the coroner."

I caught a glimpse of Mrs. O'Keefe from the corner of my eye and saw that she'd gone quite ashen, her eyes red with tears.

"Surely, Mr. Pendragon," Eldon forged on, "a man of your renown can connect two such obvious events in a straight line? I cannot imagine why my mother would be paying you were that not the case."

"Stop it!" Lady Arnifour howled as she struggled to regain her composure.

"Come now, Mother." Eldon's face flushed red. "Surely even you can see the correlation. Elsbeth's dead and Nathaniel's gone missing. Now if that pompous ass you hired and his trained monkey aren't willing to venture a presumption of the obvious then I should think they're no better than those ridiculous twits from Scotland Yard."

"Eldon," she hissed, this time in a low, flat tone.

But Eldon was not to be silenced. "I'm beginning to wonder if we can even accept Mr. Pendragon's word of Elsbeth's demise? Perhaps he's too recklessly—"

"*Enough!*" she bellowed, bolting to her feet as she snatched up a small marble ashtray and heaved it at her son's head. Time played its trick one last time as the leaden object careened toward Eldon, missing him by a fraction before imploding into the mirror above the mantel. The sound of its strike was deafening, not because of its volume, but because of the ferocity and intent with which it had been hurled. The tinkling of a thousand tiny shards of glass punctuated that fury as they rained down to the floor.

Eldon recoiled, as he was surely meant to. And when the last of the fragments settled to the ground I became aware that Mrs. O'Keefe was gone. The door to the kitchen was left swinging to and fro in a silent arc as though marking the retreat of some ghostly aberration that had gone unnoticed by this roomful of hysterics.

"I am sure, Mr. Pendragon . . . ," Lady Arnifour's voice was raw and taut, ". . . that you will be able to see to the authorities without my help."

"Of course." He nodded. "We shall take care of everything. You must try to get some rest."

She did not acknowledge his words but kept her eyes fixed on the doorway as though getting out of the room were the only thing that mattered. I glanced at Victor and thought he looked on the verge of going after her, but before he could seem to make up his mind she had already whisked herself out of the room as suddenly as her housekeeper had. He stared after her a moment, the slump of his shoulders signifying his distress, and then he too made for the door without so much as a word to the rest of us. There was nothing he could say, yet I feared his silence hinted at his own doubts about Nathaniel.

"She tried to kill me!" Eldon growled as soon as Victor was gone. "She bloody well tried to kill me!"

"You *can* be trying . . . ," Colin tossed off as he fished a perennial crown out of his pocket and blithely rolled it around his fingers.

"She's the devil's slag," Eldon carried on shrilly. "All she ever did was piss on Father. You'd have thought she'd earned her inheritance herself the way she carried on."

"Did your parents often argue about money?"

"Look around, Mr. Pendragon. She makes us live like we're on our last pound. But don't be deceived. She's got plenty. She simply prefers to dole it out. Gives her control and keeps us under her wretched, hateful thumb." He stalked back to the bar.

"But what about your father's business dealings?" I spoke up. "I thought you said your father squandered a great deal of your mother's money?"

"A man has to do *something*," he shot back, pouring himself another glass. "I'm done in. I've nothing more to say. And the only thing I want to hear from you is that you're going to throw that old shrew behind bars. She's the one who's really capable of murder," he seethed as he turned and stormed out of the room.

Colin heaved a burdened sigh and sat down next to me, the coin still sliding effortlessly betwixt his fingers. Long shadows, too numerous for the oil lamps to allay, were cast against the walls in a flickering tableau. "What do you make of all of this?"

I shook my head. "It's all very sad. There's enough vitriol here to suspect all of them and I don't even think we've heard the worst of it."

"I'm afraid I agree."

My voice hitched as I turned to him. "I'm so sorry I let you down tonight."

"Let me down?" He stilled the coin as he looked at me. "You never let me down, my love."

"It's my fault Nathaniel was able to sneak into Elsbeth's room. I fell asleep. I gave him the opportunity to . . ." I couldn't even finish the thought.

"To what? Watch her die? Because I'm quite certain that's all he did. Elsbeth died without anyone's assistance tonight. You only had to look at her to see that she was neither smothered nor strangled. You'll see when the coroner arrives."

"But . . ." And then I realized he was right. I hadn't even looked at her. I hadn't checked for the bluish hue of smothering or the telltale marks of strangulation on her neck. It had never even occurred to me since I'd been so intent on my own culpability. "Really?!"

He squeezed my hand as he offered a sad smile.

"Then why did Nathaniel run off?"

He shook his head. "Why indeed?"

CHAPTER 17

"As you can see, we're in the embassy district," I said as though Colin hadn't already figured that out for himself. We were headed down the side street where I'd followed Mademoiselle Rendell days earlier. It was all familiar, if markedly drearier, in the early afternoon sun.

"To be more precise," he pointed out, "these would be the embassies of the Austro-Hungarian nations. The Austrians, Hungarians, Bulgarians, Romanians, Bohemians, Moravians, Silesians, and Galicians are all here. And if I'm not mistaken"—and we both knew he wouldn't be—"the Russians are here as well."

"All right then." I yanked open the plain wooden door behind which sprawled the dark, elegant pub I'd followed Mademoiselle Rendell into. "Let's see which of those countries you see represented here."

"Amazing . . . ," he muttered as he took in the lavish interior. We seated ourselves at the long bar and Colin ran an appreciative finger along the magnificent wood. "I've never seen a singular piece of burl this large before," he marveled. "And given the little flags with the double-headed eagles hanging from the ceiling and the photograph of Nicholas Romanov, I would say the place is Russian, very Russian."

"Very good." I grinned. "Keen eye for the obvious. But you were the only one who realized what happened with Elsbeth last night. Even Victor looked mortified for Nathaniel, but you knew he hadn't done anything."

"Still," he shrugged, "it was nice to have the coroner confirm it."

I shook my head. "You knew."

He shrugged again and ordered us a couple of ales before spinning around on his barstool. "So which was the booth our mademoiselle set herself to work in?"

"To your left. The one near the back."

"Vaguely discreet." He snickered. "Is the barkeep the same?"

I glanced at the hairy, round-faced man pouring our drinks. "I don't think so, but he looked like that."

"And the man she met here—the foreign gentleman you insist was not Russian—is he here?"

"No."

"And tell me again why you're so certain he wasn't Russian?"

"You know this. . . ."

"Remind me."

"Back at Easling and Temple . . . ," I prodded, "I knew a lad who was from St. Petersburg. His father was an advisor to Czar Alexander."

"Ah yes . . . ," he said with more enthusiasm than was necessary, and I knew he was ribbing me. "There were a lot of Russian boys attending the academy back then. What was the boy's name?"

"I don't remember," I lied, refusing to play along with his game.

"Wasn't it something like Grigorii Yuspenovich?"

I scowled at him. "Lucky guess."

He laughed. "Well, you were only fourteen and hadn't met me yet. You had nothing to compare him to."

"I knew who you were. Everyone at Easling and Temple knew who you were. Ever the golden boy, smart . . . star wrestler . . . aloof . . ."

"Please. You'll make me blush."

"As if that were possible."

He chuckled before abruptly turning and calling out to the barkeep, *"Excuse me. . . ."*

As the burly man sauntered over to us I wondered what Colin was up to. "It appears my glass has something in it beyond the ale I ordered. While that may be sufficient for your regular clientele, it is most assuredly *not* sufficient for me. Might I get a glass that's been washed since Her Majesty's coronation?"

The man's face curled sourly as he seized the glass, his bushy eyebrows furrowing into one long, seething caterpillar. "I dun't see anyt'ing!" he snapped.

"Then perhaps I might suggest you consider a consultation with one of our fine British ophthalmologists?"

The man's eyes narrowed to black beads as he glowered at Colin. "You t'ink you're funny?"

"All I want is a decent ale in a clean glass. You wouldn't serve this to one of your diplomats if you could get one of them in here," he scoffed.

"De ambassador's staff comes here all de time." The man leaned into Colin's face. "And ve serve many staff from France and Austria and Hungary and all over the empire, so . . . ," and without another word he picked up Colin's glass and tossed it into the sink behind the bar, ". . . ve don't need you. You may leaf."

"Well . . ." Colin stood up. "It would seem that someone is always getting tossed out of this place. Must be ruddy hell on the bottom line."

"Ve have plenty business."

"So you say." He stood up. "What do we owe you? Maybe you can hire someone to wash the dishes with our payment."

"*Out!*"

The door swung shut behind us and Colin snickered as he absently rubbed his chin. "Extraordinary."

"What's extraordinary is that you just riled that man up for fun," I said as I followed him back to the main thoroughfare. "Was that really necessary?"

"It wasn't for fun—I needed some information and figured that was the easiest way to get it from him. Surely you see that."

"What I see is that the only thing we learned is that they serve a lot of diplomats."

"Yes. But at least we have narrowed down our list to the Austro-Hungarian nations. Surely you would've recognized a French accent. . . ."

I frowned. "Of course. And I could have picked up an Austrian one as well."

"Well then, perhaps the man you overheard talking to our mademoiselle was Hungarian or Moravian." He peered at me. "Are you familiar with either of those?"

"No. And what makes you think the man she met has any correlation to a diplomat anyway?"

"Because even though Nicholas married Victoria's granddaughter, you know as well as I do that relations between our countries are acutely strained, and yet, here sits a most opulent czarist pub right in the midst of our city. I guarantee it's subsidized by their government and that it serves much more than just spirits. No doubt Russia's allies partake in those favors, which would include the Austro-Hungarian Empire."

"Maybe so, but you can't be sure any of it's related to the disappearance of Michael's sister."

"Not yet, but we'll know something shortly."

"We will?"

"Indeed. We're going to Her Majesty's Foreign Ministry Office." He turned and grinned at me, knowing I would abhor the implication.

I screwed up my face. "Must we?"

"It's time we find your Slavic man, and the only way to get information about the embassy staffs is through the Foreign Ministry Office."

"It could take us days to look through all the files for those countries. There'll be thousands of them. We don't have the time."

He looked at me with grim determination. "Unless you have a better idea . . ."

But I didn't, so within the hour I was stepping into the Foreign Ministry Office. It isn't that I have anything against our esteemed Minister Randolph Fitzherbert; he is an elegant, thoughtful, and intelligent man who has served our commonwealth admirably. Rather it is the effusive woman one must endure to procure a visit with Mr. Fitzherbert: one Adelaide Crouch.

Colin and I had barely crossed the threshold from the bustling hallway when the young woman leapt to her feet as though her chair had spontaneously combusted. With her hairpin curves and froth of blond hair piled atop her head she looked like a confection better suited to a bakeshop than a government office. She hustled around her desk with her eyes glued solely on Colin, wearing a smile that seemed about to cleave her head at any moment.

"Mr. Pendragon!" she squealed. "What a pleasure to see you." As she gripped his hands she slid her eyes to me and half-heartedly allowed, "Mr. Pruitt."

"Miss Crouch." I conjured up a small smile, but she'd already returned her gaze to Colin.

"Always a pleasure to see you as well, Miss Crouch," Colin said, leaning forward and kissing her lightly on each cheek, which sent her into a bray of twitters. He was incorrigible.

"Please, Mr. Pendragon." She batted her eyes at him even as a foolish grin spread across his face. "I keep telling you to call me Adelaide."

"But of course. Is Randolph in?"

"Stuck in Parliament, I'm afraid. I don't expect him in for the rest of the week. You know how those old Whigs can be." She chuckled.

"That I do. I've sat through enough of those sessions listening to my father. Dreadful. But tell me, might we impose upon you to show us a file or two in Randolph's absence? You know I wouldn't ask if it weren't important." He flashed his dimples again and I knew we were about to see just how intoxicating she really thought his charms to be.

"Well, I really shouldn't," she said as she smoothed the front of her dress in a nervous gesture that nevertheless managed to amplify her undeniable endowments. "What sorts of files are you looking for?"

"We could start with your personnel file, little one, so that I can write great good things about you."

"Mr. Pendragon..." She laughed and waved him off as I wondered how he came up with such inanities. "You're just playing with me."

"You must forgive me," I interrupted, afraid I would lose my lunch if I did not stop these two, "but time is of the essence here and we really are in great need to see the Minister's files on the Austro-Hungarian embassy staffs. Most specifically the Romanians, Bohemians, Moravians."

She flicked her gaze to me as her smile dropped. "Ever about business with you, isn't it, Mr. Pruitt. You really should learn to enjoy yourself like Mr. Pendragon." And her eyes once again sought his as another smile eased across her face.

"I'm afraid he is right." Colin sighed as though I had ruptured some delicate mood, and perhaps I had. "The spectre of reality always seems to rear its inexorable head."

"Well, no harm's been done," she said as she continued to stare into his eyes. "You know I understand. It must be such a burden to have harpies badgering you all the time."

Had Colin not been standing between Miss Crouch and me I would have seriously considered reaching out and backhanding her. But Colin *did* present bodily interference in that moment, and as my better nature kicked in I settled for giving him a sharp poke to the small of his back to signal the end of my tolerance.

"You give me too much credit." He chuckled, and I knew I had played into his ego, which only galled me more. "But I *am* in need of a gander through Randolph's embassy files for the Austro-Hungarian Empire. If we could start with the Hungarians? I promise I shan't remove a thing."

"It's going to take days, Mr. Pendragon."

I saw a flicker of concern flit across his face before he cracked a tight smile and said, "All the more time to spend in your company."

"Oh, Mr. Pendragon . . ." She smiled. "Well, I suppose it would be all right. I've never known the Minister to refuse you any request and I would never want to be the one to stand in your way." Her voice had suddenly developed a huskiness and I began to wonder whether I was missing something. "We keep the Hungarian and Austrian staffs up here, but the rest are down with the clerk." She finally disengaged herself from Colin and headed to the door of an attendant room filled with tall wooden filing cabinets.

"We won't need to see the Austrian staff, but I'm afraid we

likely need to look at the rest," he called as she disappeared from sight. *"Are you out of your mind?!"* He rounded on me in a harsh whisper. *"We need her cooperation. Would you please try to control yourself?!"*

"She called me a harpie," I shot back.

"Then stop acting like one."

My jaw dropped, but I managed to keep from uttering what had streaked across my mind as Miss Crouch returned with a great stack of files cradled in her arms.

"Here are the dossiers on the Hungarian staff." She heaved the pile onto a low table across the room. "If you'd like to see any complete files just let me know and I'll have Record Keeping pull them. It can take a day or two, but you know I'll do everything I can to get it expedited for you, Mr. Pendragon. I'll have to go and have the rest pulled for you. What order do you want them?"

Colin shrugged uncomfortably. "Alphabetically? Shall we say the Bohemian staff next? Perhaps we can sort through two countries a day?"

She smiled. "That will take quite some time."

"Yes . . ." And I noticed he didn't sound nearly as enamored as she did.

"I'll go and fetch the Bohemian files for you."

"I'll come with you," he piped up with renewed vigor. "You certainly can't be expected to haul those files around by yourself."

"So chivalrous, Mr. Pendragon," she said, and I knew I'd been set up. "And perhaps I could interest you in some tea while we're downstairs? It'll take a few minutes for the clerk to collect the dossiers anyway. . . ."

"A brilliant idea." He gave her a generous smile as he turned to me. "You know the man we're looking for. . . ." He didn't bother to say the rest; he didn't need to; he hadn't seen the man with Mademoiselle Rendell; only I had. No matter, I'd be happy to have the two of them away from me anyway. "I'll fetch you a cup."

"Oh no, Mr. Pendragon, you mustn't," Miss Crouch said with a distinct note of pleasure. "If anything were to spill on the files it would be the end of me. The Minister would be livid."

"Don't worry about me," I chirped a bit too merrily as I took a seat at the table.

I'd hardly gotten the words out before Miss Crouch inserted her arm through Colin's and ushered him toward the hall. "The café is right by the clerk's office," she purred. "They have the best nibbles there."

"I'll get you a nibble." Colin smirked at me. "You can eat it after we're done."

"No thank you. I don't need a thing. Please, just go." And with that Miss Crouch swept him out the door.

The vacuum left by their absence was refreshing even as I stared at the daunting task before me. I hoped I would recognize Mademoiselle Rendell's companion if I saw him. A handful of minutes at the back of a poorly lit pub were hardly the best of conditions under which to remember a face. Nevertheless, I flipped open the first folder and set to work.

The first photo showed a great bulbous-faced man with a dimpled chin and more hair sprouting from his ears than the top of his head. This, the attendant description stated, was the Hungarian ambassador's attaché, a career politician with more vowels in his name than consonants. It was not the man I'd seen huddled with Mademoiselle Rendell, and while I wasn't surprised by this immediate failure, I wondered why the fruits of a search are never borne out beneath the first leaf overturned.

I threw the file aside and plunged into the next few, saturating myself in a world filled with men named Bela, Adelbert, Fodor, Lasio, and Vilmos. None, however, proved to be my bearded target.

The work was proving as tedious as I'd feared, made worse by the fact that facial hair was obviously de rigueur for Hungarian men. It seemed the axiom was proving to be true that we all eventually begin to resemble one another based on our overwhelming desire to fit in. My spirits sank with the flip of each new tintype.

I glanced up at the clock and saw that an hour and a quarter had already passed. The Hungarian files before me were barely more than half-exhausted and I began to wonder where Colin and Miss Crouch had gotten to. A cup of tea and few triangles of bread with cucumber or watercress could hardly take more than a half hour or forty-five minutes to consume at the outside. And as for the Bohemian dossiers, Miss Crouch had said they would take a few minutes for the clerk to pull, not better than an hour. I only hoped she and Colin were having fun as I grudgingly flipped open the next file before me.

A sudden burst of high-pitched laughter turned my gaze to the hallway. It seemed the indolent duo was back. I glanced at the photo in front of me and found myself staring at yet another pair of deep-set, black eyes, this time belonging to a man with enough facial hair to resemble a bear. No details could be garnered on either the shape or depth of his face given its almost complete carpeting of fur.

"We have returned," Colin announced with high spirits, his arms cradling another huge load of files.

"Smashing," I groused as I flipped the folder shut.

"Have you had any luck?"

"No!" I snapped in spite of my efforts not to.

"Then I have good news for you." He beamed, his voice sparkling in defiance of my mood. "While the clerk was collecting the files from Bohemia, I had the most interesting conversation with him."

"Oh, it wasn't him," Miss Crouch fairly gushed. "You figured it out by yourself."

He gave her a quick smile before turning back to me. "The man is practically a historian. He looks like he's worked there for longer that I've been alive. He reminded me of the alliance between Russia and Bulgaria seventeen years ago."

"Bulgaria?"

"Forged by Czar Alexander the Third. Do you recollect your history lessons?" he prodded.

"I think I was otherwise occupied that semester," I drolled.

"He freed the Bulgarians from Turkish rule," Miss Crouch said. "Everybody knows that."

"Well, at least the clerk downstairs does." I smiled acerbically.

"When he said that it suddenly struck me that if we're looking for someone involved in illicit doings being run out of a Russian-backed pub, you can be sure the Russians would want to remain beyond reproach should the activity ever be discovered."

"So what's your point?"

"That's why the man you heard wasn't Russian. Deniability."

"Okay. So what does that have to do with the Bulgarians?"

"Bulgaria owes the Russians for their release after five hundred years of Turkish oppression. If the Russians are up to something, you can be sure they're funneling it through their most grateful ally. That man you heard wasn't Hungarian or Bohemian or Moravian. . . ." His grin stretched across his face.

"He's Bulgarian," I answered, finally understanding.

"We shouldn't have any more files to go through than these." He set the pile down in front of me, revealing the Bulgarian insignia on their cover.

We both began poring through the stack of files, Colin flicking them open and shoving them under my nose while Miss Crouch hummed at his shoulder when not leaning over him in a feigned attempt to be useful. More than twenty minutes elapsed in that way, fraying my nerves to the point of rupture, when I suddenly caught sight of the face we'd been searching for. Heavily bearded, darkly complected, black eyes set within a full, round face, he looked like so many of the men I'd been sifting through, yet there were distinct differences here. His nose was broad and flat and his forehead short, and I knew it was the man I'd seen in the booth with Mademoiselle Rendell.

I hoisted the photo into the air and practically shrieked that we'd found him. "Outstanding." Colin beamed, and for a moment I thought he might be about to hug me.

Only Miss Crouch looked disappointed.

"So what do we do now?" I asked.

"Let us learn all we can about . . . ," he leaned in over the file, ". . . Vitosha Harlacheva. I believe he'll be the person through whom we shall lure Miss Rendell."

"Who?" Miss Crouch asked with a note of displeasure in her voice.

"A woman caught in some nasty business," he muttered.

"How terrible," she said, but there was no fervor in her words.

"So you think this man has something to do with Angelyne's disappearance?"

"He's the first person she went to see after our visit. Mr. Harlacheva is the key. I'm certain of it. But right now . . . ," he looked over at me, ". . . we must pay a visit to the late Earl's partner, Warren Vandemier. If you're up to it."

"Of course I am," I answered too quickly.

"Good," he said, but his eyes hesitated a moment too long. "Because I suspect he has some information that will help. I'm not at all pleased with our progress on that account. Every day that goes by makes the trail colder, and I will not be stymied by that infuriating family."

"Why, Mr. Pendragon," Miss Crouch enthused, "are you investigating the murder of the Earl of Arnifour?"

"I'm not investigating it." He turned to her. "I am solving it."

CHAPTER 18

A light rain had begun to fall in direct opposition to my mood, which had begun to rise the moment we'd left the Foreign Ministry Office.

Once Colin had been able to study Mr. Harlacheva's slim dossier we had made a hasty exit, much to the disappointment of Miss Crouch, who was even further vexed to realize that we would not need to come back over the ensuing days, either.

I tugged the brim of my hat farther down over my forehead to keep the rain off my face while I waited for him to hail a cab. The inclement weather had succeeded in driving nearly everyone into a carriage and I began to wonder if we were going to have to walk. I was just beginning to resign myself to such a fate when Colin suddenly lunged into the street and seized the reins of a passing horse, tugging it to the side of the road.

" *'Ey!*" the driver bellowed from under his tiny awning. "Wot in the bloody 'ell do ya think yer doin'?"

"Official business!" Colin bellowed right back. "You will take us across town and you will do it quickly and safely."

"Like 'ell I will. Piss off. I'm done fer the day."

"You will take us where I say or you'll be done for good," Colin said as I grabbed the carriage's door and leapt in before he could get it moving again, and despite the withering look I received as I ducked inside, I was grateful to be out of the rain.

"It'll cost ya extra!" the man growled back at us.

Colin shoved in next to me and hollered back, "Move!"

Twenty-five minutes later we had gone all the way across town and were back in Whitechapel, a distance that should have taken us twice as long. Five minutes after that we were sitting before the well-cluttered desk in the tight, slovenly office of Warren Vandemier.

The late Earl's associate was a man of middle years, probably not more than a handful ahead of Colin, though harder looking in every way. Heavy lines creased his face into a perpetual frown that confirmed Warren Vandemier had led a difficult life. He was jowly, but not fat, though there was a noticeable bulge about his midsection. His brown hair was short and curly, with a liberal infusion of gray flecks along the crown of his face. To me he looked exceedingly tired, the weight of the existence he'd managed to scratch for himself having taken its toll in his rounded shoulders, hollow eyes, and leaden manner. Yet, when he spoke, he lit up with the passion of a much younger man, winking and gesturing with great animation. He seemed to come alive only when thusly engaged, for as soon as he shut his mouth his demeanor once again collapsed in on itself.

Mr. Vandemier's official occupation was property manager, the collector of rents for the noble gentry who did not dare venture down to the flophouses and sweatshops that comprised at least some of their financial holdings. But we were here about his unofficial trade.

"... and the Arnifours ... ," he'd been blathering on about inconsequential inanities from the moment we'd sat down, as evidenced by the crown sailing between Colin's fingers for the last several minutes, ". . . also had a fair bit of property at one time in this neighborhood." He smiled like an overzealous teacher who has no idea that his class is trading spitballs behind his back. "That's how the Earl and I became acquainted. I managed a few buildings for him. I'm the best there is, you see." He leaned forward and winked for what seemed the hundredth time. "I have a way with the scrubbier classes. I was born here. Right around the corner, in fact. My success is all my own." He leaned back in his chair with a satisfied grin, though it was a bit hard to decipher given the ruts creasing his face that begged to belie his good fortune.

"I'm sure your mother is proud," Colin muttered.

The man's brow caved in, an expression that seemed far more customary than his gregariousness, and then he broke out in a laugh that sounded as false as his prior gusto had been. "Very good, Mr. Pendragon. Perhaps I *have* pushed the point a bit far."

"Let me be honest, Mr. Vandemier—"

"I would expect nothing less."

And without even realizing it Warren Vandemier had handed Colin the freedom to proceed with the delicacy of a charging rhino.

"Very well." He flashed a tight smile as he quickly tipped his shiny silver crown back into his vest pocket. "Then we should like to dispense with this twaddle and hear about your opium business."

"Opium?!" The man's eyes popped so unnaturally wide that it looked as though a charge of lightning had ripped through him. *"Opium?!"* His voice squeaked again. He cleared his throat. "I'm afraid I have no idea what you're talking about."

"It's a narcotic, Mr. Vandemier. Derived from the poppy."

"I know *what* it is." He frowned, pushing himself to his feet in a great blustering display. "But I find your inference to be an offense."

"We are not fresh from the womb, Mr. Vandemier. Please do not suppose you can deceive us with your hackneyed indignation."

"You have no reason to accuse me," he blustered, but with less vigor.

And this time I knew it was my turn to speak up. "When I was a foolish lad," I said in as cavalier a tone as I could muster, "I lived for a time just around the corner on Limehouse. For room and board I did the bidding of a woman whose opium club was the most prominent in the city. So let me assure you that I can smell its residue in your hair and clothing, and given your heavy-lidded look, I would say that your last use of it was less than two hours ago."

"You worked for Maw Heikens?!"

"I did," I answered brusquely, aware of Colin's disapproving glare on the side of my face.

"Then you've got nothin' on me!" Vandemier snapped. "Room and board my ass."

"Look," Colin interrupted with evident distaste, "I really don't give a good bloody hell how you earn your living. I just want a few answers to some simple questions."

"Well, just because I run an opium club doesn't make me a murderer," he shot back.

"A murderer?" Colin glared at him. "Have I accused you of being a murderer?"

Mr. Vandemier narrowed his eyes as he glared at Colin. "I know why you're here. I know what you think."

"You know what I think?!" Colin replied, glancing at me with a smirk. "I'd bet my life that you don't."

"I had nothing to do with Samuel's death . . . or that whore niece of his, either."

"A man who's not afraid to have an opinion." Colin's smile disintegrated. "May I remind you that I've not accused you of

anything. We have only come here in search of some information."

"Well, there's nothing for you here. Samuel and I had our
disagreements over the years, but I sure as hell didn't want him
dead. Do you know that he owed me money? That old sod was
into me for a pretty pound."

"Was he . . . ?"

"Damn right he was! Seed money, Mr. Pendragon. We'd just
opened the club. The finest supplies, private rooms for the
wealthiest patrons, the most beautiful women to tend to a
client's every need. Better than anything Maw Heikens ever
did." He slid his eyes to me. "But that old witch Samuel was
married to kept her devil's eye on him. She refused him so
much as a farthing unless she knew exactly what he meant to do
with it. Which left *me* to put the money up *myself*. All of it. His
share *and* mine. Bastard swore he'd pay me back." He hawked
into a spittoon sitting on the floor by his desk. "I was a bleedin'
fool. I should've known Samuel would be as worthless as his
title."

"Then why did you go into business with him?" I asked.

He swung his exasperated expression in my direction, his
eyes squinting to near pinpoints. "I had no idea what a useless
turd he was until *after* I'd fronted him the money. Before that
he'd been throwing cash around like he grew it on his estate. It
was a sham. All he had was what that shrew wife doled out to
him. And all he did with *that* was chase whores. I don't believe
she really gives two shites who murdered him. Good riddance,
I say. But I sure as hell didn't do it." His narrowed eyes raked
our faces several times as if daring us to refute him before he
added, "And you can both bugger off if you think you're
gonna pin it on me."

"You must have an extraordinary alibi," Colin said.

"I was at the club same as I am every night. Plenty of people saw me. Plenty."

"Users?"

"What?"

"Are you asking me to accept the addled remembrances of addicts? That's your defense? I'm not sure what a magistrate would make of that."

"I've got nothin' to hide." He leaned forward eagerly. "Ask me anything."

And once again I saw the whisper of a sparkle in Colin's eyes. "How accommodating." He stroked his chin. "When was the last time you spoke to the Earl?"

"About a week before he got himself killed. He was supposed to bring me an overdue payment, but of course he showed up without so much as a blasted shilling. Had some slag in his carriage and a load of piffle about needing more time. I told him he had a fortnight or I'd damn well tell that harpy wife of his everything. Then he got himself killed. Anything ta toss me outta my money."

"Such disdain. Makes it hard to imagine why you persisted in your dealings with him."

"What was I supposed to do? You think a titled man comes along every day looking to get into the opium trade? I thought he'd be able to open doors for us. Get us noticed by a better class of people." He turned and assaulted the spittoon with something he'd hacked up. "Played me for a ruddy fool." He glared at us from beneath his furrowed brow. "I tell you what, I wish I *had* killed him. God bless the man who did."

"Touching," Colin muttered. "And why should we believe you didn't *hire* the man upon whom you are so happy to impart the good Lord's blessings?"

"He owed me money, Mr. Pendragon. Haven't I made that clear?!"

"Ah yes . . . money. So one of the mightiest motives for murder happens to be *your* saving grace."

Warren Vandemier rose to his full height and scowled fiercely down upon Colin's towhead. "This conversation is over!" he growled with as much menace as an opium user can muster. "I have nothing more to say to you."

"That may be," Colin stretched his legs out languorously, "but I am not finished with you, Mr. Vandemier. Now sit down, because you do *not* want me to stand up." He delivered his last sentence in an offhanded, playful sort of way, but I knew he meant it, and so did Mr. Vandemier, who gave a petulant *harrumph!* as he dropped back into his seat, folding his arms across his chest as if to demonstrate some measure of defiance.

"I will thank you to conclude this interview quickly!" he snapped. "I have work to do."

"Mr. Vandemier . . . ," I started to say, hoping to dispel a bit of tension.

"Sod off!" he barked at me. "I'll not be attacked by the likes of you."

"The likes of me?! I walked away from opium years ago. You're still an addict."

"An addict never walks away!" he growled back, inciting my deepest fear.

"You'd best watch yourself, Mr. Vandemier," Colin cut in, leaning forward and fixing his eyes on him. "I'll not tolerate you speaking to Mr. Pruitt like that."

Warren Vandemier rubbed his eyes with the heels of his hands and I knew he was in dire need of something to soothe his rattled countenance. Which meant that what was left of his resistance was likely on the verge of collapse. "May we please finish this?" he pleaded.

"If you can contain your theatrics then I'm sure we can be

done quickly. I only have a few more questions—for the moment."

"The moment?!" He looked positively apoplectic as he sagged in his chair. "Get on with it then. . . ." He made a rotating gesture with his hand as if that were going to have any impact.

Colin drew in a slow, languid breath. "Who was the woman you mentioned who accompanied the Earl the last night you saw him?"

"The woman? I have no idea. She didn't come up. You oughta ask Abigail Roynton. She'd probably know. She's the one he tossed over for the new one."

"Ah . . . ," Colin muttered. "We haven't had the pleasure of meeting the Arnifours' neighbor yet."

"She's somethin' else." He let out a low, wolfish laugh. "And I'm not just referring to Samuel, either."

"You aren't suggesting . . ."

"Oh, but I am. . . ." He leered at us.

"Eldon?"

"The prodigal son himself!" he sneered with great enthusiasm, seeming well pleased that Colin had followed his accusation. "The lovely widow is not known for being discerning. She'd probably even give *you* a go."

Colin leapt to his feet and seized the man by the lapels and yanked him nearly the full way across his desk. "You are a reprehensible little turd, Mr. Vandemier," he snarled within a hair's breadth of his face.

"I haven't told a single lie," his voice cracked.

Colin heaved him away and stepped back, allowing the flustered man to recoil slightly as he fussed with his clothes as though to reengage his dignity.

"A last question then, and I will caution you to remember your place. Why did you disparage the Earl's niece earlier?"

Mr. Vandemier took several mincing steps back in a clear attempt to avoid any further molestation. "She came to the club on several occasions, Mr. Pendragon, and not always under the tutelage of her uncle. And in spite of the pride I have for my business, I presume you will agree that it is not a place for a young girl of breeding."

"Elsbeth came to your opium den?!"

"More than once."

"And Eldon and Kaylin?"

"Eldon and his father rarely spoke. Samuel seemed to have little use for his son. As for Kaylin . . ." An uncomfortable look crossed his face. "Have you met her?"

Colin nodded.

"Then I should hardly think you'd need to ask the question."

"And why would that be?"

"Because the only reason Kaylin Arnifour would go to an opium club would be to liberate the whores and burn the place to the ground. Now please, Mr. Pendragon, are we finished here?"

Colin continued to glare into the man's fretful eyes. "For now, but you can be sure we'll be back to see your club within the week."

The man frowned and shook his head. "I don't like it."

"I don't care."

CHAPTER 19

W̲ere it not for Colin's pocket watch it would have been impossible to tell the hour by the time we finally took our leave
from Warren Vandemier's office. The rain had stopped for the
moment, but the temperature had dropped in tandem. With the
addition of saturated horse droppings, rotten produce, and as-
sorted other leavings littering the streets it was all I could do
not to cringe as I pulled my cloak tighter about myself. Even
still, it all smelled better than the residual of opium that had
hung about Warren Vandemier.

"We aren't more than fifteen minutes from Stepney Green . . . ,"
Colin said, flipping his own collar up. "Fancy a walk?"

"Well, I suppose," I answered. "So long as the rain holds out."

We came to a halt in front of Michael and Angelyne's walk-
up and all I could think about was going inside to get warm.
Even the stale residue of opium that assailed us as we entered
did not bother me. " 'Oo's there?" the familiar voice of Mademoiselle Rendell barreled out in response to Colin's knock.

"Mr. Pendragon and Mr. Pruitt."

There was a great sigh as a flurry of locks and bolts were unlatched before she abruptly halted and called out, "Talkin' don't pay me bills."

"This time it will."

"Two cost extra."

Colin leaned forward and placed his mouth close to the door. "Let us in and I shall make it worth your while. Persist in keeping this sorrowful rectangle of rotting wood between us and I'm afraid I shall have to tear it down and we'll converse for free."

"All right . . . all right . . ." Another dead bolt unseated as Mademoiselle Rendell finally yanked the door open. "We ain't all born to the colors, ya know."

"Whatever that means, I'm sure it's a good thing," he muttered.

I tried to ignore the scowl she leveled on me as I followed him inside. We remained on our feet awaiting an invitation to sit down, if such a space could be found, but none was forthcoming anyway. Instead she moved away from the door and said, "Wot?"

"May I?" Colin gestured at her well-worn divan still cluttered with all manner of papers and magazines.

"If ya must."

"Not feeling hospitable this evening?" He smirked as he shoved the mess to the end of the couch and sat down, motioning for me to do the same, which, grudgingly, I did. "We haven't come here to set you in a foul state. If you'd rather not be given the opportunity to respond to the statements of your Bulgarian friend . . ." He shifted a blank gaze to me.

"Vitosha Harlacheva," I filled in, wondering what he was up to.

"Yes. Mr. Harlacheva. We can just take his word."

" 'Oo?" Her stance remained unwavering, but her voice betrayed a hint of vacillation.

"He's one of the couriers for the Bulgarian attaché. Rather a broad-faced, bearded gentleman whom you met at the pub by the Russian embassy the other night. The one who informed you that your mutual business was finished for the foreseeable future."

"Toshy?" She blurted the name out as a furrow creased her brow. "And what did that shite say about me?"

"That you're blackmailing him," Colin replied.

"You're lyin'." She shook her head and laughed, but her eyes remained wary.

"Am I? Perhaps you'd like to come with us to the Bulgarian embassy and confront Mr. Harlacheva?" I admired his bold stroke given that I thought it likely she might choose to, but she did not. She *harrumphed* and stalked across the room, tossing a pile of garments to the floor as she sank into a chair and wound her arms tightly around herself.

"Go on," she said.

"Your friend . . . your Toshy . . . ," he flashed a smirk, ". . . has been under surveillance by the Yard for some time now."

" 'E ain't no friend a mine," she sneered.

"Nevertheless, it would seem he may be involved in everything from the illegal drug trade . . . ," I noticed he had slowed his speech and was keeping a watchful eye on her, ". . . to passing sensitive government information, and quite possibly involvement in a child slavery ring he claims *you* spearheaded."

She bolted up, her face a cloud of rage. " *'Ow dare 'e!* That weren't my idea, it were *'is*." She began pacing and cursing under her breath. "I've a right mind to go down there and kick 'is bloody, lyin' arse."

"Why don't you just help us get Angelyne back? Doing a good turn will get you high praise from me and I'm sure Inspector Varcoe will . . ." Colin let his voice trail off as Mademoiselle Rendell swung around and glowered at him.

"I see 'ow it is," she sneered. "I must look like a right dumb slag ta you, but I know what you're up to."

He pursed his lips and leaned back. "And what would that be?"

She wagged a finger at him, shaking her head and chortling with great self-satisfaction. "Toshy didn't tell you no bollocks 'bout me headin' nothin'. You're just tossin' about for information on that pissant little bitch."

"She's only twelve."

"I 'ad me a list a clients long as me arm by the time I was twelve. So what?!"

"And look how well you turned out."

"This is getting us nowhere," I jumped in, stopping her before she could say anything further. "The choices you've made for yourself are your business. You'll hear no judgments from us. But doesn't Angelyne deserve to make her own too?"

"I ain't makin' no apologies!" she snapped.

"None are warranted," Colin said.

"There's a need fer what I do."

"Of course . . ." I could hear his patience ebbing.

"I weren't born no 'ore."

"Education is the backbone of every profession."

"That's right."

He smirked as he leveled a gaze at her. "Did you deliver Angelyne to Mr. Harlacheva?"

"Don't you look down on me!" she fired back.

"My dear . . ." He turned his head away. "I shan't even look at you at all."

She glared at him as though trying to gauge whether he was still playing her for the fool and I doubted this ploy would work, either. Nevertheless, he neither moved nor slid his eyes back to her, holding himself with remarkable stillness. I hardly knew where to look myself, so I settled on dropping my gaze to the well-worn floor, heavily stained with the accumulated remnants of too many people. " 'E pays me real good," she finally confessed to my amazement.

"How many have there been?"

"Seven."

"And where does he take them?"

"I don't know. I never see 'em again. It ain't me business. I don't ask."

He turned back and looked at her. "Thank you for telling the truth."

"A girl 'as ta make a livin'."

"As we all must, but at what cost?"

"A livin' don't cost nothin'."

He stood up and moved to the door with me close on his heels. "Yours will cost you your freedom if I ever find you involved in business like this again. If you wish to prostitute yourself that's your right, but you will *never* make such a decision for another human being again. *Especially for a child.* Do I make myself clear?"

"Are you threatnin' me?"

He gave a tight smile. "Absolutely."

CHAPTER 20

By the time we got outside again we discovered that the sky had finally begun to let loose its watery burden, which meant that we were well wet by the time we reached the Bulgarian embassy. Though he'd managed to flag a carriage without too much trouble, it turned out to have a tear in its roof the length of my hand, which had allowed the pelting rain access throughout the entire fifteen-minute journey. When we finally reached the embassy and I took proper refuge under the building's huge stone portico, I turned back just in time to see Colin thrust his hand up through the gash in the roof to hand the driver his fare.

We hurried inside the colonnaded foyer and I was struck at once by its grandeur. Massive inlaid teak panels stretched all the way to the ceiling two floors overhead and wide swaths of jade green marble lay beneath our feet. Freedom from Turkish rule had clearly done the Bulgarians some good.

"We are here . . . ," I heard Colin addressing a dark-eyed beauty behind an ornate counter across from the entrance, ". . . to speak with one of the ambassador's diplomatic couriers. A Mr. Vic—" His voice abruptly wound down.

"Vitosha Harlacheva," I filled in as I came up behind him.

"Do you hev an appointment?"

"Colin Pendragon and Ethan Pruitt."

The young woman's eyes drifted up and were as black as the waves of hair falling about her shoulders. "Vot?"

"Our names . . . Are we in the appointment book?"

"You do nut know yourselves?"

"Would we have come all this way on such a dreadful evening without an appointment?" Colin smiled easily.

The woman glanced over at one of the two apathetic young guards posted on either corner of her desk, but neither returned her gaze. I wondered if indifference was a Bulgarian trait before realizing that it was likely neither spoke much English.

"Vot is your nem again?" Exasperation had crept into her voice.

"Colin Pendragon. I'm with Her Majesty's Foreign Ministry Office. I investigate accusations of improprieties at the embassies. I'm sure we'll have no such issues here, unless there's some problem with my addressing Mr.—"

"Harlacheva," I quickly piped in.

The woman flicked her eyes between Colin and me before finally saying, "You vill vait here."

"As you wish."

She exited through a door behind her desk, leaving us to slowly accumulate small puddles around our shoes. I tried to figure out where he meant to go with this ruse and then wondered if he even knew himself. I shot a quick glance at the two guards and decided it was safe to press him while we waited. "What are you going to say to this man if she lets us in?" I said in a sort of half whisper just to be sure. "You can't just walk in there and accuse him on the word of Mademoiselle Rendell."

He shrugged. "Something will come to me. It always does." He turned to the guard standing closest to him. "Might I trouble you for the time?" The man's eyes slid to Colin's face, but there was no comprehension in them. "No?" He glanced at the other man. "How about a pistol? Am I allowed to bring a pistol in with me?" Again there was no response, the second guard not even bothering to shift his gaze.

"They can't be much use if they don't even understand what anyone's saying."

"All they need to understand . . . ," Colin smirked, ". . . is that if you make a move to go through that door uninvited, you are to be stopped."

"That's all good and well, but didn't you find Mademoiselle Rendell too eager in confessing her sins?"

He looked at me. "Whatever do you mean?"

"She took your word on Mr. Harlacheva without much of a fuss."

"Why would she trust him? It's all a dirty business."

"She earns her keep with her cunning."

"She earns her keep on her back."

I shook my head and chuckled. While he had a point, he could be sorely mistaken if he presumed that truth made her imprudent. Maw Heikens was living proof of that. I considered reminding him of that fact even though I knew he would curl up his nose at the mention of her name, but the receptionist suddenly popped her head out from behind the door.

"You vill follow me," she said before barking a harsh, guttural command at the two guards. The men stamped their feet in unison, bounced the butts of their rifles off the floor, and stepped back from the desk to allow us to pass.

"Nicely trained." Colin snickered.

We followed the young woman down several plain corridors, the embassy's budget clearly having been exhausted in the foyer. A series of short, squat guards stood at loose intervals along the hallway, making me suspect that as the budget for the building went, so did the dimensions of its soldiers. We were led through successive halls until I began to fear that we were about to be ushered right out the rear exit, but to my relief, the receptionist made an abrupt right turn and brought us into an empty conference room.

"You vill vait here," she said without further explanation, gesturing us to seats around a table at the room's center. As soon as we settled in, she took a practiced step backwards and pulled the door shut, leaving us on our own.

"Well . . . ," I glanced at him, "at least we've made it this far."

"We've got quite some way to go yet," he answered distractedly. "Do you have a notebook with you?"

"Don't I always?" I passed him the little leather folio I carry about with its small nib of pencil. "What are you going to do?"

"I have a thought," he answered smoothly as he began to scribble something onto several sheets.

"Is that Latin?"

"Very good." He smiled cannily just as the door opened to reveal a tall, broad-shouldered man wearing full military regalia. As he strode in I realized he was *not* Vitosha Harlacheva.

"Zer is no Pendragoon at ze British Foreign Ministry Office," the towering man informed us as he scowled from across the room. "Who are you and vot do you vant?"

Colin stood up but made no effort to move toward the man, a wise choice since he was easily half a foot shorter than him. "My apologies to the great and honorable nation of Bulgaria for having used subterfuge to gain entry." The man's brow furrowed with noncomprehension. Colin smiled. "I did indeed fabricate that story, but only because there is a most urgent and personal matter that I must discuss with Mr. Harlacheva."

"All matters vit Mr. Harlacheva must go through me." He bit the words harshly.

"Of course." Colin nodded. "I did mention that it is of a personal nature?" he said, letting his voice trail off and giving me a sudden inkling as to what he was up to and why he'd written in Latin.

The giant man flicked his eyes between us, his great bushy brow furrowing deeply. "You vill see nothing but ze alley unless you discuss your matters vit me."

"Very well . . ." And now Colin did step closer to the man. "We're from the London Lock Hospital and Rescue Home on Harrow Road and your Mr. Harlacheva came to our offices the other day. He was complaining of some discomforts. . . ." He gestured below his waist and then flipped open my little notebook and thrust it under the man's nose. "You can see from the results of the tests we've run that Mr. Harlacheva is suffering from the French disease. The syphilis. And—" He got no further before the man stepped back, unconsciously dropping his hands in front of his nether regions.

And then he uttered two words I would never have dreamed I'd hear: "Mademoiselle Rendell," he gasped.

"It's a misnomer, you know," Colin barreled on. "It doesn't just strike the French." He glanced at me and chortled in a way that urged me to do the same. "Be that as it may, we will need to retest Mr. Harlacheva to see if there's been a mistake. That does happen from time to time. And we'll need some information regarding the possible genesis of his condition." Colin eyed the man. "Who was that woman you just mentioned?"

"Vait," was all the great bear said before disappearing out the door with a dexterity that would have rivaled a prima ballerina.

"How did you ever come up with that?!" I shook my head as Colin tossed my notebook back at me.

"It seemed like a good way to get a man's attention." He shrugged.

I started to laugh but quickly turned it into a cough as Vitosha Harlacheva came stomping into the room. It was obvious by the rapidity with which he joined us that he'd been hovering close by. I wondered if he hadn't suspected meeting with us was likely to be unavoidable. It was hard to say, and his heavily bearded face gave little away.

He had broad shoulders and was of average height, much like Colin, but the similarities ended there. Mr. Harlacheva's eyes were dark and rooted deep within his broad, flat face, and his expression truly was nearly impenetrable, buried as it was within the wiry hair that seemed to spring from his cheekbones to the collar of his shirt. And while Colin's frame is solid, revealing no softness or paunch, Mr. Harlacheva had a layer of fleshy padding that covered the circumference of his frame. While I did recognize him from his tête-à-tête with Mademoiselle Rendell, if pressed I would have said he was taller, handsomer, or at the very least more presupposing than this square ape of a man. Nevertheless, he permeated a gravitas that I could not deny.

"Vat is this about?" he growled.

"It's about an abomination." Colin remained where he was, his shoulders squared and his chest puffed out in his own rite of domination.

"You haff no authority here. You are standing in Bulgaria just now."

"That may be. But this Bulgaria is in the heart of Her Majesty's England. And I happen to have a great deal of authority here. I would be happy to demonstrate if you'd like." He flashed a humorless smile.

"I have done nothing."

"Seven young girls have been handed over to you by a woman . . . a whore. She goes by the name of Rendell."

"You haff me confused with someone else. Good day."

The man turned and made to leave before I spoke up. "I saw you. I followed Mademoiselle Rendell two nights ago to that pub by the Russian embassy. You told her your business with her was over for now. That you were leaving the country for a time."

He stopped but did not turn back. It was as though he was trying to determine how best to react in order to effect the quickest end to the conversation. "You are a liar," he finally said. Which was not the best choice.

With barely an intake of breath Colin hurled himself down the length of the table and punched Mr. Harlacheva in the kidneys, dropping him in a gasping heap before the man even realized what had happened. "You will *never* speak to Mr. Pruitt that way again," he seethed through gritted teeth. "Nor will you waste our time one second more or else I'll tear your ruddy kidneys out with my bare hands."

"*Help!*" the man gasped in a pitifully small voice.

"Allow me." Colin stepped over him and yanked a handkerchief from his pocket. He pressed it over his mouth and pulled the door wide to reveal the towering military officer standing just outside, clearly waiting to be summoned if the need should arise. "This man is contagious!" Colin shouted into his face. He stood back and gestured with his free hand. "Quarantine. *Kapahtnh! Now!*"

The security officer nearly tripped on his feet as he stumbled backwards, his eyes as big as a fawn's. He only kept himself upright by virtue of some gravitational anomaly that I would have bet against, spinning on his heels and disappearing down the long hallway with all due haste.

"*Ka-pat-nah?*" I repeated as Colin slammed the door.

"It's Russian. I don't know any Bulgarian." He dropped down beside the panting Mr. Harlacheva and whispered into his ear, "In about four minutes that officer is going to return with a phalanx of guards whose sole function will be to keep you locked in this room until I can have you properly hauled away. Or maybe they'll just come in here and shoot you and put an end to the whole feral mess. It makes little difference to me. Unless you start talking. Now."

To his credit Mr. Harlacheva squeaked out, "I spit on you."

"Unless that's a Bulgarian custom meaning you're about to purge your conscience"—Colin fished a small knife wrapped in a bit of cloth from his breast pocket—"then we shall have an issue." He leaned forward and waved the knife over the man's lap. "Seven little girls," he said.

"Go to hell," came the wheezing reply, a thin film of sweat shining on his forehead like a grease slick.

Colin's hand flashed like a striking serpent and for a moment I didn't know what he'd done. Mr. Harlacheva gave a short, high-pitched yelp and my heart rocketed as I tried to see if Colin had actually stuck him.

"I shall cut your bits off one at a time," Colin seethed into the man's closest ear, "and then fix it so you have to squat to piss. That'll teach you to mess with children."

My eyes shifted south and I finally spotted the knife tucked up between the cowering man's legs, the point obviously being driven home in a most convincing way, since Mr. Harlacheva was not moving a hair. Colin gave another quick jerk and sheared through the crotch of the man's slacks and undergarments, releasing his cowering genitals.

"You are devil," he started to blubber.

Colin poked the scalpel up against his tender flesh. "I won't ask again."

"They are gone. They vent on ship."

"What ship? To where?"

"St. Petersburg. Ve make papers for them and they go vork for Russian nobles. Not bad life."

"I'll bet. What's the name of the ship?"

"*Ilya Petrovina.* But is too late."

"It's never too late. I'm bloody British, we don't believe in failure. Nine hundred years of squabbling royals have taught us that much." He leaned directly over Mr. Harlacheva and twitched the hand wielding the knife just slightly, but it was enough to make the Bulgarian release a fresh torrent of sweat.

"We shall take our leave now." Colin spoke slowly. "And you will take your leave of this kingdom." I saw his hand twist almost imperceptibly and thought for a moment Mr. Harlacheva was going to swoon. "And should I *ever* see your face in this city again, I shall make good my threat by whittling pendants of your bits. Do you understand?"

The man blinked his eyes and I realized he was too afraid to speak.

"Excellent."

It took only a second more for Colin to move his hand away and spring to his feet. Vitosha Harlacheva scrambled to cover himself as best he could, the color slowly returning to his face. He looked beaten, desperate, and I should have recognized that fact sooner than I did, but I was unnerved myself and didn't realize what was bound to happen.

Colin sneered as he started for the door, but before I could even begin to follow, Vitosha Harlacheva leapt to his feet and threw himself fully at Colin's back, colliding hard and sending the two of them careening into the nearest wall. I threw myself forward to try to pull the burly man off Colin, but he'd already half-twisted around, and then I heard Mr. Harlacheva cry out, and just that fast it was over.

The bearish man fell to the floor like a gutted fish, his hands covering his exposed crotch as a river of blood flowed through his fingers. It took another moment before I spotted the small dark lump of fuzzy flesh on the floor near Colin's shoe and realized what it was.

"Come on!" he barked at me.

I didn't need to be told twice as I hopped over the man and fled out the door, slamming it shut behind me. We were well down the hallway when he suddenly barked at me, "Put your handkerchief over your mouth!" doing so himself.

I heard the drumbeat of quickly approaching men as I clutched my kerchief to my mouth and nose just as the security officer came jogging around the far corner with three men on his heels. They looked wary and not at all happy when they spotted us. "Vat is happening?" The officer slowed down, staring at our handkerchiefs.

"It's bad." Colin kept up a brisk pace, forcing the man and his troops to fall in behind to hear what he had to say. "His flesh is dying. Falling away. You mustn't touch him or go near him. Stay away. We're going to get help."

"But ze ambassador . . ."

"*The ambassador will be fine!*" Colin shouted. "Just keep everybody away from him until we get back."

"Yes . . . yes, of course."

The officer and his soldiers gradually slowed as we bolted back out to the foyer. The receptionist looked startled as we rushed out, handkerchiefs pressed tight against our faces. "Too much cologne," Colin muttered as he tucked his away. "Nasty business."

"Nasty," I repeated absently, already vexed about how we were ever going to stop the *Ilya Petrovina* from reaching St. Petersburg.

CHAPTER 21

The sky was as dark as pitch, a layer of brooding clouds obscuring all signs of the moon and stars. The storm of the night before, the night spent grilling the vile Vitosha Harlacheva, was returning. It was only a matter of when.

Colin and I were sitting deep within the confines of a hansom cab. We had a blanket across our legs and my collar was turned up, but even so, the night's incessant cold was beginning to worm its way through to my flesh. Colin's right hand was bare as he absently spun a crown through his fingers, and I couldn't imagine how the metal wasn't freezing his skin. We'd been sitting like this, well back in the thickets down the road from the Arnifour estate, for over an hour. I couldn't imagine how the driver was tolerating the dense chill from his perch above us. We would need to slip him an extra wage at the end of the evening.

"How long do we have to sit here?" I asked, fearing that he meant to spend the whole of the night. "It's just that I'm worried we might get a return communiqué from the Foreign Ministry Office tonight . . . ," I started to say, but I could see by the look he flicked at me that he knew better.

"Let's give it another ten minutes and then we'll call it a night. Given the storm that's coming on I doubt any reasonable person would be going anywhere, including Victor Heffernan."

"Well, that's a relief," I leaned against him, "because I'm freezing."

"Me too," he sighed, finally shoving the coin into his pocket and slipping on his glove. "Besides, we have a previous engagement."

"A previous engagement?"

"Indeed. We're due at the Roynton estate at half past nine this evening. The comely widow is expecting us."

"Abigail Roynton? She invited us to her residence? Whatever for? And who says she's comely?"

He laughed. "I'm guessing she would have to be, given her ability to attract both Arnifour men."

"Any woman with a bit of money and a reserve of spirits could attract the Arnifour men."

"You have a point."

"Why would she contact us?"

"Actually, I sent her a message this morning informing her of our investigation. I told her we hoped she might be able to offer some insight. Her answer came as we were leaving tonight—she said she'd be charmed."

"Charmed? Seems an odd word given we're conducting a murder investigation."

"But you forget," he arched an eyebrow, "she is a scorned woman. Remember what Warren Vandemier said about her being recently replaced in the Earl's affections."

"Do you really put much stock in what *he* says? He hardly seems a reliable source."

"True. But ask yourself: Who among that coterie of character witnesses is any better? Should we really dismiss his word any quicker than that of the Earl's family or staff?" I had to concede that he had a point. He yanked out his watch and glanced at it. "I do think that's enough for tonight," he said as he rapped his free hand on the metal rib of the cab's top.

"And what about Victor? Varcoe's got a dragnet across this whole area and I told you there was a photograph of Nathaniel in the *Times* today. It all but accused him of the killings. If he's spotted he's liable to be lynched without a second thought."

"I've got some lads who'll take over for us. Not to worry. *Hello?*" he called out again. "We'd like to go to the second address, please."

"Aye!" the man shouted back, snapping his crop at the lone horse and guiding us out of the thicket.

"We'll let the boys fill in for the rest of the night." And sure enough I caught sight of a young man settling in by a hedge, his collar pulled up to cover the better part of his face as though he was hunkering down for a lengthy stay, which undoubtedly he was. I only hoped it wouldn't rain. "They'll come by in the morning for their stipend," Colin added.

"I'll give them something extra if it rains." They would earn their money this night, but at least we were keeping them out of their usual mischief for one evening.

"Unless Victor makes a move to go to Nathaniel tonight we're going to have to stop by tomorrow and apply more pressure. He's got to do something before that incompetent inspector blunders onto the boy. They're as likely to shoot him as arrest him. They like nothing more than to tidy up a case—damn the details."

Our cab passed beneath the imposing gates of the Roynton estate, quite literally the next home over from the Arnifours', if some considerable distance away. Given the increasing moodiness of the night sky with its dense scent of rain, I was grateful we made good time.

The horse clacked down the cobbled drive through a forest of trees that led along a sharp curve before finally revealing a glimpse of the house. The difference between this home and the Arnifours' was startling. It wasn't simply the architecture, the Roynton estate having been built in the style of a French château with four rounded turrets topped by steep pointed roofs of black slate delineating the corners of the palatial structure. No. What immediately struck me was that every one of the scores of windows dotting the massive stone-block façade was ablaze with light, making it look as though the house must surely be filled with a thousand people. Even the half-moon forecourt hugging the face of the building was lined with gas torchieres that broke the night's austerity with their warm glow. And the building was immaculate, from its cream-colored walls rising four stories without a mar to the cement spiraled colonnades encasing the front doors and large paned windows stretching across the entirety of the ground floor. The Roynton residence was precisely tended and full of life. It was, in effect, the antithesis of the Arnifours'.

The cab came to a gradual stop in the forecourt.

"We shouldn't be long," Colin said as we climbed out. "A couple of hours at the most."

"Right then. I'll be waitin' under the portico if it starts ta rain. Just give us a whistle when yer ready."

"Fine." The cab clattered off to the side of the building as we climbed the half-dozen steps to the expansive porch. "It would seem the widow must have something against the dark, as she clearly keeps her staff busy banishing it from her home," Colin said as he grabbed one of the knockers, a great brass lion's head with a ring clutched in its teeth, and heaved it. In less time than it had taken us to climb the steps, the doors swung wide to reveal an elegantly dressed white-haired gentleman with the stiff manner and regard of one of the Queen's own staff.

"Mr. Pendragon." He nodded at Colin before throwing me the usual vacant stare. "And guest," he added.

"Ethan Pruitt," Colin corrected with a nod to me, but offering no further explanation.

"Madame is expecting you," he answered blithely before ushering us inside and taking a careful moment to firmly bolt the doors behind us. I couldn't help wondering if that wasn't a habit put in place in light of the recent murders at the Arnifours'. "If you would follow me, please."

The man's face remained unreadable as he led us through the foyer where a massive double-spiraled staircase wound in and out of itself all the way up the full four stories. Yet, as is so often the case when Colin and I are shown in, we were deposited in a library filled with leather-bound books, overstuffed furniture, and a lifetime of collectibles. In this case the collection consisted of tiny porcelain figurines placed on every conceivable surface, including the mantel top, which encased such a roaring fire that I was sure it was being fed by a steady stream of gas.

We were offered drinks, which we both declined, and with his duties thusly completed were shut inside the giant, yet somehow claustrophobic, room.

"He had about as much personality as Mrs. O'Keefe." I snickered.

"If you'd grown up in an atmosphere as stuffy as this one," he muttered as he began poking through the books, "you would find our Mrs. Behmoth a great deal more agreeable than you do."

"I wasn't born on the streets, you know," I shot back.

"I know. . . ." He waved me off. He knew I'd not been raised an urchin. That had come later. That had been my own doing.

"I'm sorry to have kept you waiting," a smooth, husky voice filled the silence. I turned to find the storied widow, Abigail Roynton. I no longer recollect what I'd been expecting her to be like, but it was definitely not the radiant woman who stood at the door in the reflection of the warm, honeyed glow of the gas lamps. She was tall and slender, and held herself with a bearing that spoke of an upbringing above even that which Colin had known. Her face was round and open and as flawless as fresh-fallen snow, not simply the result of her age, which I knew to be in her middle thirties, but because she had clearly lived a pampered life free of anything more than a passing familiarity with the sun.

Her hair was a lush and curly black, spiraling down the sides of her face even though it was pulled up in back. She wore a dress of deep greens and gold, striking for both its simplicity and the way it accentuated her meticulously trim figure. The smile that parted her lips was warm and genuine, and I was taken aback to think that perhaps this might prove to be the one person of substance among the many schemers in the late Earl's life.

"You've not kept us waiting at all." Colin nodded, a master of diplomacy when it served him.

She moved into the room as though she were floating above the floor. "I trust you both were offered a drink?"

"We were." Colin waited for her to settle herself on a settee near the fireplace before following suit. "I apologize for having to bother you on such a matter as this. We're grateful you've consented to meet with us and shan't stay a moment longer than is necessary."

"Don't trouble yourself. There is no bother. Your note mentioned the murders of the Earl and his niece, and as you can imagine, I am anxious to help in any way I can. I'm afraid I'm unlikely to be of much use, however, as I haven't seen either of them for some months."

"Ah . . ." Colin rocked back in his chair. "Was it months, then?"

The door to the library opened delicately and a young woman in a black serving uniform eased into the room causing no more distraction than a slight wisp of air. She carried a silver tray upon which sat a split of champagne in a silver bucket and three crystal flutes. Drinks, it seemed, were destined to be a part of this interview.

"Perfection!" The lovely widow beamed as the girl set the tray on a side table beside her before uncorking the bottle and pouring a glass for each of us. The solemnness of our topic was momentarily banished with peculiar ease.

The drinks were served with Colin and me accepting ours as etiquette dictated. A silent toast was offered by means of thin smiles and bobbed heads as the serving girl retreated from the room, and only after we'd all had a sip did Colin persist in pushing ahead.

"Do you happen to recall the nature of your last visit with the Earl, Mrs. Roynton?"

"Do call me Abigail." She flashed an easy smile. "I simply cannot bear undue ceremony."

"Abigail then." He returned his own generous grin. "Do you recall, Abigail, your last visit with the Earl?"

"I most certainly do." She smirked at him as she paused long enough to take another languorous sip of champagne. "Samuel was bringing about an end to our trysts, and quite badly, I might add."

"Trysts?!" Colin nearly spat the tug of champagne he'd been taking.

She threw her head back and laughed. "Come now, don't tell me I've shocked you?"

"I would say . . . ," I spoke up, fearful that Colin might yet choke on the swallow he was still wrestling to contain, ". . . we're simply not used to such forthrightness."

Abigail continued to laugh as she saluted me with her glass. "Yes, I would suppose not. Most people are too busy trying to bury the truth beneath a veneer of respectability. I can never figure the point in that. No matter what one does, the tongues will wag. It seems to me one should simply claim their reputation."

"Honorable," I said, and easy for a person of her means to say, I thought.

"Not really." She winked, setting off her throaty laugh yet again.

"So the Earl—" Colin cut in, having finally managed to regain himself.

"You mean Samuel," she corrected. "He had no claims to that title. One of his forebears did a turn for a balmy king and a hundred years later his progeny gets to wave around the pedigree. It doesn't sit well with me."

Colin took another nip of champagne. "Samuel then," he said with a bit less grace. "Samuel was ending your affair?"

"Affair?" She gazed off toward the fireplace for a moment, a distracted look on her face. "To me the word 'affair' suggests foreign travel and clandestine meetings in romantic places. That's not what Samuel and I had. We had trysts. Right here. No travel, no romance, and only the barest nod to the idea of being clandestine. Really, Colin . . . ," her voice dropped lower, hitting a timbre that threatened to raise the hairs on the back of my neck as she turned her considerable focus back on him, ". . . are you truly such a prig?"

He held her gaze as he cocked his head to one side. "Now there's something I've never been accused of." He slid his eyes to me and I gave him a look that I hoped would warn him to say no more. I didn't particularly like this woman, her familiarity and unflinching zeal to speak her mind. I couldn't see what made her any better than Mademoiselle Rendell and yet knew she would be aghast at such a suggestion.

"My apologies." Colin tipped his flute in her direction. "Do tell me then, how long was it that you and Samuel were having it off?"

"Two and a half years."

"Indeed?! That's quite the extended tryst. And to what end were the two of you carrying on?"

"The usual, I should think." She fluttered her eyelashes coquettishly.

"My point . . . ," he pressed on, ". . . is that I'm trying to understand if you and the Earl, your Samuel, had been entertaining any sort of more permanent plans? Marriage perhaps?"

Once again she threw her head back and roared with delight, the curls on top of her head shaking appreciably as she rocked back and forth. "*Marriage?!*" she gasped as she took a sip of champagne and tried without success to regain her composure. "Now why in the Queen's name would I *ever* want to marry that insolvent, self-absorbed, lecherous old bore? I simply will not believe that you're being serious."

"Am I missing something?" Colin leaned forward and I could tell from his stiff posture and the slight pursing of his lips that he was finding this a great deal less amusing than she was. "Would I have found you so disparaging had we met in the midst of your *inflagrante delicto*?"

"Oh!" She brought a delicate hand up to her mouth. "Latin. Everything sounds so much better in a dead language." She snickered.

"I'll have your answer, please."

"Will you?" She kept her eyes on him as she emptied her glass. "My late husband left me a very wealthy woman. And as I'm cursed with childlessness . . . well, I think you can imagine how tiresome such an existence can become. I abhor gossip, which means that gallivanting about with my peers in their saber-toothed decimation of one another is out of the question. And you simply *cannot* expect me to take up with the servants, although I hear that's worked for some of the neighbors." One side of her mouth curled up as she continued to smirk at him. "I don't know what more to tell you other than Samuel was available and I was crushingly bored. He was also exactly the man I described to you. Perhaps not at first, but even a chameleon shows its true color eventually. I even let him swindle me out of a bit of money just as he did to everyone else." She shrugged. "Rather like paying him for his services, meager though they were."

"Under what pretext did he take your money?"

"He called it an investment. Turned out to be opium. So banal."

"You're talking about his business with Warren Vandemier?"

She gave a start. "Well, you really are as clever as they say."

"You flatter me."

"I doubt it."

"What can you tell me about Mr. Vandemier?"

"Mr. Vandemier?" She curled her lips as she picked up a little bell and rang it delicately. Instantly the young woman who'd brought the champagne came back, moving to refill her mistress's glass. We were also topped off before she neatly plunged the bottle back into its bucket and made a hasty retreat, once again pulling the doors quietly shut.

"Now let me guess," Abigail started again. "I'd be willing to wager a considerable sum that upon your meeting Warren he told you that Samuel came up with nary a farthing to start their venture, leaving him to front the entire enterprise himself. Am I correct?" She waited for Colin's nod. "Tell me you didn't believe the boorish little shit?"

"It seemed unlikely."

She grinned. "Very wise."

"I also wonder if perhaps he didn't decide to end your dalliance rather than pay you back. That would relieve him of a financial obligation you'd have had a sorry time trying to collect anyway. Am I close?"

Abigail Roynton looked positively buoyed with astonishment at Colin's having reached so obvious a possibility. "You clearly *are* a man worthy of his reputation." She chuckled, but this time I knew she meant it. "And do you know *why* I let Samuel talk me into giving him that money?"

"Not for love." He smirked.

"Heavens no. *Never* for love."

He studied her a moment and I wondered if he was trying to divine an answer or determine whether he should share whatever else he suspected when he suddenly blurted out, "Because you are a shrewd businesswoman."

She smiled wickedly, leering at him as people will do when they share a devious secret. "Do go on."

"Opium," he said.

She clapped her hands. "Yes, yes." She shrieked with laughter. "You've got it!"

And indeed he did. For there is no more loyal customer than that of an opium dealer. Once an addict is hooked, you almost always have them for life—however long that proves to be.

Her amusement soured my mood. I was beginning to find this woman a great deal less principled than Mademoiselle Rendell.

"Shrewd," Colin said dully.

But she didn't seem to catch his tone. "I thought so. So when it was over between us it wasn't so much that I'd lost the occasional afternoon's amusement as that I'd gained a share in a burgeoning business. Warren's only trying to peddle his story of self-funding because he thinks he can nip me out of my share of the profits. But he is sorely mistaken. He'll soon learn he can't play *me* for a fool."

"I'm certain of that," Colin said. "And would you happen to know who took your place in Samuel's bed?"

"Bed?!" She leaned back in her chair and rolled her champagne flute absently across the exposed skin of her plunging neckline. "Please don't think me so old-fashioned."

"Nevertheless . . ."

"Of course I know." She raised her glass and sipped from it, glaring at him from over the rim, the gleam in her eyes almost as hot as the embers in the fireplace. "But you won't believe me if I tell you."

CHAPTER 22

Foreign Minister Randolph Fitzherbert sent word the next morning that the men from Her Majesty's cutter the HMS *Renard,* had succeeded in running down and boarding the *Ilya Petrovina,* where it was discovered that she not only carried the cargo listed on her manifest—tobacco, spare carriage parts, and an assortment of fine ladies' undergarments—but also sixteen young girls ranging in age from nine to thirteen with nary a traveling document among them. The *Ilya Petrovina*'s captain had immediately accused them of being stowaways, but Her Majesty's naval staff had not been so easily deceived. With the information provided by Colin and transferred through Mr. Fitzherbert's office to the commanding officer of the *Renard,* the *Ilya Petrovina*'s captain had been placed under arrest and the ship was being escorted back to Dover. The expected arrival date was five days hence. We had no way of being certain that Angelyne was one of the girls, yet the odds were in her favor and at the very least we were still rescuing sixteen innocents.

Colin sent word to Michael at once, so there was little surprise when he presented himself at our flat within the hour. He came bounding up our stairs as soon as Mrs. Behmoth opened the door, leaving her to trail along behind him in great huffs of annoyance. "Ya 'aven't been properly inerduced," she snarled as she lunged into the study well behind the young man.

"Never mind, Mrs. Behmoth." Colin gave her a nod as he sent the dumbbells he'd been wielding onto the floor.

"It ain't right," she groused, but nevertheless withdrew.

"Right . . . wrong . . . ," he chuckled as he turned back to Michael, "who among us is fit to judge what is and what isn't?"

"*Bugger off!*" she hollered back.

I rolled my eyes, but Michael seemed to take no note as he hurried across the room to pepper Colin for news of his little sister.

"I can't tell you beyond all doubt that she is on her way back," Colin said. "But I am fairly confident she'll be among those arriving in Dover next week."

"Bless ya, Mr. Pendragon, Mr. Pruitt." Michael grinned. "Ya've been most kind. I'll not trouble ya no more."

Colin gripped the young man's shoulder a moment. "We're here anytime should you ever need us again."

Michael shuffled his feet exactly as I would have done at his age and demurred quietly. How well I understood this boy, which was why something at the back of my mind kept niggling at me.

"We shall see you Tuesday then," Colin muttered as he turned to his knife play.

"No, no." He stopped on the landing and turned back to us. "I couldn't ask ya ta do that. Ya've given me too much a yer time already. I'll collect me sister and we'll pop round so's you can see 'er."

"As you wish." Colin shrugged, setting the knife back onto the mantel and snatching up his dumbbells again, curling them steadily as he sat back down.

"Thank you then." Michael nodded and tipped his cap before bounding down the stairs.

"Sounds like a blasted 'erd a wild boars!" Mrs. Behmoth bellowed as the front door slammed.

"More like a jackal," I muttered.

"You're seeing too much of your own past in him." Colin snickered as he continued to roll the dumbbells back and forth. "Can't you give the lad a bit of slack?"

"Hmmm . . ." I knit my brow. "I rather think that's what he's hoping for. That boy is almost certainly a pickpocket, a thief, a pimp, and probably a drug addict. I'll wager you his sister hasn't disappeared, he's probably sold her and has now received a better offer."

"How very cynical."

I scowled. "Tell me I'm not right."

He chuckled as he kept the weights smoothly curling, but didn't say a word.

CHAPTER 23

By the time twilight was nestling outside our windows and the sounds of Mrs. Behmoth rattling pans downstairs in preparation of the evening's meal amplified, I could tell Colin's thoughts had moved somewhere far away. He'd long since given off tossing the dumbbells about and had reverted to shining the same knife blade he'd been working on so that its gleam was becoming nearly solar. For myself, I could not leave go of my wariness of Michael's story even though I had nothing more concrete to offer than my own intuition. I was familiar with him, I knew who he was, and I knew he was up to something.

"You seem preoccupied," Colin said after a while.

"It's that little rogue, Michael . . . ," I mumbled.

"Still doubtful of his motives."

"I am."

"And what if he is hiding something? Does it really matter? No matter the details, something *has* happened to his sister and we need to get her back. What happens when we do will be a topic for a later conversation. Assuming she's not come to some harm."

I shook my head, remembering how many young girls I'd seen disappear so very long ago, most of whom were never accounted for again. "Tragic . . . ," was all I said.

He set his knife on the table and sighed. "Well, we're sure to get your mind off it for the night when I tell you what I've decided."

"And what would that be?"

"I think it's time for us to drop in on the dubious business of Warren Vandemier and the Earl. Tonight. With neither invitation nor notice."

"Sounds perfectly underhanded." I smiled, aware that his reticence was correlated to the yoke that had once tethered me so many years ago. I wanted to tell him that he needn't worry because I feared enough for the both of us, but instead muttered, "Mr. Vandemier will be livid if he finds out."

"You know . . . ," he looked at me keenly, "I can go alone. You needn't come."

"Don't start that," I said with finality. "I shall be at your side as always."

And so it was that we found ourselves standing in a urine-soaked, litter-filled alley in Whitechapel not an hour after eating dinner in the warm solace of our humble Kensington flat. It was a staggering contradiction and one that set an ancient and familiar chill rattling through me in spite of my determination to deny it.

"Wretched place," Colin muttered as he picked his way deeper into the alley toward the single scrubby gaslight hanging above a nondescript red-lacquered door. "Let's hope this club of Mr. Vandemier's looks less infective inside than it does out."

"Not likely—" I started to say, before clamping my mouth shut and letting the thought go unheeded.

We reached the door and Colin took a moment to tug at his coat and tie as though anyone inside would notice or care whether he was suitably attired. He raised his fist to knock on the door but pulled up short, sliding his eyes over to mine as he stood there, arm coiled, and said, "You really don't have to do this."

I reached out and pounded the door myself. "Don't be ridiculous."

He gave me a crooked smile.

A small rectangular slot rocketed open to reveal a pair of almond-shaped eyes. "Who sent you?" a thin, gentle voice demanded.

"Warren Vandemier," Colin answered at once.

The slot jerked shut and the door instantly swung open to reveal a delicate Oriental woman. She smiled generously, bowing her head as she waved us inside. Behind her stood two glowering, dark-haired Irish blokes who were clearly meant to intimidate, and did. Neither of them spoke or paid us much heed as we were led past by our diminutive hostess. I glanced back just in time to see another young woman slide onto the stool by the door, there to wait for the next guest's arrival. I'd rarely seen the custom before and knew Warren Vandemier was serious about setting his establishment above the rest.

Our exotic guide took us down a short hallway lined with doors on either side that I presumed led to private rooms for the gentry Mr. Vandemier had referenced. Even in a drug-addled state the city's aristocrats would find it anathema to mix with the commoners who frequented these sorts of clubs: sailors, stewards, mountebanks, shop men, beggars, outcasts, and thieves. All of them found a way to afford the pleasures promised by the seductive vapors once they'd woven their spell upon the addicts' receptive minds. Most of them could be counted on to prefer the ragged smoke of opium to food, leaving many of them to look as emaciated and near death as they truly were.

We rounded a corner at the end of the hallway and entered a large, dimly lit room in which numerous swaths of gauzy fabric hung around tight clusters of cushions and reclining benches. The floor-to-ceiling fabric afforded a semblance of privacy, further raising the standard of the establishment. None of the furnishings were marred or discolored, though unless they were swapped out regularly it was only a matter of time. Yet the draw of these clubs was specific and singular and had little to do with the décor, for it was at the apex of this room that the gentle coaxing of the drug became obvious. Its dry, stinging odor permeated the air like creosote from a poorly venting fireplace. I could feel it squeezing my throat and nudging at my temples, and felt one of my eyelids quiver. Yet I also knew that none of those effects would last long as slowly, stealthily, like a hunter shadowing its prey, the drug would begin to caress the mind, and lure its victim deep within its web. Even as I stood on the threshold of this vast partitioned room, I could feel it tugging at me.

"You want company tonight?" the young woman asked.

"We do." Colin gave a roguish smile and for a moment I thought I could see a haziness easing in behind his eyes as well.

"This way."

She wound us through the middle of the room and down two steps to a sunken area where five men and two women were sitting. At the center of the group stood a large water pipe with a dozen flexible tubes sprouting from its sides. One of the women was stirring a black viscous mixture over a small open flame. After a moment she scraped the sticky, bubbling mess into a small metal bowl perched near the top of the pipe. She lit it for her six cohorts, all of whom were only too eager to drag the swirling vapor from the nearest mouthpiece. As I stood there staring at them, remembering the enfolding embrace that was assuredly fingering its way into their willing minds, I thought I could see them losing fractured bits, not of their consciousness, but of their very beings.

"Please . . ." Our escort gestured us to a pile of cushions still available in the midst of this decaying circle of addicts.

We sat down and Colin reached into his breast pocket and pulled out the wad of cash I'd pressed on him before we'd left our flat. He peeled off some bills with a great, showy flourish and handed them to our hostess. "I presume this will get us started?"

She looked at the notes as though he were offering something untoward and I knew this sort of business preferred payment at the end of the evening when the revelers were well past giving a whit about the expenses they'd incurred. That, of course, assumed they'd not already been picked clean by the hostesses themselves. Either way, it all ended up in the proprietor's pocket by the end of the night. "If you wish," she said, delicately lifting the stack of bills from Colin's hand. I had to admit: Warren Vandemier's club was proving downright genteel.

We were left with the group of strangers and I felt my heart quicken the moment the man next to me shoved his mouthpiece in my direction. "Help yerself," he said.

"Not just yet." I smiled uneasily, aware that the dense smoke was already wiggling about my brain. "I'm rather in need of a drink first."

"I recommend the whiskey," my neighbor offered with a lopsided grin. "With a splash of water if you must."

"Save the water for the pipe," I shot back to great guffaws, suddenly struck by the feeling that I'd said that somewhere before. I glanced over at Colin, looking for some comfort in his solidity, and was caught by the nearly apoplectic look on his face—the result, I realized, of the proximity of the mouthpiece to my hand. In that moment I realized he'd been right, I shouldn't have come. "Can I get you something?" I squeaked as I fought the rising urge to flee.

"Go," he answered quietly. "Let Mrs. Behmoth draw you a bath. I'll tend to things here and meet you across the pillows later."

As I gazed into the glacial blue of his eyes, seeing the concern nestled within made me determined not to fail here. I could do this. I would do this. "No. I'm fine," I said with a strength that surprised even me. "You've nothing to worry about." I pushed myself up to get us something to drink, convinced that if I could just clear my head a moment I would be able to maintain my sanity.

He reached out and grabbed my arm, pulling me close. "You've nothing to prove," he hissed.

"I know," I said, but knew he was wrong. I had spent nearly the whole of my adolescence and early adulthood hiding in places like this among the alluring opiate fumes and tattered lives of other addicts. Each of us hiding some secret, some compulsion, driving us to alter our consciousness as often as we could while all the while convincing ourselves that we chose to be here and could leave it behind at any time, but we were fools. These places—this habit—wound themselves around our lives so completely that if one was lucky enough to stumble upon redemption it was impossible to accept. I know it was for me. And just like that, even thirteen years later, I couldn't be sure that enough time had passed yet.

I girded myself to the task at hand and before long returned with two glasses filled with overpriced, watered-down tea to simulate the color of whiskey. I passed Colin a glass and almost laughed when I saw the look of relief dart across his face as he tasted it.

"Spot-on," he said with a nod and a grin. "I have been speaking with these fine people in your absence," he continued cheerfully. "It seems they're all familiar with our Mr. Vandemier."

"E's in 'ere every night," one of the men volunteered. "Smokes up 'alf the profits if ya ask me."

Everybody laughed, including the two women, one of whom continued to take it upon herself to keep the pipe filled and circulating. She, I figured, was almost certainly his employee.

"But the most fascinating thing . . . ," Colin leaned forward as though on the verge of sharing some tasty secret with our bleary band of eager fellows, ". . . is that most of them are also familiar with his late partner, the Earl of Arnifour."

"Familiar?!" The redheaded woman on Colin's far side leered. "That's one way a puttin' it."

Once again all seven of them howled with laughter. It appeared the Earl's proclivities did not even exclude his clientele. Only the relighting of the pipe quieted them as the seven snakelike mouthpieces were once again put to use. Colin and I subtly demurred the opportunity to imbibe, but it was only a matter of time before we would need to at least appear to join in.

Colin shot me a grin. "Vanessa here was telling me she was *quite* close to the Earl at one time," he said, referring to the redhead.

"Close?" She shrugged as she sucked in another hit from the pipe. "We 'ad it off a time or two if ya call that close. But then I'd shag his ruddy wife if it'd earn me a round in 'ere," she cackled merrily. "I ain't no different than most a the birds in 'ere. I bet we all 'ad 'im sooner or later."

"Until recently?" Colin prodded.

"Sure." She let go of the mouthpiece and sank back on her cushion, clearly trying to steady herself as the opium seized her mind and seemed to arc it up and out of her body. "He changed a while ago. Tryin' ta set an example for 'is latest rummy that I was tellin' you about."

"That one was a right chipper." The man on my right shook

his head and snorted. "Comin' in 'ere all tarted up like she owned the place."

"And she weren't all that." The man across from me spoke as he struggled to hold in a lungful of smoke.

"She knew 'ow ta fix up what she 'ad." My neighbor cut him off. "She knew what a man likes."

"Every woman knows what a man likes," the redhead mumbled toward the ceiling, her head tilted back, eyes staring up as though waiting for something to appear out of the smoky haze. "No bloody mystery there."

"Who . . . ," I whispered to Colin, figuring he'd been able to get from this group what he'd been unable to extract from Abigail Roynton, ". . . are they talking about?"

Colin flicked his eyes toward mine and flashed that roguish grin. "Why, his late niece, Elsbeth."

"I don't remember being told you two were coming tonight?" a familiar voice growled from over our shoulders.

We both turned to find Warren Vandemier standing there. He was as pale as the smoke wafting around his head and almost as ethereal. From our position on the cushions, sunken two steps below the main floor, I was struck by how curiously foreboding he looked, his harsh, angular frame towering above us with a mixture of accusation and fury. The woman who'd seated us hovered just behind him, obviously having been warned to summon him whenever anyone bandied about his name at the door.

"We didn't want to bother you." Colin stood up. "We just wanted to see if your establishment lives up to its vaunted reputation."

"And? " There was no suggestion of a smile on his face.

"It is *indeed* a step above," Colin smiled, "but then a snake pit is still home to vipers."

Warren Vandemier's face showed little reaction. "I shall thank you to leave," he said.

"In that I am happy to accommodate you." He smiled again as we started to move off before he suddenly turned back and added, "By the way, Abigail Roynton sends her regards, though she does find your accounting methods rather disagreeable."

"She's a lying slag."

"Odd . . . ," he locked his eyes on Warren Vandemier, "she said much the same about you."

Nothing further was said as we left the premises. I sneaked a peek back and caught Warren Vandemier saying something to the Oriental woman who'd initially welcomed us. I knew there would be no such greeting were we to come back. I hoped Colin had gleaned what he'd come to learn.

"You all right?" he asked as soon as we were outside.

"I am," I answered with conviction in spite of the fact that my head was swimming toward a certain migraine. "And now we know who replaced Abigail Roynton at the Earl's side."

"Ah . . ." He chuckled. "We know more than that."

"We do?"

"While you were off fetching cold tea in a glass, which, by the way, was inspired, I not only learned of the Earl's trysting with his niece, but also that Elsbeth might not actually be a relation of his at all."

"What? But Lady Arnifour said . . ." And even as I heard myself say those words, I knew how foolish I sounded.

"Indeed." He chuckled as he stepped into the street to hail a cab.

CHAPTER 24

Three days passed since our foray to Warren Vandemier's opium club, which left only two more before the *Ilya Petrovina* was due to return to the docks at Dover. Colin spent most of his time wrestling at the gymnasium or doing calisthenics in our flat, and when he wasn't slaving away at one of those rituals he would sit in front of the fireplace and either sharpen, polish, or gaze blankly at one of the knives in his collection as though whatever answers he sought might possibly be coaxed from out of its cold, hard metal.

Each night we would venture forth to plant ourselves in a cab among the hedgerow down the road from the Arnifour property, waiting to see if this might be the night Victor went to Nathaniel, but he never did. It was our fourth night running, the silence in the cab full between us with only the sound of the horse flicking its tail and shifting its hooves to interrupt the incessant trill of crickets.

"I wonder . . . ," Colin startled me as he flipped open his pocket watch and checked the time, ". . . how Nathaniel felt knowing the woman he pined for was involved, so to speak, with the Earl."

"What makes you think he knew?"

He lifted an eyebrow to me as he switched his pocket watch for a crown and began teasing it slowly around his hand. "I think we'll find that nearly *everyone* knew who the Earl's momentary favorite was. And if you'll recall, Victor told us that the night of the attack he overheard Nathaniel arguing with Elsbeth. Nathaniel said himself he tried to talk her out of going. He knew what she was up to."

"You can't know that."

"I think I do," he said pointedly, palming the crown. "Remember the afternoon Victor took us to see the remains of that stable?" I nodded. "Remember my telling you there were two sets of horse prints?" I nodded again. "I told you that one set belonged to the killer because I could see where he'd run the Earl down, and the other set were deep, suggesting a heavy load: Elsbeth and the Earl."

"I remember."

"Nathaniel would have realized by the condition of her horse whenever she went out alone. When she returned, there would have been a marked difference in the beast's level of fatigue between carrying that slight woman as opposed to both her and a man with the girth of the Earl."

"Well, that's true...."

He smirked at me as he set the coin in motion again. "Elsbeth and the Earl met up at some prearranged place, no doubt their habit whenever she got out alone, and rode down to that stable together to avail themselves of its privacy. It explains how a man of the Earl's age and physical condition could have covered such a distance in so short a time. It also explains *why* he would have done so." He stared out into the night. "Consider that not one person in that household believed the Earl capable of covering such a distance on his nightly jaunts, and yet none of them has offered that explanation as a possibility."

"Which means what?"

"They all knew what was going on."

"You can't be serious."

"Deadly serious."

"Then you think Nathaniel followed Elsbeth and attacked her and the Earl in a jealous rage?"

"That *is* the rub." He knit his brow as he gazed up at the starry sky. "I think Nathaniel is innocent."

"Innocent? Then who do you suspect?"

Colin suddenly bolted upright, seizing the crown in midair. "Victor Heffernan."

"*Victor?!*" I was stunned by his accusation, especially given that he'd repeatedly insisted Lady Arnifour would never have hired us if she weren't confident of his innocence. And that's when I heard the frantic clatter of horse hooves bolting along the opposite side of the hedge we were hiding behind. "Oh," I mumbled. "You meant *that* was Victor Heffernan."

Colin gave me a sideways glance before leaning forward and pounding on the cab's roof. "Here's your chance, man," he called out. "Don't lose him and for heaven's sake, don't let him see that we're following him."

The driver jerked the reins and quickly guided us out onto the cobbled street that led back to the heart of London. Victor had already achieved some distance, making it unlikely that he'd take any notice of us, though I did worry we could lose sight of him once traffic picked up. Our driver proved himself adept, however, guiding the horse with equal parts skill and strength as he maintained an easy pace in Victor's wake. Nevertheless, Colin remained ratcheted forward in his seat, keeping a steely gaze on our quarry's dark, hunched back.

We were not forced to slow down until we'd reached the

narrowed streets of Whitechapel, the very same neighborhood as Warren Vandemier's opium club. It occurred to me that Victor could be headed there, but I rejected the notion as I knew he wasn't a user and couldn't imagine Nathaniel having anything to do with it, either.

Our cab careened around a dimly lit corner at a preposterous speed as I scanned the area ahead while waiting for gravity to grip our wheels again. I was relieved to catch sight of Victor among the throng cluttering the slim thoroughfare, dismounting and tying his horse to a post in front of a sorrowful-looking storefront. Our driver had also spotted him from his vantage point above and was bringing the cab to a smooth stop some distance from where Victor was still fiddling with his horse.

"Expertly done." Colin handed the man the entire fistful of notes I'd given him earlier. "You needn't wait for us."

"I'd be 'appy to," he assured, beaming at his earnings.

"Another time," Colin called back, and headed down the street, his eyes locked on Victor. "I never forget a helpful face."

As Victor ducked down an adjacent alleyway, Colin took off at a measured pace, forcing me to nearly break into a run to keep up. He slowed as he neared the corner and came to a stop, peering cautiously around the building's edge. He stood that way: morbidly still, his head cocked slightly, and all I could think was how glad I was that we were in this section of the city, as anywhere else his unorthodox stance would have attracted notice.

"Where's he gone?" I whispered in spite of the din in the street.

"Through a metal doorway on the left. Looks like a tenement building. I think we've struck gold."

"Suppose this turns out to be a pied-à-terre for Victor and Lady Arnifour?" I blurted out. "What if we walk in on something unseemly?!"

"Perish the thought." He pursed his face. And then he was off again, striding down the center of the alley with his eyes fixed on the doorway he'd seen Victor disappear through.

I followed as quickly and casually as I could, wondering how he intended to determine which of the building's flats was the one Victor had gone into. He entered the scrubby, dimly lit entryway and stopped in front of the bank of mail slots, slowly running a finger across each of the names. He skimmed each of the thin slips of paper until he reached the bottom and then, without the slightest hesitation, stabbed his finger at a name just shy of the midpoint.

"What?" I asked, my heart pounding in my ears.

"Desiree Helgman," he answered. "I think you were right."

"What?" I stared at him uncomprehendingly. "Right about what? Who's Desiree Helgman?"

He chuckled. "Doesn't the name Helgman rattle something in your brain?"

"Helgman?" I parroted in an effort to jog my gray matter.

He grinned. "It *is* rather inside out." He pointed to the letters in a seemingly haphazard order, one after another: "*L-a-n-g-h-e-m.* Langhem. Lady Arnifour's maiden name."

My jaw slackened and I laughed out loud.

"And Desiree, a derivative of the word 'desire,' is no doubt an unsubtle homage to how this place was used. Rather pedestrian."

"I just hope it's Nathaniel we find."

"Indeed."

We started up the narrow staircase hugging one side of the small foyer. Nothing about the building offered even a hint of gentrification, paling even in comparison to the faded austerity of the Arnifour estate. This was a place of profound desperation, of prostitutes and addicts. It seemed inconceivable that

Lady Arnifour would have come here for any purpose, let alone the one so clearly advertised on the mail slot.

"Do you suppose . . . ," I spoke softly as we creaked up the sagging stairway, ". . . that the Earl might have found out about this place and tried to blackmail his wife? That's one way he could've gotten his hands on her money again."

"The inestimable value of one's reputation," he muttered. "You could be right. There's certainly nothing that matters more to the titled set." We came to the third-floor landing and he waved me back. "Stay away from the door." He spoke quietly as we approached number 304: Desiree Helgman's flat. "We'll not be knocking." He glared at the door as he pulled a small pistol from the breast pocket of his overcoat.

He backed up, gripped the doorjamb with one hand, raised a foot, and then stopped, looking at me with his leg dangling in midair. "If they're having it off," he whispered, "I'll pluck my eyes from my head." And then he crashed his boot against the flimsy knob.

Given the ease with which it sprang open I surmised that either the Earl had never had the occasion to follow his philandering wife or else she simply didn't care. Whichever the case, it gave way like a prostitute at last call, slamming so fiercely against the receiving wall that it left spidery fissures where the knob collided with it.

The room beyond was not well lit and it took a moment for my eyes to adjust, though I was aware of frantic movements almost at once. Colin didn't hesitate, however, but careened immediately inside. There was a rapid succession of shouting followed by the heart-seizing report of a gun.

And then there was silence.

No motion, no words, not even the life-affirming sound of a breath being drawn, for what felt an eternity until I became aware of someone pounding on the opposite side of a nearby wall and shouting, "*Shut the bloody hell up in there!*"

That muffled voice finally propelled me inside the tiny one-room flat once I'd done my best to seat the damaged door back into place. I came up behind Colin, standing no more than ten feet from where I'd been rooted, and saw that he had his gun leveled on the room's only window. Nathaniel was slumped on its sill, one leg out but the bulk of him still inside, his father standing beside him. I thought he'd been shot even though I couldn't see any blood before finally realizing that Colin had only fired a warning. He'd wanted to stop Nathaniel from fleeing down the fire escape and been persuasive with that one shot.

"Swing around, Nathaniel." Colin's voice was as calm as if he meant to discuss the night air. "And have a seat on the bed."

The young man did as he was told, pulling himself out of the window and dropping onto the large bed that dominated the room. As my heart began to settle I noticed that the flat was much more than what the dilapidated building seemed to suggest. While undeniably discreet in size and design, it was freshly painted and immaculately clean, and its sparse furnishings were as comfortable looking as they were new. Even the commode and sink, partially hidden behind a silk flat-panel screen, appeared to be pristine, as though they'd only recently been installed. The place was indeed fit for a lady, a lady and her paramour.

"You're makin' a dreadful mistake, Mr. Pendragon," Victor said in a pitifully beseeching voice. "Nathaniel didn't do anything. The boy's innocent."

"Of course. Innocent men always run."

"You're wastin' your time!" Nathaniel snapped. "Let 'em hang me. I don't care anymore."

"*No!*" Victor stepped toward Colin, his eyes blazing. "I will *not* let you accuse my son of something he didn't do."

"May I remind you, Victor, that I've yet to accuse your son of anything. And that's despite his proximity to Elsbeth's bedside the night she died."

"I didn't kill her, you tosser," Nathaniel spat. "I loved her. If you were half as smart as they say, you'd already know that."

"Nathaniel . . ." Victor shrank back.

"The boy's right." Colin shoved the gun back under his vest. "I suspected it but haven't been able to find any proof, and without proof all that's left is supposition, which is really little more than overinflated rumor. But the one thing that keeps nagging at me is why the son of a groundskeeper would ever fancy himself a suitable match for a potential heiress to the Arnifour estate? How is it you thought the family would ever look kindly upon such a union?"

I caught Nathaniel stealing a peek at his father, but neither of them answered.

Colin rubbed his chin as he began pacing the short distance between the window and the door, being careful to keep himself placed to avoid giving Nathaniel a second opportunity to attempt an escape. After a couple moments of idle wandering with nary a breath from either of the Heffernans, Colin started up again. "Nothing? Then let's talk about your decision to flee the night Elsbeth died. Running off like a guilty man. Why would you do that if you've nothing to hide?"

"The inspector—"

"—is an ass who wasn't even there." Colin waved him off. "The coroner confirmed she died of the wounds sustained the night of the attack. She wasn't asphyxiated by you or anyone else. While your guilt in the initial attack may still be a matter of consideration, you have most assuredly been exonerated of any misdeeds the night she died. And you knew that. But you still ran off." Colin turned back and settled his gaze on Nathaniel. "So why is it I think you're still not going to be returning home?"

"Home?" Nathaniel said the word as though it was bitter on his tongue. "That decaying mausoleum is not my home."

"Nathaniel . . . , " Victor pleaded. "You mustn't say that. It isn't true."

"Of course it's true." He rubbed his forehead. "I don't belong there. I never have. You do. Elsbeth did. But I never fit in. I need to make my own way."

"No." Victor shook his head but made no move to reach out to his son. "Your future's there just as it's been for the past three generations of our family."

"Eldon's got no use for me. And Kaylin . . . ," he gave a slight shrug, "I don't think she has much use for any man."

"But Lady Arnifour—"

"Won't live forever." He stared at his father. "She only cares about me because of *you*," he added with surprising gentleness.

"She loves you—"

"She loves *you*." He glanced at Colin. "I'm sure that's no surprise."

"Just a moment," he interrupted, his brow deeply furrowed. "You just said you never fit in the way your father and Elsbeth did. And you've proclaimed that you loved her—*loved her*. But I've misconstrued your intent all this time, haven't I? You loved her, but not in the way I've presumed."

Nathaniel looked away as Victor raised his eyes to reveal them rimmed with red. I glanced back at Colin and tried to fathom what I'd missed. "Tell me . . . ," Colin said evenly, ". . . who was Elsbeth to you?"

Nathaniel's shoulders caved as he closed his eyes. "My half sister."

Victor collapsed onto the bed as I suddenly realized with the swiftness of undeniable truth how that could be.

"Lady Arnifour . . . ," Colin was saying, ". . . was Elsbeth's mother."

Victor did not speak as he buried his face in his hands, but I couldn't help thinking Nathaniel looked relieved as he shifted closer to his father and draped an arm across his shoulders. I was certain given the depth of Nathaniel's release that he alone had been privy to this information outside of his father and Lady Arnifour.

"You mustn't be angry with me," he said to his father with remarkable tenderness. "They were gonna find out. It's why I warned you about lettin' her hire them in the first place."

"She was worried about you." Victor sounded wounded by his shame.

"No. She worried about you."

"I've disgraced her," Victor choked.

"You've done no such thing," Colin spoke up. "But I will say—it's a marvel the way you were able to keep such a thing secret."

"But we didn't." Victor looked up, pale and drawn. "The Earl knew right off and he wasn't of a mind to help by claiming any such baby his own. No ... ," he shook his head as he pulled away from Nathaniel, "he forced her to go away as soon as the morning sickness took hold. Told people she was off helping a sister suffering with child. When she returned she brought our Elsbeth back. Claimed her sister had died in child-birth and the husband couldn't care for the infant alone. It was a good story. No one questioned it."

"How did Lady Arnifour get her husband to agree to raise Elsbeth as their niece?"

"Money."

"Of course. . . ." Colin shook his head. "And does anyone else in the household know? Mrs. O'Keefe?"

"No. No one."

"And how did Nathaniel come to the truth?"

"I told him," Victor mumbled as he wrapped his arms

around himself. "I'm the only family Nathaniel's ever had. I wanted him to know the truth in case something happened to me. I owed him that." His face was etched with regret.

"Is it possible Elsbeth knew? That she'd figured it out?"

"No." He sucked in a stilted breath. "Elsbeth had little interest in me. I couldn't see what good telling her would do. I knew she was happy believing she was one of them. . . ." He let his voice trail off.

"Why?"

Victor stared at his hands as though searching for the answer in the calluses and lines therein. Just when I thought he wasn't going to respond, Nathaniel spoke up. "She had no use for him," he stated. "She treated him like rubbish and acted like she was better than us. Always lookin' down on us. I wish you *had* told her. It woulda served her right."

"Nothin' good would have come of it," Victor muttered.

"And so Lady Arnifour paid her husband to keep him quiet," Colin repeated.

"She did. He spent the whole of Elsbeth's life forcing money from her. You've seen the estate. It's fallin' apart. And now there's only the few of us left to look after it. It's a disgrace." He shook his head again.

"Then you must be glad he's gone," Colin said.

"No you don't!" Nathaniel leapt off the bed. "You aren't gonna scab this on my father. Better you take me. The inspector—"

"Oh, to hell with the inspector," Colin shut him down. "Stop bringing that bloody wretch up and stop confessing to a crime you didn't commit. You're growing tiresome." He glanced back at Victor. "I assure you I would never try so obvious a way to entrap you if that were my intention."

Nathaniel dropped next to his father again.

"I *am* glad he's gone," Victor finally said. He looked small and inconsequential next to his lanky son, but there was a fire behind his eyes as he spoke. "He was a vile and hateful man who took some great pleasure in making his wife miserable."

"A man isn't guilty for wishing something to be so!" Nathaniel growled.

"Of course." Colin slid his gaze to me for an instant. "Though I suppose that depends on how badly he wants that thing." He came over to me. "In this circumstance I agree with you, Nathaniel. As I have repeatedly told you both, I am not accusing either of you of anything. I am only gathering information." He paused, but neither of the Heffernans even glanced at him. "There is one more thing I should very much like to know, Victor. You claim the Earl extorted money from his wife for years to remain silent about Elsbeth's progeny, yet he seems to have suffered from a reputation for being endlessly short on funds. How do you explain that?"

"It was a ruse, Mr. Pendragon."

"A ruse?"

"To demonize his wife."

"Ah . . . ," Colin said in a tone I recognized to be fraught with skepticism. "Then that is a thing he must have wanted very much, for it seems to have cost *him* as well."

"You don't know how much he hated her," Victor muttered. "A man like that cuckolded . . ."

"Ours can be such an unforgiving gender." Colin smirked as he turned on Nathaniel. "I think you're right to stay here, Nathaniel. Despite the coroner's findings, I doubt Inspector Varcoe would be of a mind to allow you to return to the Arnifour estate."

"I have no intention of ever going back."

Victor glanced at his son but kept quiet. He'd either lost the will to argue or finally come to understand the irrefutable truth of what Nathaniel had been saying.

"Stay out of sight," Colin warned as we headed for the door. "But I'll expect you to remain available should I wish to speak with you again."

"I'm not going anywhere," he muttered tersely. "Not yet anyway."

CHAPTER 25

The next morning Colin and I rode out to the Arnifour estate without the courtesy of any advance notice. He was eager to catch the lot of them at home, unsuspecting, to see what we might discover. As we clattered across the forecourt I caught the shadow of a face peering out at us from between the curtains of an upstairs window. The sight reminded me of just how many places this enormous house offered a person to hide. In effect, it made Nathaniel's flight to Whitechapel seem redundant. He would probably have been safer hiding in the moribund wings of the estate.

"You needn't wait," Colin said to the driver. "We'll make our own way back." I was puzzled by his pronouncement and wondered how he meant for us to get home again, but decided not to second-guess him. If this was to be a day of the unexpected, and we were certainly starting it out that way, then I was determined to allow things to unfold as they would.

I climbed the porch steps and pounded on the door as Colin came up beside me, the rhythmic clacking of our cab's wheels receding as we waited for the dour Mrs. O'Keefe to answer my knock. It took several minutes, as it inevitably does when unannounced visits are made, as nothing is at the ready and the staff can seldom be counted on to make haste. And why would they? Certainly no one of consequence would *ever* arrive without proper notification.

"I should've guessed," Mrs. O'Keefe said when she finally pulled the door open. She stepped back, wearing the disparaging look of a headmistress, her black eyes glittering with disapproval.

I was needled with discomfort as I walked past her, and yet Colin appeared quite oblivious. "You will announce us to your mistress, please," he said, and though he bothered to use the kindness of a pleasantry, it was obvious he did not mean it as a request.

"Madame has only *just* risen." Her note of scolding was unmistakable.

"I'm sure," he muttered as he moved across the foyer. "We shall wait in the study as always."

"Of course," came her clipped reply. "Most unorthodox," she stated in full voice as she turned on her heels and headed for the foyer staircase.

"And so it is," Colin called after her. "But we Brits are too conventional anyway. Perhaps more of such behavior would serve us better."

"Must you antagonize?" I hissed under my breath.

"Antagonize?" He looked wholly innocent as we settled before the unlit fireplace in the study and he began rolling his usual crown between his fingers. "Is that what I did?"

"And what would you call it?"

"Yes . . . well . . ." He shrugged. "She really should learn her place."

I started to laugh, the incongruity not lost on me between Mrs. O'Keefe's behavior and that of Mrs. Behmoth, but before I could say anything, Colin shoved the crown into his pocket and jumped up, a warm smile spreading across his face as he said, "Lady Kaylin..."

I turned to find Kaylin standing in the doorway wearing crop pants, a crisp white blouse and hunter green tailcoat, and high black boots, her delicate features alive with a most welcoming smile of her own.

"Kaylin," she chided. "What a pleasant surprise."

"The pleasure is ours." Colin nodded his head.

She waved him off with a laugh as she took a seat across from us. "Such a flatterer. Emmeline says a man who flatters intends only to deceive."

"I assume you're referring to Mrs. Pankhurst?"

"I am." Her smile grew.

"I rather think she is correct . . . at least most of the time. Yet she's wrong where I am concerned, for what possible motive could I have for idly filling the head of such a charming woman as yourself?"

"Perhaps you interpret her statement in too narrow a context?"

"Do you suppose? It would seem to me that Mrs. Pankhurst had only the most literal intent in mind."

"And I believe you underestimate her. She *will* make a difference one day, Mr. Pendragon. She will be remembered as a pioneer for the rights of *all* the oppressed."

"You must forgive me," he smiled, "I don't mean to disparage, but I think the only way your Mrs. Pankhurst will be remembered is if she chains herself to the gates of Buckingham."

She scowled. "And I would have thought you to be a more forward-thinking man."

"One cannot be progressive without first taking into account reality. For instance, I think you will agree that it's impossible for a solitary man to push an ox up a hill. The trick is to convince the ox that the top of the hill is where it wants to be."

"I do hope she's not lecturing you about that wretched sisterhood again. . . ." I turned around to find Eldon leaning against the doorjamb with his arms folded across his chest. "She does go on so."

Kaylin remained rigidly still for a moment, looking as though she were taking in her brother's disheveled appearance through the back of her head. When she finally deemed to turn to him, however, I could see her face begin to tighten. "Suffering from those dreary tremors again this morning, Eldon?" she scoffed.

He did look very much the worse for wear, having clearly slid on a pair of slacks that appeared to have spent some considerable time in a wad, and a shirt dotted with a mélange of stains, its tail fully asunder. I don't think his hair had even had the benefit of a quick run-through by a hand, and yet he was able to rouse his perpetual rogue's grin as he padded barefoot across the study to the small bar. When he swept past his sister I could see how morbidly pale he looked in contrast to her flushed, healthy glow.

He took a quick shot of something and smirked at her. "How like Mother you're becoming. It's so unflattering." He moved out from behind the bar and glared at me and Colin. "Tell me, gentlemen, have you managed to hunt down that scoundrel Nathaniel yet?" I glowered back at him. "No?" he continued when neither of us answered him. "Let me guess. I'll bet you're still concentrating on interviewing everyone this family has ever spoken to. You'll be wanting to dig up my pet rabbit, Cecil, I'm sure. I used to tell him all sorts of horrid little secrets."

"I have no interest in Nathaniel at this point," Colin answered.

"Really?! Do tell." Eldon's lack of earnestness was matched by the smirk blemishing his face.

"You can be such a bore!" Kaylin snapped.

"Now, now . . . if you please . . ." Colin leaned back in his chair and I could almost hear his eyes rolling. "I presume you're going for a ride?" he said to Kaylin.

"I am. The horses don't get enough exercise with Nathaniel gone. I don't think they should suffer for the things we've done."

"Speak for yourself," Eldon groused. "Do you need me, Mr. Pendragon? Because I have an engagement this morning."

"I do have a couple quick questions." He stood up and moved over to the fireplace, squaring himself off between the two of them. "How old were you when Elsbeth was brought here?"

"Elsbeth? What difference does *that* make? You think she killed our father and then beat herself senseless to cover her tracks?" He snickered, but to her credit, Kaylin kept still.

"Humor me."

"How the hell am I supposed to remember something like that? She's been here forever. Isn't that enough?"

"I was almost three," Kaylin spoke up. "Mother told me I was almost three when she brought Elsbeth home. That would have made you six."

He shrugged with disinterest and slouched back to the bar. "It amounts to most of our lives. I assume that's what you're getting at. She was like our sister. . . ." He waved his arms expansively. "She was like the dear sister I never had." He laughed.

"And what of her parents?" Colin pressed. "What happened to your aunt and uncle?"

"Dead." Eldon came around and flopped into a chair. "A yachting accident. Or maybe it was boredom?"

In an instant Kaylin stormed across the room and slapped her brother across the face with a crack that echoed in the confined space. It was startling, and even more so when the red-hot print began to rise on his cheek. "Have you no respect for *any-one?*" she seethed. "Has your drinking robbed you of all decency?"

He pushed himself to his feet, towering above her, and for a moment I thought he might pummel her back, but he only stepped around her and stalked back to the bar. "We all have our crutches," his voice was low and flat as he refilled his glass, "whether it be drink, drugs, pleasures of the flesh, or that women's claptrap you subscribe to, so I wouldn't point fingers."

She stared at him with a mixture of fury and revulsion before storming out of the room.

"Insufferable bitch," he said as he downed a shot.

"What are you talking about?" I turned at the sound of Lady Arnifour's voice to find her standing in the doorway, a vision of hurried preparations, her thick makeup indelicately applied, her dressing gown clutched tightly in a thin hand, and her dark wig the slightest bit askew. "What have you been telling them?"

"The truth," he sneered. "But I do hope that doesn't cause you to lob another grenade at me."

She didn't flinch. "You confuse the venom you find at the bottoms of your bottles for truth. Now get upstairs and pull yourself together."

He glared at his mother like he was staring at muck caught between his toes, but she didn't waver the slightest as she scowled back at him, and after a moment he had little recourse but to storm from the room with what dignity he could muster.

Lady Arnifour closed the doors behind him with a look I couldn't quite gauge before turning back to us with a forced smile that failed to contain a shred of welcome. "I'm afraid I must apologize for my son's behavior yet again. It seems he is always displaying the worst of himself when the two of you are here."

"You mustn't," Colin replied as he flashed his own hollow grin. "After all, we did descend upon you without notice."

"I'm sure you have your reasons," she said, moving into the room and perching on the edge of a chair like someone who didn't expect to be there long. "Do you bring news?"

"I've not solved the murders if that's what you're asking, but I have come into some information which I simply must discuss with you."

Lady Arnifour flicked her gaze to me before abruptly springing to her feet and going to the windows. I was certain I'd spotted a look of concern in her eyes so was not surprised when she kept silent for a few minutes. I peered over at Colin and found him focused on her back and knew he meant to wait her out. And so we stayed that way until I heard the sound of a galloping horse draw near and caught sight of Kaylin bolting past. In the brief moment it took her to cross my field of vision I recognized the skill with which she drove her handsome mount. Lady Arnifour also seemed to soften as she watched her daughter thunder by, and although she did not turn back to us, she did finally begin to speak.

"Poor Kaylin has suffered the sole responsibility of caring for our horses since Nathaniel's disappearance. Victor just doesn't have the heart for it."

I took note of her informal, almost intimate use of Victor Heffernan's name and realized, in that one small gesture, that everything had changed.

"I would appreciate your providing me a closing statement, Mr. Pendragon," she continued, "as I won't be requiring your services any longer."

"A closing statement?" He lurched out of his chair. "But I haven't finished my investigation. I haven't solved the ruddy case."

She persisted in staring out the window in spite of the fact that Kaylin had long since passed from her view. "I understand all of that, Mr. Pendragon, but as I brought you into this sorrowful mess, so I am now removing you from it."

His face soured. "May I ask—"

"You may not," she cut him off. "I don't owe you an explanation, only the remuneration for your services."

"You're making a mistake."

"Perhaps. But it is mine to make."

"I *will* solve this case."

"Not at my expense." And with that she turned from the window and faced us, her expression as tight as granite.

"I see," he said grimly. "Then am I to understand that you're no longer interested in seeing justice served in the deaths of your husband and daughter?"

I almost gasped as he flung the question at her and could tell by the mortification on her face that she was equally stunned.

"How *dare* you . . . ," she blustered, but it was evident that the comment had struck bone.

"You hired me to discover the truth and that's exactly what I've been doing."

"I hired you to prove the innocence of a man and you have done that. Nathaniel's flight speaks for itself. The inspector has men searching the city for him and in time, perhaps, he will be found and brought to justice. I suggest you accept your success, Mr. Pendragon, and take heed with such wild innuendos."

"You know as well as I do that Nathaniel is innocent."

"Your presumption is offensive."

"My presumption is no more offensive than your willingness to allow that boy to pay for a crime he did *not* commit," he snarled at her.

She stormed across the room and flung the doors wide. "We are finished here," she seethed. "I will thank you to leave."

He took his time walking to the door, holding her gaze with

his own. "Very well," his voice was measured and flat, "but know that I'll not allow him to be turned over to the Yarders and I would caution you against doing the same."

"You forget yourself, Mr. Pendragon!" she snapped.

"I do no such thing," he answered. "I do no such thing."

CHAPTER 26

———✦———

I followed Colin without a word before remembering that he had released the cab upon our arrival. I couldn't believe that he meant for us to walk all the way back to town and so hung my hopes on the probability that he'd already formulated a plan. But as we continued to storm down the driveway without the slightest falter, I began to give up hope. And then we crested the driveway's second hill and he abruptly turned right and plunged into the woods without so much as a backwards glance to see if I was following. He knew I would be.

We continued in silence, crashing through thick brush that clawed at my trousers until we emerged onto a promontory that overlooked a velvety green meadow. Colin stopped and leaned back to draw in a deep expanse of morning air. "Spectacular," he said breezily. "Why is it the moneyed are the last to appreciate what they have?"

"Well . . . ," I sucked in my own deep breath, ". . . because it's impossible for a person to value that which they've never had to do without."

He chuckled. "Profound."

"Tell me . . . ," I said as I gazed out to the horizon, "did you remember you'd let the cab go when you stalked out of the house?"

He shrugged. "Not exactly. But I can't remember everything. You are certainly free to contribute whenever you think it might be valuable."

"I shall remember that the next time you're crossing words with a client who lives out in the country."

"Crossing words?" His nearest eyebrow shot up. "Is that what you think happened?"

"Didn't it?" I couldn't help chuckling. "Wasn't that you who just threatened her about giving Nathaniel to the Yard?"

"I suppose so." He waved me off and started barreling across the field, leaving a trail of bent grass in his wake, which I followed. "I'm not really angry with Lady Arnifour," he called back, "because I'll solve this case anyway. I don't need another farthing from her."

"So you don't care about being fired?"

"Fired?!" He curled his mouth with distaste. "I prefer to call it *freed*. Can we leave it at that?"

"Still . . ."

"Let me ask *you* a question." He tossed back a rogue's grin. "Did you notice at what point in our questioning of Eldon that Lady Arnifour arrived?"

"I haven't a clue." I laughed.

"We were talking about his earliest memories of Elsbeth and what had happened to her parents. He was reciting the story he'd been told as a boy. Lady Arnifour knew where I was leading him. It's why she stopped our conversation and sent him slinking upstairs. And I've no doubt she knows exactly where we got that information from."

"Because the Heffernans are the only other ones who know."

"Precisely. And she likely fears that if we can get those delicate details out of them, then there isn't much else we won't be able to extract." His pace slowed as he continued to move diagonally across the field toward another stand of trees. "She knows we've discovered where Nathaniel is hiding." He exhaled slowly. "I suspect we've become something of a threat to Her Ladyship. No doubt we've discovered far more than she ever intended. In fact," he nearly growled, "we have learned everything about this blasted case except who the bloody hell killed her husband and illegitimate daughter, and why?"

I was startled by the intensity of his frustration as I stared at him. "How can we be a threat to her? We're trying to solve these murders. I mean, it's one thing that she didn't care about her husband—that marriage had soured years ago—but Elsbeth was her own flesh and blood!"

"Yes. And she was born of an illicit union that caused Lady Arnifour a lifetime of grief."

"That's deplorable!"

I could tell he was struggling not to laugh at my indignation. "Not everyone harbors the same sense of propriety that you do. And that is exactly what has kept us employed all these years: the rabble who believe they are either above the law or smarter than it."

"But we're talking about love. We're talking about family bonds—" But even as the words fell from my mouth, I recognized the intricacies of what I was saying. I knew better. My own childhood spoke of something very much different from the whimsy I was trying to float.

"Where have you gone off to?" I heard him say, and allowed him to impel me back. "Work awaits," he announced, gesturing toward a rocky outcropping a short distance away. I followed his gaze and spotted Kaylin Arnifour seated on one of the boulders, her horse tied to a willow tree off to one side. She was staring away from us, gazing resolutely at the vast grassy lands stretching beyond her. "Did you know she'd be here?" I asked.

"I hoped she would. I've been following her trail since we left the house. Surely you knew that?"

"Trail?"

"Bent grass, snapped underbrush, fresh hoofprints. Have you not noticed any of it?"

I shrugged. I had no better answer to preserve my self-respect.

"Well, where did you think we were going?"

I shrugged again.

"Such devotion." He laughed.

"So what *are* we doing here?" I asked, eager to stop feeling the fool.

"We've come to gain some clarity." He started moving toward the promontory Kaylin was perched upon. "And to get a ride home."

It was my turn to laugh, as I knew that had *not* been part of his original plan, and that's when Kaylin turned and spotted us. She waved as though pleased to see us, which I doubted given the desolation of her chosen spot.

"I hope you don't mind the intrusion," Colin called as he picked his way across the boulders.

"Not at all. You're both welcome to my bit of refuge any time you feel the need. You'll find me here often, I'm afraid."

"It is a beautiful place," Colin said as he achieved the summit.

I pulled myself up behind him and was shocked by what I saw. The lush field was indeed remarkable, dotted with great stands of oaks and willows in a haphazard harmony that only nature can produce. Yet off in the distance to the left, sitting like a smudge on an otherwise flawless panorama, stood the scorched remains of the barn her father and half sister had been murdered beside. It was an unnerving sight that could only be ignored with considerable effort.

"Is this where you seek your solace then?" Colin asked as he dropped down next to her.

"Elsbeth and I used to ride out here all the time. It was our sanctuary. I haven't been up here since . . ." She pulled her knees in tight and hugged herself. "It doesn't help to be able to see that." She nodded toward the charred remains. "I've decided to face this direction for the time being," she said as she half-turned so she was facing Colin.

"Once that's torn down and hauled away you'll see the earth heal herself," he reassured. "There'll be no trace. You'll have this to yourself again."

"I know," she sighed. "But at the moment I can't imagine that will ever be true."

"Never discount the resilience of either nature or the human spirit."

"I'm afraid my family's spirits come mostly in a bottle."

"So I've noticed."

"Don't judge us too harshly, Mr. Pendragon." She sighed again as though the effort of defending her family were more than she could bear.

"I don't judge you at all. I must admit to living something of an unconventional life myself," he said, flicking a glance at me that was thankfully missed by Kaylin.

"But you uphold the standard that everyone is expected to live by, Mr. Pendragon. The standard of law."

"I suppose I do." He leaned back on his hands. "But only those laws that make sense to me."

"Are you telling me there are laws even you will break?" She grinned.

"There are laws I break every day." He smiled back.

"May I ask you something?" I interrupted, eager to steer the conversation to safer grounds. "Are you and your neighbor, Mrs. Roynton, well acquainted?"

"Abigail Roynton?" She looked at me curiously. "We speak whenever we happen to attend the same engagements, but I would never call her a friend. I find her indiscretions to be the sort of vulgar behavior that sullies the reputation of all women. Never mind that my father fell prey to her. Men can hardly be blamed for what they have no control over. And I mean no offense." But I could see she meant exactly what she'd said. "And why do you ask such a thing?"

"Because while I also found Mrs. Roynton unconventional to be sure, I thought there was something rather liberating in her ideals—"

"Liberating?!" She nearly choked as she glared at me. "If behaving without scruples can be construed as liberation, then I suppose you're right. I find her boorish and nothing less than despicable. It does nothing but impede the good work of the suffragists."

"Of course," I demurred, though I was actually wondering whether she thought Abigail Roynton capable of complicity to commit murder.

"Don't fall out of step with the movement and get left behind," she continued to persist. "We are at the precipice of a new millennium and with it will come a world where men will no longer be allowed to accommodate their every whim at the expense of women. I'm sure I needn't remind you that without women there would *be* no men."

"Yes. We figured that out some time ago." Colin flashed a tight grin. "But do let me ask you about Eldon. . . ."

She grimaced. "I must apologize. I behaved badly with him and I'm terribly sorry. Eldon's always had a tougher go of things. Our father was forever demonstrating his disapproval and I'm afraid Eldon took the brunt of it."

"And what was it your father was perpetually disapproving of?"

Kaylin stared out across the landscape for a moment before answering. "I always remember Eldon being an awkward boy, terribly shy, hanging around my mother's skirts, having no interest in his studies or hunting. For the longest time my mother promoted that. She protected him. But she got distracted as we grew older and eventually . . ." She let her voice drift off.

"Your brother's travails notwithstanding," Colin said with a noticeable lack of empathy, "there is something weighing on my mind that I hope you might be able to explain." He steadied his gaze on the side of her face. "As I'm sure you are aware, your father had a reputation for being kept on a tight financial rein by your mother. Nevertheless, I've come to believe that he may in fact have had access to considerable funds throughout the years. If that proves correct, what do you think he might have done with any money he was able to amass?"

"Considerable funds?! My father?! That's absurd. He had what my mother gave him, and that only begrudgingly."

"I'm not so sure that's true."

"No one would have given him money. I'm sorry, Mr. Pendragon, but that doesn't make sense."

"Even so, for sake of the exercise, I'd like to hear what you imagine he might have done with a ready supply of cash?"

She looked at him a minute, and then turned to me as though I might see the folly in what he was suggesting, but I knew he meant to have an answer. "I can't even fathom such a possibility. My father was horrendous with money. I'm afraid you've struck upon a preposterous notion. Whoever told you such a thing was deceiving you. It isn't true."

"Well then . . ." He smiled easily and turned his gaze back across the field. "I'm only trying to ensure I follow every possible supposition."

"A noble goal." She stood up and stretched. "But I'm afraid I must be getting back to the house. I have four more horses to run today."

"Of course, but might we trouble you for one more thing?"

"I'll do whatever I can," she said as she nimbly picked her way down off the boulders.

"We find ourselves without a way back to town. Could you possibly?"

She glanced up at us, a generous smile parting her lips. "I'll have to take you one at a time."

"Certainly."

She let out a satisfied laugh. "I very much like this. For once the damsel gets to come to the rescue."

CHAPTER 27

I admit that I was surprised. After Kaylin dropped me off I had assumed Colin would be no more than an hour behind, so when he arrived three hours later reeking of lavender perfume and champagne I was not particularly pleased. He explained that he had decided to visit the widow Roynton while waiting for Kaylin to come back for him, and that Mrs. Roynton had sent him home in her own carriage. "She's really just an old flirt." He snickered.

"I should hardly think anyone would refer to her as *old*," I replied with perhaps a touch more sarcasm than I had intended.

It got another snicker out of him just the same. "Shouldn't you be asking if I learned anything of value?"

"I was getting to that," I said. "It's just hard talking to you when you smell like a wine-soaked floral shop."

He sniffed at his coat as he pulled it off. "Hmm. I suppose you have a point."

I could only shake my head. "She helpful then?"

"Helpful?!" he repeated as he dropped to the floor and began a quick succession of push-ups. "I'm happy to report that the lovely widow admitted several things to me," he said without missing a beat. "Not the least of which is that she can absolutely believe our noble Earl had access to money he didn't let on about. She insists there was no limit to his levels of deceit. Yet she professes no idea as to what he might have done with any such sizeable fortune. Nevertheless . . . ," he jumped up and rotated his arms with a satisfied sigh, "she suggested someone who she believes shares the late Earl's lack of conscience and just might have an idea."

"And who would that be?"

He grinned as he snatched up one of his dumbbells and began curling it effortlessly while pacing. "Poor, carping Warren Vandemier. She thinks the Earl's partner has far more up his sleeve than he is letting on."

"But all he did was prattle on about how the Earl cheated him."

"Precisely. He put up such protestations that it reminded me of that Shakespeare quote."

"What Shakespeare quote?"

He cocked an eyebrow and glanced at me. "You know the one: *Methinks he doth protest too much*?"

"*The lady.*"

"What?"

"*The lady doth protest too much*. Hamlet's mother says it."

He shrugged, switching the dumbbell to his other hand. "Details."

"So now you're tying your deductions to the intrigues of literary characters?"

He shrugged. "Good literature, by its very definition, casts an unwavering eye on the truth of humanity. That's what gives it its profundity."

"This from a man who never reads."

" 'Ay?" Mrs. Behmoth hollered. "Ya got comp'ny comin'. Stop yer cluckin'."

"Ever so gracious," I muttered.

"*I 'eard that. . . .*"

Colin hurried to the window and gazed down onto the street. "Well now, here's an unexpected turn. Eldon Arnifour has come to pay a visit."

"Lock the liquor cabinet."

"Perish the thought," he said as he rolled the dumbbell under the settee and took a seat. "It's important that he have plenty to drink lest he harbor any hesitancy about saying whatever he's come to say."

"*Lord Eldon Arnifour comin' up!*" Mrs. Behmoth yelled from the bottom of the stairs.

"I hate when she does that," I grumbled.

"I should think you'd long be used to it by now."

Not a moment later Eldon appeared on the landing in his typical disheveled fashion, sporting a crooked grin that undoubtedly spoke more to the amount of drink he'd consumed than any sense of good mood. "Have a seat," Colin said magnanimously. "Make yourself at home."

"I don't think you really mean to say such a thing to me." He chuckled as he dropped onto the same settee his mother had collapsed upon the day she hired us. "I'm afraid home has no particular fondness for me. But could I trouble you for a drink?"

"I assume you're not referring to tea?"

"Not unless there's a fair amount of scotch in it."

"We could do that if you'd like or we could just forego the tea completely," Colin said, producing our bottle of scotch from its eternal resting place in the cupboard.

"Now there's the best idea yet. No wonder your services are so well respected, Mr. Pendragon. And anyway, I'd hate to force that delightful woman downstairs to tote a tray of tea all the way up here."

"And for that I know she would thank you." Colin poured three small glasses, giving Eldon the most, and handed them out. If Eldon noticed that his glass was fuller than ours he certainly didn't seem to care. "So tell me . . . ," Colin sat down and casually placed his untouched drink on the table between us, "to what do we owe this unexpected pleasure?"

"I'm tired of being censored by my mother every time we try to have a conversation. The old harridan thinks she controls everyone, but she doesn't toe the line on me. Oh no. I've come to say some things I'll wager you've not heard before," he said with great bluster before he drained his glass. "Is there a limit?" He glanced at Colin.

"Only by virtue of what's in the cupboard. Help yourself."

Eldon popped up, not warranting a second invitation, and refilled his glass. "Did you know, gentlemen, that my esteemed father once had quite the dalliance with that charming bulldog Mrs. O'Keefe?" He laughed coarsely. "Just imagine *that*, if you will."

Colin slid his gaze to me, but I couldn't tell if it was doubt or disbelief in his eyes. "And why would that bear any interest? It seems to me your father rutted just about anyone who would let him."

Eldon wandered back over to us, the whiskey bottle clutched firmly in one hand. "Ah yes, it is a curse of the male Arnifour progeny. It is a need, not a desire, that we elevate to an art. Surely you must be able to understand that, Mr. Pendragon. You're something of a strapping man yourself. I'm sure you've turned the ladies' heads many a time."

"I'm sure I haven't noticed," he drolled. "But you were talking about Mrs. O'Keefe. While I'm certain she must be a delightful housekeeper, I'm finding it something of a struggle to fathom why your father would be interested in shagging her."

Eldon chuckled as he shrugged lazily. "Availability, I suppose. My mother was indisposed carrying Kaylin and where else could the poor man turn? We didn't have any other female help at the time and she's always made such a fuss over him.

Anyone can see it. I wasn't quite five at the time and I knew she was keen on him." He winked and tipped his glass at Colin as he took another sip.

"Well, this is all very fascinating . . . ," Colin said as he got up, "but I fail to see—"

"Then stop interrupting," Eldon sniped as he stabbed his glass onto the table in front of him. "You are missing the point, Mr. Pendragon, because you have not let me finish."

Colin snatched up the hunting knife he had left on the mantel and began buffing its blade with a handkerchief he pulled from his pocket. "Forgive me," he said with more sincerity than I could have achieved at that moment. "By all means . . ."

Now that Eldon knew he'd earned our fullest attention, or at least the closest we were ever likely to accord him, he made a great show of pouring another two fingers into his glass and settling back before continuing. There was also a rakish grin teasing the corners of his mouth. "My mother was quite ill when she carried Kaylin. She kept to her room nearly the entire time, which left my father to chase Mrs. O'Keefe about like a middle school boy. This *is* quite some time ago." He chuckled and allowed himself another sip of his drink.

"While I was certainly very young, I was not blind to the incongruity of my father and Mrs. O'Keefe sneaking about, especially with her giggling like a coquette whenever my father was nearby. It was all very appalling, which is precisely why I remember it. Why is it that such things stick in our brains while that which is most cherished is as fleeting as a cut rose?"

"Are you asking me?" Colin asked as he continued to buff the knife blade. "Or am I still just listening?"

Eldon's brow furrowed. "Really, Mr. Pendragon, you're being most uncivil when I've only just come to tell what I know."

"Yes, yes," he muttered. "Very obtuse of me."

Eldon seemed to ignore Colin as he held his glass up right in front of his eyes with a look of great enticement. "I should think you would find it interesting to hear that our dear Mrs. O'Keefe began putting on weight while my own poor mother was lying about upstairs trying to ensure the safe arrival of our Kaylin. I remember it because I said something to my nanny about the suddenly expanding Mrs. O'Keefe and was quite soundly thumped for my cheek. It was only some years later that I realized what had likely transpired." He leered.

I clamped my mouth shut to keep my jaw from unhinging, certain I must be misinterpreting his meaning. Even Colin kept still for a protracted period of time before finally screwing up his face and asking, "Are you suggesting that Mrs. O'Keefe was with child at the same time as your mother?"

"Ah . . ." Eldon grinned roguishly as he tipped his glass. "There's the sleuth the papers adore."

"And you're saying your father was responsible?"

"Come now." Eldon took another sip as he stretched out on the settee. "Is that really so hard to believe? We've already established his propensity for a tryst, and you cannot deny that he was fully capable." He swept a hand across his body with a flourish, clearly meaning to present himself as the truth of that statement.

"How old were you at the time?"

Eldon heaved a sigh as though bothered by such a banal thought. "I was just about six and very precocious, and would've remained so if I hadn't been driven to spirits by the time puberty seized me." He scowled. "Mrs. O'Keefe got fleshy," he continued after a moment, "and then she was gone."

"Gone?"

He looked up at us and in that instant his usual derision had returned. "Packed off like the embarrassment she had become," he said gleefully. "She was gone for about four months. Who the hell can remember. But it was a bloody long time, that's for sure. Certainly long enough—" He let the sentence hang in the air.

"Where were you told she'd gone off to?"

He seemed to consider the question a moment as he cast his gaze about and pursed his lips. "I don't really remember anymore. Sisters? Aunties? Dog pound? Hard to say."

"I see . . . ," Colin muttered, and I could practically hear his brain whirring. "Suppose she *had* gone off to have a baby . . . what of it?"

"Well, there's the thing." Eldon nearly crowed his enthusiasm. It was evident he was taking great merriment in our skepticism, which I could not help but find unsettling. "Not long after Mrs. O'Keefe went missing—it couldn't have been six or eight weeks later—I awoke sometime in the night to a great deal of commotion. Dear Mother was not well, you see. There were all manner of people bustling about, and my cursed nanny kept trying to shoo me back to bed. But I wasn't having any of it. I hid in the shadows of the hallway until I saw them carry my mother past on a stretcher. There was a great crowd of people around her, so I couldn't see her face, but I could hear her crying. I remember being quite terrified." He let out a caustic laugh. "Can you imagine?

"My father finally noticed me lurking about and yanked me back to my bedroom with his usual brute affection," he chuckled again, "but not before I caught sight of the blood. There was a towel heaped on the floor of my mother's room that was saturated and a puddle of it near her bed. A young boy remembers a thing like that." He lifted his glass slightly and twirled its contents around a moment before deciding to continue. I couldn't tell whether he was drawn to the memory or repelled by it. "And do you know what my father told that snot-nosed, weepy-faced boy after pulling him back to his bedroom? He said: *Buck up, you little turd—your mother might not make it and we can't have you sniveling about.*"

I don't think I had really expected to hear anything much different, yet it remained striking just the same.

"I suppose your father was practical if nothing else," Colin said as he set the knife he'd been buffing back onto the mantel and stooped to poke at the fire. "But your mother did return and she brought Kaylin with her." Colin stood up and turned to Eldon. "She did bring Kaylin with her?"

A sly grin slowly grew on Eldon's face. "So clever, Mr. Pendragon. Kaylin came. Eventually. About a fortnight after Mother had returned from the hospital and just days before Mrs. O'Keefe made her own discreet homecoming. They told me dear sister had been sick and almost died, but as I got older and remembered all that blood, I began to wonder who was fooling whom."

Colin moved around and dropped back into his chair. "If what you're insinuating is true, why would your mother agree to such a ruse?"

"And that's the thing." Eldon finished off his scotch and pounded the glass onto the table with finality. "I believe this was perpetrated on my mother without her ever having the slightest notion. She wasn't around to see Mrs. O'Keefe's gradually burgeoning shape. And once my mother was in the hospital it would have been easy for my father to control what information she received. How he must have loved having her raise his daughter as though she were her own."

"Why would any doctor agree to such a sham?"

Eldon laughed. "Oh, come now, Mr. Pendragon, don't you know they're the worst type of addicts? They've got access to every sort of drug. And doesn't it take one addict to recognize another? That fact would never have been lost on my father." There was an odd note of pride in his voice.

Colin fished a coin out of his pocket and quietly began flipping it between his fingers. "Of course," he said after a moment, "this is all strictly conjecture on your part. Long-ago memories of a very little boy."

"Guilty." Eldon winked. "But surely a man of your prowess

has noticed how Mrs. O'Keefe dotes on little sister. And even now she remains the only one of us who gives a whit that Father's dead. Wouldn't she just be forever grateful that she had been able to tend to her own daughter all these years, even if the poor, stupid girl didn't know the truth."

"So why are you telling us this now?"

"Suppose my mother recently found out the truth? Suppose she discovered the fraud he'd been perpetrating on her all these years. How enraged do you suppose she would be?" He beamed with mischievous delight.

"So you are suggesting she may have had something to do with your father's murder then?" Colin's tone remained smooth and steady even though the very idea that Eldon had come to dangle such an accusation was entirely repellent.

"Oh," his smile dropped, "I'm more than suggesting it. My parents were a venal pair. If it wasn't for my inheritance I would have left that horrid place years ago."

"And how have you fared with your inheritance?"

Eldon shoved himself off the settee and stretched. "Everything my father owned has reverted to me."

"And Kaylin?"

He waved Colin off. "She inherits in name only."

"What specifically?"

"Everything."

"Your sister is a part owner of an opium den?" I blurted out, unable to contain myself.

"In name only, I said!" Eldon barked. "She has some ridiculous notion about liberating the women who work there. I told her to stick to her bloody horses and leave the rest to me. In fact, I think I may just go to the club tonight to claim what's rightfully mine from that maggot my father was in business with."

"Indeed." Colin's face turned grim. "Then perhaps we should come to your club tonight as well."

"Oh," he flushed, "you really must. Warren Vandemier had best beware, for tonight he will be made to pay. . . ."

I detested the idea of watching a surly and intoxicated Eldon Arnifour harangue against an equally addled Warren Vandemier. Even more so now that Eldon had so joyfully come to implicate his own mother. But most of all, I dreaded the thought of being inside an opium club again.

CHAPTER 28

W e arrived just after eleven that evening, both dressed plainly in an effort to be inconspicuous, although we'd had to use Eldon's name to get in. Colin had managed to refrain from asking if I was certain about accompanying him here again, but I could tell by his surreptitious glances that the question did not hover far from his lips. Everything looked familiar: the dense and seductive haze that wound through the scattered groups of people sharing pipes and the occasional loners randomly huddled about. Most of the doors to the private rooms lining the entrance hallway were closed, with the sheer drapery hanging around the main space affording what little privacy the rest of the clientele was accorded.

"You like company tonight?" asked the lovely Oriental hostess who ushered us inside.

"We would." Colin tossed her a dazzling smile. "Might *you* be available?"

She giggled behind a hand as she threw a glance toward the overbuilt man seated behind the door. "You funny," she giggled again, "but I only let customer in tonight. I find someone special for you." She looked at me. "You want two?"

"One," Colin answered. "We needn't be greedy."

She giggled yet again as she led us to a small area at one side of the room where several unoccupied lounges were arranged. We made ourselves comfortable, an easy task in such a setting, while she struck off to arrange a companion for us.

"The trick . . . ," Colin leaned in close to me, ". . . will be to get our new friend to partake without actually doing so ourselves. Tell me you're okay."

"Now don't start that," I warned.

He offered a wry smile. "All right then. Then I shall concentrate on worrying about myself."

"No worries!" A beautiful Oriental woman with the slightest figure I'd ever seen sidled up to us. She had delicate features and straight black hair that fell below her waist. "You relax," she said as she settled onto the lounge across from us, setting the water pipe she was carrying next to the candles on the table. "I take care everything."

Colin passed her a few pounds as she pulled a small pouch from the bodice of her dress. The pouch was little more than a tiny piece of fabric tied together at one end to form a teardrop shape. I knew she would be carrying more than a handful of these. Business, and her pay, depended on it.

She carefully set the little package on the table between us and tugged at the string binding it, revealing an oily black goop at its center. I was mesmerized as I watched her scrape the gummy substance into the thimble-sized metal holder also strung around her neck. With a practiced hand she slowly waved it over the open flame of a candle.

After no more than a minute she pulled a hairpin from behind her ear and gently coaxed the mixture into a thick, honey-like paste. As the pungent aroma gradually rose and drifted between us, swirling about and deftly stealing into our minds, she tipped the contents into the pipe's bowl and smiled at us.

"Who first?" She turned the pipe toward Colin.

"The honor is yours." He smiled back at her. "I must insist."

"No, no, no . . ." She shook her head and thrust the pipe out again. "Not right. Honor belong to customer."

"I insist." He snatched one of the candles and tilted it toward the bowl. "Now don't make us wait. . . ."

The young lady flicked her eyes left and right, clearly checking to see if anyone might catch her breaking what was certainly a house rule. Evidently satisfied, she quickly leaned forward and took a tug off the pipe without so much as touching it. She collapsed back onto her chaise and held the smoke deep in her lungs, her head lolling back as she stared up at the ceiling. After a few moments a gentle burst of smoke shot straight up from her mouth, mixing with the already murky air. "Wunnerful," she sighed. "Now you."

Colin snatched the pipe from her and made a great show of lighting it himself, bugging his eyes and alternating a sort of sucking and blowing combination that seemed to succeed in releasing a great deal of smoke without his apparently inhaling much. Still, it was more than I thought I could bear given the already toxic atmosphere swirling about my brain. So I was greatly relieved as I watched Colin push the pipe back toward our flushed attendant.

"No, no . . ." She giggled. "Not my turn. Is turn for friend." And as if to illustrate her point, she picked up the candle and waved it toward me. "You next. You have fun too."

"My friend started earlier this evening," Colin smoothly informed her as he lifted the candle from her hand and turned it, and the pipe, back in her direction. "Your turn. We have to catch up." He winked at her, sending her into a second round of soft-pitched giggles. This time, when he leaned the candle toward the bowl our companion didn't even bother to demur, but quickly swooped in and took a great, long pull.

"You very kind," she said, smoke leaking from the sides of her mouth. "I do you service in return." She smiled boldly, glancing from Colin to me. "I get us room. Show you trick with smoke."

Despite my foggy head, I managed to keep from laughing as Colin leaned forward and patted her knee. "No services. We've got that covered. What we'd really like is a little information. Could you help us with that?"

She looked deflated, since that was money that would have gone directly to her. "But I best in club. I please everyone."

"I'm sure you do. But what would be most pleasing is if you would tell us a little about the club's owner."

The woman scowled and shook her head. "I not like that. I work in club. Make people happy." She pushed the pipe toward me and gestured determinedly with the candle. "Your turn. No say no. Trust me. No talk about owner. Tonight, you owner."

"You misunderstand." Colin lifted the pipe from her hand and put it up to his own mouth, leaning forward and giving his elaborate show of smoking. "I'm a friend of Mr. Vandemier's. I just want to make sure he's treating you well." He sent a great discharge of smoke into her face, which she instinctively inhaled.

"Oh." She smiled. "No worry. Sometimes people say bad things, but I have no bad things to say." She took the pipe from Colin and pressed it into my hands. "You have some. Way past time for you."

"Way past time . . . ," I repeated numbly, lifting the pipe to my lips as I leaned in toward the nearest candle. I clenched the metal nipple between my teeth and tipped the candle forward, and instantly a rush of familiarity overwhelmed me in a sickening yet somehow welcoming way. With the sound of my heartbeat rocketing in my ears, I sucked on the pipe until I felt the first smooth tendrils of smoke curl into my mouth. It tasted soft and soothing, like a dear friend who'd been gone too long. My lungs struggled to reach up and draw it in: one inhalation . . . one weedy taste . . . just one . . . but before I could be thusly seduced Colin yanked the pipe from my hands and ground his heel into my foot. I yelped, expelling the smoke in a single coughing burst.

"There, there," he muttered with mock concern, slapping my back a bit too heartily. "Let's not be greedy."

"No," I stammered, my eyes watering as I looked up and spotted the concern behind his eyes. "No," I repeated, more for myself.

"Would you say Mr. Vandemier is a good man?" Colin turned his attentions and the pipe back to our young attendant. "Is he fair? Kind?"

"He not owner. He only manage. You say he friend . . ." She slid the pipe out of Colin's hand and began to refill it. "How come you not know that?"

"He told me the club was his." Colin hiked an eyebrow as he watched her. "Has he been feeding me a line of trifle?"

The young woman giggled. "He no own. Owner dead."

Even with the miasma fingering about my mind I understood the profundity of her words. If she was right, if she was telling the truth, then Warren Vandemier had far overstated his value in the enterprise. There would be a great deal more for him to explain.

"Are you certain?" Colin pressed as he snatched up the candle and lit the refreshed bowl for her.

"Oh yes. Everybody know he dead. Somebody kill him."

"I meant Warren Vandemier. Are you certain he's not the owner?"

She shrugged as she took another tug on the pipe. "He always getting yelled at. Make him mad. He take it out on us.

With owner gone now he happy. Say he own place, but he still only manage."

"Then who's the owner?"

"Owner dead."

Colin smiled and leaned forward, tipping the candle to relight the pipe for her. "But if the owner's dead . . . ," he said with remarkable patience, ". . . then who's the owner now?"

"Why don't you ask someone who knows?" came the tight, grating voice of Warren Vandemier.

I turned to face him and caught a glimpse of the hostess who'd seated us the first time lurking in the shadows. She had done us in—again. I wondered whether she'd recognized us or if perhaps she'd caught us ministering to our young companion's obvious habit.

"I thought I'd put an end to the two of you skulking about!" Mr. Vandemier growled.

"Skulking?!" Colin stood up and smiled. "And since when is availing ourselves of a public establishment considered skulking? I thought you'd be glad for the business."

"Perhaps you'd prefer to cease this charade and speak to me. It seems such a waste of your time otherwise."

"Not a waste at all," Colin answered. "You'd be amazed at the things one hears in a place like this."

Warren Vandemier scowled irritably. "Let me be clear, Mr. Pendragon, I neither need nor care about indulging your business. So unless you'd like to be escorted from the premises . . . again . . . ," he nodded toward the entrance hall, ". . . then I would suggest you come with me. We can attend to whatever questions you have and then I shall ask you to leave for the last time. You . . . ," his brow furrowed deeper as he threw a sideways glance at me, ". . . and Mr. Pruitt are not welcome here."

"Well . . ." Colin smiled, "I'm almost hurt. Come then, it would seem there's to be no leisure for us."

I stood up and had to take a moment to steady myself before I could follow Colin and Mr. Vandemier to a side door that led to a plain wooden staircase that was clearly not for regular customers. "Go on. Go on up," Mr. Vandemier said with a thick amount of impatience. "I'll be there in a minute." We'd gotten no more than halfway up when he bellowed out, "And I'll thank you not to go mucking about my things!"

"As though I would do such a thing," Colin called back with a chuckle. "I explore . . . ," he muttered under his breath. "I do not muck about."

The door below slammed shut, offering its own stinging retort.

"I don't trust that man," I said as we reached the cramped office at the top. "And I doubt he's ever said a word of truth to us."

"I'm sure there's truth to be found around the edges," he answered, and started right in poking about the enormous desktop.

I sat down and attempted to get comfortable in one of the straight-backed chairs clearly not crafted for comfort. "He is working every side against the other, which makes me suspicious."

"I would hope so." He glanced at me with a smile as he pawed through a mountain of papers on one corner of the desk. "But there's nothing of interest here."

He abandoned his rummaging and set to peeking behind the small, smoke-stained paintings of scantily clad women that hung on the walls. There was a lone filing cabinet shoved in one corner and I reached out and found that the drawers willingly sprang open. As I began to paw through them, it quickly became evident that there was no need to lock what no one else could decipher. Cryptic notes on files containing no other discernment than a single letter were not going to reveal a thing.

"Anything?" he asked as he settled down beside me.

"I'm afraid he's too clever for that."

The sound of the door below was followed by the plodding

of footsteps on the stairs, and a moment later Warren Vandemier stomped in. "I hope you're happy," he snarled as he sat behind his desk. "You've cost that girl her job."

"That seems a bit harsh—" Colin started to say.

"Not in the least." He leaned forward and locked eyes with Colin. "I don't hire addicts."

"Come now. . . ." He smirked. "Even you must realize you've got nothing *but* addicts working here."

Warren Vandemier stiffened. "Why are you here?"

"We've been hearing stories about money, Mr. Vandemier. The Earl's money to be precise. And more than a few rumors about your partnership. And most astonishingly, these stories bear little resemblance to what you told us a few days ago. I'm left quite disconcerted. I've decided I owe you an opportunity to reconsider some of the bollocks you've been trying to sell us."

To my amazement Mr. Vandemier broke into an easy smile, looking at us with considerable disinterest and an obvious lack of concern. Something was most assuredly amiss. "Such a generous gesture on your part, Mr. Pendragon, especially given that your services for Lady Arnifour have been dismissed." And there it was then. That news had traveled fast. "Under the circumstances . . . ," he stared at us with beaming self-satisfaction, ". . . I hardly think I owe you an explanation about anything."

"Though I am no longer being compensated," Colin glared back at him, "you can be sure I will still solve this case. Do not underestimate my determination, Mr. Vandemier."

"Perish the thought." He chuckled. "I'm sure I wish you all the best, but you'll get nothing more from me." He flashed his crooked yellow teeth at us. "I've nothing more to say to you. Ever."

"And that is curious. Because I can't understand why an innocent man would be unwilling to answer a few questions?"

"A few questions?! Is that what you have? Then tell me, why would you be twiddling about downstairs, doping that stupid girl, if all you wanted was to ask me a few questions? Now really, Mr. Pendragon."

"I had no idea you'd be so magnanimous with your time," Colin answered smoothly. "So let me ask you, if the Earl was as flush with cash as I now believe him to have been, why are you insisting he never paid his share in this establishment?"

Mr. Vandemier pursed his lips and snatched up a half-smoked cigar from an ashtray filled with them. Only after the stink of it had been suitably sucked into his lungs did he finally deem to answer the question. "I had to protect myself," he said.

"Whatever from?"

"This may come as a surprise to you, Mr. Pendragon, but not all of the late Earl's family is particularly fond of me."

"Pray tell. . . ."

"His son's a turd and that nettlesome daughter of his—"

"Lady Kaylin?"

"I believe he only had the one." His sarcasm was wholly evident on his face. "She would sooner slit my throat than look at me when it was *her* father who bankrolled this. I wanted the lot of them to think I fronted the old stiff the money so they'd piss off and leave me alone. I knew none of them would make good on any debt they thought he owed me." He snickered. "Now that you're no longer taking his old widow's wages—" But that was as far as he got before the door below abruptly slammed open and was followed by the panicked footfalls of someone rapidly assaulting the steps.

"*MR. VANDEMIER!*" A terrified pasty-faced young man rose into view. "It's Li Shen. She's gone daft. She's set the club on fire."

"*What?!*" He bolted to his feet and rushed around the desk, catching himself sharply at the hip. "*Dammit to bloody hell!*" he bellowed as the first wafts of acrid smoke began to overpower the opiate scent clinging in the air. "Those blasted idiots were supposed to get her out of here."

"She was acting crazy." The young man kept flicking his eyes nervously about the room. ". . . Clawing . . . scratching . . . screaming. And then she set one of the curtains on fire, and then another, and then another—"

"*I get it!*" He nearly punched the man as he shoved past him. "If this club suffers any damage you and the rest of those idiots will pay every farthing to repair it!" he hollered as he flung himself down the stairs.

The young man stared at us slack-jawed a moment, looking like a terrified alley cat, before he suddenly gathered himself and went bolting back down the stairs. I'd done no more than turn my gaze back to Colin when Warren Vandemier and his young liege came thundering back up. Mr. Vandemier now looked a great deal more distressed than angry, and I knew it was bad.

"The whole place is ablaze," he blurted out.

"The door?" Colin said as we scrambled to our feet.

He shook his head. I looked back and noticed the first black wisps of smoke beginning to waft up the stairwell. My eyes began to sting and I felt my heartbeat surge as I realized time was quickly running out.

Colin pushed past Mr. Vandemier and the young man, seizing the chair he'd been sitting on and heaving it out the room's only window. "I would suggest . . . ," he said with steely calm, ". . . that we find some way to climb down while we've still got the chance." He shoved me toward the window. "You first."

I didn't need to be coaxed, though I am not especially enamored of heights. I crawled out onto the window's thin ledge and tried to keep myself focused to allay my fears. All I knew was that I would be leaping down onto unforgiving cobblestones and a steadily increasing band of sooty, gagging people who even now were stumbling from the club's door. There had to be some way I could lower myself at least partially, and that's when I spotted the shutters hanging just below me.

I shifted my weight and jockeyed around so I was facing the inside of the building and then with both hands clutching the windowsill I slowly lowered myself, flailing my legs until I felt the top of the shutters just below. Colin scrambled out the window as soon as I'd cleared the ledge and quickly worked himself around as I had. He started to lower himself and I was able to reach his feet to help him gain purchase. He let go of the ledge just as Warren Vandemier scuttled onto it, and then we both knelt down and gripped the top of the shutters.

"Drop!" I yelled. And without another thought I did just that, careening down onto the cobbled street and landing heavily on my backside. It was not as far a drop as I'd thought, but it was enough to flush the stale air from my lungs.

"You all right?" Colin dropped close to me and squeezed my arm.

"I'm fine," I stammered, pushing myself up. "You?"

"Perfect."

Warren Vandemier slammed down on my other side with a cry and a crack that I knew meant he'd broken something. I stretched, grateful that everything felt fine, then looked back up to see if I was in the way of the young man who'd been with us . . . but he wasn't there. All I could see was the lapping of flames against the windowsill that only a minute before had been my perch.

"Colin . . ." I stared around at the throng of stilted, somnambulistic people stumbling around the alleyway.

"I know . . . ," he said, grabbing my arm and pulling me away. "We have to go. There's nothing we can do."

The distant sound of clanging bells and windup horns that reached my ears mixed eerily with the groans and sobs of the disoriented crowd, and I knew he was right. And that boy . . . that thin, sallow boy . . . never came out.

CHAPTER 29

We stumbled two or three blocks before it became apparent that we were being followed. The horse-drawn fire coaches had already careened past, clanging and screeching their warnings, and in the vacuum they left behind it was clear that ours were not the only set of footfalls on the cobbles. Yet each time one of us would glance back, the advancing footsteps halted in tandem, revealing no one behind us. I was finding it increasingly unnerving, though Colin didn't seem the least concerned. I knew pickpockets didn't work uncrowded alleyways and thugs never worked alone, but someone was still matching us step for step and that was rarely a good thing.

We continued our measured pace for a while longer before Colin asked, "What was the name of the woman who sat with us at the club tonight? The one who started the fires?"

"Li Shen."

"Well then, I believe Li Shen is following us," he announced with certainty. "And rather badly at that."

"Li Shen? You think it's her?" I started to turn to see if I might yet catch a glimpse, but Colin seized my arm and kept me from doing so.

"Don't look. Just keep moving. We'll get her to come to us."

I knew what he was up to, so as soon as we turned the corner I ducked in the notched alcove of a darkened storefront and yanked him in after me. "Don't make a sound," I cautioned him with a chuckle as he maneuvered around in the tight space.

Almost at once someone came scurrying out of the alleyway and a second later the silhouette of Li Shen came into view as she paused, no more than a few feet away, and scanned the street.

"Lose someone?" Colin cooed as he stepped out. She released a stifled scream and looked as if she was about to run when she abruptly collapsed against Colin's chest and began wailing like a child. "There, there . . . ," he said stiffly, his eyes finding mine to reveal his discomfort.

I patted Li Shen's back and allowed him to pass her to me. She sobbed until I thought she must surely need to stop for air. I knew it to be an effect of the drug and as I held her I was suddenly overcome by the realization that at least one person had lost his life tonight as a result of her drug-addled rampage. It seemed unconscionable to offer her succor when she'd shown so little care herself just a short time ago. And yet she had not been in her right mind then, and that was because of us.

"We mustn't tarry," Colin warned. "Mr. Vandemier will be crying for his pound of flesh as will the authorities once they find out what happened."

She pulled away from me and wiped her eyes with the sleeve of her dress. "I no trouble you," she said in a thin voice. "I fine. You go."

"We'll not leave you here. You'll come with us," he said.

She shook her head. "I no have business with you. You go. Leave Li Shen."

"No." He took her arm and began to get us all moving.

"You will come with us if I have to carry you all the way to Kensington, which I am *not* in the mood to do. I'll not hear another word on it." He slid his gaze to me.

"Absolutely." I pasted on what I hoped was a welcoming smile even though I did not relish having her in our flat. "Not another word."

"Bless you." She bowed repeatedly. "You most kind. A thousand blessings on you both."

"Fine. Lovely. But we really must get moving . . . ," Colin prodded again as he tried to get her to pick up the pace. "It won't do us much good if we're found wandering about the area by the authorities."

I held Li Shen's arm, who only now seemed to be comprehending what she had done. Her frail body was shaking as though she were walking barefoot across a patch of ice and I knew it was only a matter of time before the drug fully receded to leave her alone with the consequences. When we reached Fleet Street Colin gestured for us to stay out of sight while he hailed a cab, and only after he'd done so did the two of us dart from the shadows and leap inside.

None of us spoke the entire way back, and I could smell the burnt sulphur and thick pungent musk of opium on all of us. We would need to bathe with herbs and oils to remove these residues from our skin and hair, and I could only imagine what Mrs. Behmoth was going to say.

" 'Ere now . . . ," she did not disappoint, "ya couldn't give me some notice that you were bringin' someone 'ome?" Her hair was in rollers under her knit cap and she was wearing a long flannel robe and well-worn slippers that had long ago molded themselves to her feet. "Come on then. . . ." She held the door open and watched curiously as Li Shen drifted across the threshold. As she passed by Mrs. Behmoth her nose curled up and I could tell she knew where we'd been. "You better not smell like 'er." She pinched my arm as I tried to brush past her.

226 / Gregory Harris

"It's all right," Colin exhaled wearily. "I chaperoned. We haven't done anything we need regret."

Li Shen started and turned to Colin, and immediately dissolved into tears again. She sagged back into me and I held her a moment before hastening her upstairs and away from Mrs. Behmoth's questioning glare.

"I'd say ya'd best speak fer yerself," I heard her mutter to Colin as he started up after us.

I settled Li Shen onto the settee and poked the fire back to life while Colin pressed a brandy on her. She sipped at the drink and eventually exchanged her sobbing for a series of protracted sighs and an occasional hiccup. It was easy to see by the heaviness of her eyelids that the opium was loosening its grip on her, and I knew that before much longer the truth of what had happened—of what she had done—would finally poke into her conscience and demand its due.

"You must get some rest," I said to her.

"Yes." Colin seated himself across from her, his own face drawn. "We'll talk tomorrow. We'll decide what needs to be done then."

"No rest for Li Shen," she whispered. "No rest."

"Leave it be," I tried to soothe her. "There will be time enough to think on it all tomorrow."

"But I start fire. I *want* fire. I try to destroy man who want to destroy me, like owner's woman. She come to club and want to destroy everything too. Wave lamp around. But she not really do it, only Li Shen did it."

"What woman?" Colin's brow knit.

She shook her head and took another sip of brandy, staring at the amber liquid as though hoping to find some solace within its honeyed glow.

"How long ago was this?" he persisted.

She gave a slight shrug.

"Two weeks? Six weeks? Six months? Surely you can remember something?"

Mrs. Behmoth shuffled into the room startling all three of us. "I made up the guest room for the young lady. I 'ope you won't be keepin' her up 'alf the night. She looks as if she's 'ad enough. It ain't right ta keep at 'er—"

"Thank you!" he snapped, sending a frosty glare in her direction. "We appreciate your thoughtfulness. Please don't trouble yourself any further. We'll see that our guest gets down to her room."

Mrs. Behmoth folded her arms across her chest and stared right back at him. "Yer a pip," she said flatly. "Ya jest see that she does." And with that she turned and lumbered back down the stairs.

"Forgive the intrusion." He flicked his eyes back to Li Shen. "How many times did you see the woman at the club?"

"*That* woman?" Li Shen pointed to our empty doorway.

"No, no. The owner's woman. The one who was threatening to burn the club down."

"Couple time. She very mad. Shouting . . . scaring client. Say she burn everything down. Bad for business."

"What did she look like?"

"Young. Small like Li Shen."

Colin glanced at me. "That rules out Lady Arnifour and Abigail Roynton, which leaves us with Elsbeth. But why would she threaten to burn down the club?" He looked back at Li Shen. "Was the Earl there when it happened?"

"Earl who?"

"The owner. The Earl of Arnifour. The one who was killed."

"He there. He have bad night. Have fight with man and then girl come in. He try to calm girl down. Want to take her upstairs. She not happy, screaming and yelling. She crazy. Everyone say so."

"Man? What man?"

"Owner son. He say bad things. Then he leave and girl come in and—"

"I know. . . ." Colin waved her off. "You've been quite clear about the girl. But what about the son? What kind of things did he say?"

Li Shen shrugged tiredly. "He hate man."

"Which man? What man?"

"Father. Owner. Say he teach him lesson. Why he want to teach lesson to father he hate?"

Colin shook his head with a noticeable lack of interest and sighed. "And what was Mr. Vandemier doing during all this?"

"He not there. Too early for him. Not climb out of pig pit yet."

"And how long ago did this happen?" he repeated, his own exhaustion catching up to him.

"Sometime . . ." She didn't even bother to finish her sentence. She wouldn't be able to. Opium steals time. The months she'd spent in that club would forever be one continuous span. She yawned and set her brandy down. "Li Shen tired. No feel good."

"Of course." Colin rose and I did the same.

"If you'll come with me," I said, grasping her arm and leading her down to the room beside Mrs. Behmoth's own. Everything had been arranged so that this seldom-used space looked inviting. She had turned down the bed and pulled open the armoire to reveal extra covers and some nondescript nightclothes. She'd even managed to scrounge up a small vase of pale pink roses that she'd placed on the bedside table. I bid our guest good night and hoped she could get some rest before the morning and its realizations came roaring in.

I found Colin reclining in the bath upstairs attempting to soak off the vagaries of the night. I lowered myself to the floor and leaned against the wall, a heavy weariness sweeping over me in direct contrast to the gentle dancing of the candles he'd set about the tiny room. It would be so easy to fall asleep but unacceptable to awaken on the floor of the bathroom.

"Is she settled in?" he mumbled in a voice as tired as I felt.

"As much as she can be," I said as I allowed my eyes to close.

"We'll have to decide what to do with her tomorrow."

"Someone died tonight because of her, maybe more. . . ."

"I know," he sighed. "But something isn't right. . . ."

"How do you mean?"

"I can't get a clear picture of Elsbeth. By all accounts she was willing to have an affair with a man she believed to be her uncle, relishing the extravagant lifestyle it afforded and allowing herself to be spotted in public with him under less than appropriate circumstances. Yet now we learn that in a fit of pique she went down to his club and shouted slanders and threats? It doesn't make sense."

"No . . ." I had to agree. But in spite of my determination to hold up my end of the conversation I knew I was fighting a battle against sleep I was unlikely to win.

"And why would Eldon have been there that night? What could have compelled him to confront his father like that?"

"Li Shen could be wrong," I said, biting into the side of my cheek to keep from yawning. "She *is* a drug addict."

"She is . . . but we have to be careful not to be too dismissive. There's undoubtedly some truth in what she's saying. And yet I can't help feeling that we're still missing something. The trigger. What drove Eldon to make such a public spectacle of himself when anyone can see he fears his own shadow? And why would Elsbeth threaten to burn that damnable place down?!"

"Eldon's a drunk. There's no explaining a man like that. Coming to our flat this afternoon to tell us that story just so he can implicate his mother. It's a disgrace."

"It could be true," Colin sighed. "Though it's hard to take

the recollections of a five-year-old with anything but caution. What may have seemed like quite a lot of blood to him then could prove quite inconsequential to an adult. Still, it is a sordid tale."

"And even if it is true, it might not change a thing. Maybe Elsbeth was on the verge of being replaced as the Earl's favorite and that's what set her off," I blathered in near incoherence.

Colin bolted up so quickly that water splashed out of the tub and onto the floor. "Of course! How foolish I've been."

"What?" I blinked vacantly as I struggled to focus. "Foolish about what?"

"What's the one thing that would have set them both off?" He stared at me, but I had nothing. If there was an answer to see I wouldn't have spotted it scrawled on the wall in front of me. "The Earl had someone else. Someone who was a threat to Eldon's inheritance. All this time . . . ," he chuckled as he climbed out of the tub, ". . . there's been someone missing from this game. Someone who set everything else in motion."

CHAPTER 30

Morning roared in with great anticipation, as did Colin. By the time I managed to coax my eyes open he was already up and dressing at a furious pace.

"Are you planning on sleeping all day?" he teased. "There's much to be done. The *Ilya Petrovina* is due in shortly and we've got to get down to the docks to see if your suspicions about Michael have any basis. And I should also like to announce that by the end of this day we will have named the perpetrator in the Arnifour murders. However, first we must question our houseguest. I'm going to have Mrs. Behmoth awaken her. I simply cannot wait another minute."

I roused myself as quickly as I could, loath to miss anything, all the while considering Colin's declaration that he was on the verge of solving the Arnifour murders. I hadn't the slightest notion how he intended to do so given the possibility of yet a more recent mistress in the picture. I couldn't even imagine how he meant to find her. If Li Shen didn't know who she was, and that seemed most likely, then we would be beholden to

Warren Vandemier, and I didn't expect we'd get much help from him anymore.

I tidied up and dressed swiftly, and was about to go downstairs when I heard the distinctive thudding of Colin trudging back up. I suspected Mrs. Behmoth had routed him for disturbing our guest at so early an hour and had sent him back up to wait a little longer.

I made my way to the study and found him stirring a fire to life. He was well pulled together and as I settled into my armchair, anxious to ward off the remnants of sleep, I was grateful to have a few minutes to collect myself before having to confront Li Shen again.

"She isn't here," he muttered as soon as I'd gotten settled.

"What?!"

"Li Shen is gone. Mrs. Behmoth found her bed empty." He tossed the poker onto the hearth with a clatter and stalked to the stairway. "Can we please get some tea up here!" he bellowed.

"Don't you 'oller at me!" she hollered back. "It ain't me fault she's gone."

Colin threw himself onto the sofa, a stern gaze clamped on the fireplace until Mrs. Behmoth finally made her appearance, the silver tray of tea and scones clamped in her hands.

"I spent 'alf the bleedin' night with 'er, ya know," she groused as she banged the tray onto the table. "She was sick the 'ole time. Chuckin' and moanin' 'til the sunrise began pokin' in through the windas. I was fagged out. It ain't no wonder I never 'eard 'er stir."

"I am *not* blaming you—"

"Like 'ell yer not."

"All I want to know is if she said anything? Did she give any indication where she might have gone?"

"Wot? In between hackin' 'er guts out?" Mrs. Behmoth screwed her face up and spoke in a high-pitched voice, "*Par-*

*don, mum, but as soon as I'm done 'ollowin' 'ere, I'll be 'eadin'
off for a pint at the local pub."*

"Fine!" he snapped. "I get the point."

"Poor little thing was sick as a cur."

"Yes . . . I've got it."

A loud rapping at the door was all that kept Mrs. Behmoth
from responding, which, given the sourness of the expression
on her face, I was grateful for. She disappeared back downstairs
muttering under her breath, and I hoped it might be Li Shen,
though I knew how unlikely that was.

Moments later Inspector Varcoe and one of his lackeys were
standing on the landing outside our study. As I stared at the inspector's self-righteous gloat I couldn't help but wonder how a
day so filled with promise just a few short minutes ago could have
so swiftly turned bad, the evidence of it standing before us now.

Inexplicably Colin did not appear perturbed in the least. I
supposed he'd been expecting this visit; it was bound to come,
though it was unforgivably early.

"Aren't we just the picture of domestic ease this morning,"
Inspector Varcoe sneered as he strolled in. "I would've brought
your paper up but didn't want to rob you of the only *legal*
recreation you're likely to have today."

"I do wish we had a dog to fetch it. I'd love one of those bull
terriers," Colin said as he sat down in his usual chair and casually flipped out a crown, starting its inevitable route between
his fingers.

"Well, you'd certainly have the time to train it." The inspector snickered. "I hear you've been fired by Lady Arnifour."

"Not fired," I shot back. "We have been paid in full for services rendered."

"Oh, I see." He chuckled again. "But I'm not here to gloat,
though it is a distinct pleasure; I'm here on official business. I
need to know where the two of you were last night."

"I'm quite sure you know exactly where we were." Colin

shifted his gaze to the uneasy-looking bobby still hovering in the doorway. "Would you care to sit down, young man? You needn't stand on formality here."

"Stay where you are, Lachlan!" Varcoe snapped. "Why did you leave the scene of a crime, Pendragon?"

"Crime?" Colin tossed the coin onto the mantel as he reached over and picked up one of the dumbbells next to his chair and began methodically curling it with his left hand. "Are you implying that the fire in that club last night was deliberately set?"

"Piss off."

"You might remember that you're in our home now," I pointed out. "If anyone is going to piss off—"

"Now, now." Colin smiled easily as he continued to pump the weight. "Perhaps if you outline your suspicions we can see if we know anything further."

"*I want some ruddy answers!*" he roared, his face morphing into the burgundy of a plum. "What were you doing there last night after Lady Arnifour *fired* you from the case?"

"It's an opium club," I said without a hint of patience. "I'm sure you can extrapolate."

"Bollocks! Don't lie to me."

"He's telling the truth," the young bobby spoke up. "It *is* an opium club."

"*I know what the bloody hell it is, you twit!*" he howled, forcing the young man to take an unconscious step backwards. "And I know that's *not* why you were there. You two may be a lot of things," he leered, "but you're not blasted addicts. So what the hell were you doing there?"

"Idle curiosity?" Colin shrugged, switching the weight to his other hand.

"Bullshit! Warren Vandemier says you went there to harass his clientele and cause him physical and monetary harm."

"Now, Inspector, Warren Vandemier *is* an addict. I'm sure you've figured that out by now—"

"That's enough, Pendragon. I will drag your ass down to the Yard if I have to, but you *will* answer my questions!"

"If you will just settle yourself a moment I think you'll find that I've answered every one of your questions thus far."

"You've been dismissed from the Arnifour case, Pendragon, so I expect you to stand down from this business and let the *real* authorities settle things," Varcoe snarled before he turned and stalked from the room.

When I heard the door slam a second time in as many minutes, it was a monumental relief. "What in the bloody hell was that about?" I asked as I leaned forward and poured us some tea. "Why did he come here?"

Colin turned back to the fireplace, but I could see that his eyes were unfocused. "I would venture we're getting nearer to the truth and someone with attachments to the authorities has sent our impressionable inspector to rile us. Someone cunning enough to use him without his being aware of it." He rubbed his chin absently. "Actually, whoever it is wouldn't need to be *that* cunning."

I laughed. "So who do you think sent him?"

His sapphire eyes drifted back to me as I handed him his tea. "There can only be three possibilities: Lady Arnifour, Warren Vandemier, or Abigail Roynton."

CHAPTER 31

———✦◦✦———

Our first stop was to visit Warren Vandemier in the hospital. We discovered that he'd broken his right femur, so if nothing else, he would prove to be a rapt audience. We found him in bed with a cast that went from his hip to the ankle of his right foot, the whole thing dangling from a sling bolted to the ceiling. Even so, he did not hesitate to make his repugnance clear the moment we strode onto the ward. "As if I'm not knackered enough already," he groused.

Colin perched on the end of his bed next to Mr. Vandemier's plastered leg. "That's the thanks we get for saving your life?" he sighed.

There was much grumbling. "I see the two of you managed to escape without so much as a ruddy damn scratch."

"We did." Colin shrugged. "Survival of the fittest and all that, I suppose. But we're not here to compare wounds—only to ask a couple of questions."

"I've had it with your bloody questions. I told you that last night."

Colin appeared to ponder that before shaking his head.

"No, I don't think you did. Perhaps you've suffered some head trauma as well—"

"Oh, just get on with it," he seethed.

"I'd like to know something about the Earl's niece, Elsbeth. Did she ever threaten your club?"

"Elsbeth?!" He looked surprised. "Now why would she do that? She partook on more than one occasion. Had a row with Samuel over it too."

"She tried opium?"

"Bloody well right, she did. But Samuel was a hypocrite. Perfectly happy to make a regular of anyone who walked in the door so long as they weren't related to him."

"Were you aware of anyone threatening your business? Threatening to burn it down?"

"Just that stupid slag last night. Are you trying to blame the fire on somebody other than Li Shen? It's your fault, you know! You plied that dragon whore with opium. You're as guilty as she is."

"Settle down or I'll see that you get a matching plaster on your other leg."

"Are you threatening me?!"

"Not very well if you have to ask. Now I'm *not* talking about last night—"

"Well, you sure as hell *should* be!" he snapped. "Because my life was as good as *destroyed* last night."

"This isn't about you."

"*The hell it isn't!*"

Colin smiled thinly as he leaned toward Mr. Vandemier. "I'm only going to ask this one more time—"

"I don't give a crap. Shove whatever twaddle you've got on your mind straight up your ass."

Colin leaned back slowly, his eyes piercing Warren Vandemier's face. He eased himself off the bed, one side of his mouth rising lazily, before reaching out and yanking the sling cradling Mr. Vandemier's leg several feet. It took less than an instant before he let out a soulful scream, his eyes rolling up into his head.

"Now don't be crude." Colin spoke softly. "Rudeness is redundant in a man like you." He released the sling and let Mr. Vandemier's leg drop back to its original position with a jolt. A second screech followed as we left the ward, a trio of nurses making a dash toward the noise.

"That was a touch brutal," I said once I'd caught up to Colin.

"He's just lucky those damn nurses heard him scream."

"Well, did you at least learn something?"

"Not what I wanted to hear," he muttered, heading off down the street.

"So where does that leave us?"

"In the middle of London," he answered with great exasperation as he stepped into the street to flag a passing cab.

I bit my lip as I climbed aboard and Colin instructed the man to take us to the docks. It was time to see how the reunion of Michael and Angelyne would play out. I hoped it would be heartwarming, but couldn't shake the feeling that something was asunder.

Colin climbed in next to me, turning and staring out the window as we got under way. It was clear there was much on his mind, so I determined the best thing I could do was leave him in peace and set my gaze on the passing scenery as well.

Upon arriving, I glanced around the small crowd milling about the wharf to see if I could spot Michael before he could catch sight of us. Even though the *Ilya Petrovina* was making an unannounced call, there were dozens of people to greet her, not the least of whom were the policemen and Yardies who'd been sent by the Foreign Ministry Office to inquire about the alleged stowaways. I started to move off, keeping well away from the crowd, certain that Michael would also want to keep his distance from the authorities lest they decide to stop his sister from returning to his care. "Now don't get ahead of me," Colin warned as I crossed perpendicularly from where the people were milling.

"I'm looking for Michael . . . ," I answered vaguely.

"I know what you're doing," he said. "We'll scout the scene before we make our presence known, but not every East End boy is as deceitful as you obviously were," he teased.

"I was not deceitful," I protested as we moved off in the opposite direction from where the *Ilya Petrovina* was set to berth. "I was clever."

"You were a drug-addled hellion."

I considered taking offense, but as I followed him behind a maze of crates and boxes littering the docks I decided now wasn't the time for it. Besides, I'd been called worse things.

As the great, hulking steamship was carefully maneuvered by a pair of rusting tugs, we took an opposing, perpendicular track until we'd reached some distance from where the front of the ship would eventually lie, well concealed among a throng of languishing cargo. "Feeling shy, are we?"

"We're going to sit here and see if your suspicions have any merit. It's my show of faith in you."

"I'm touched."

He chuckled as he settled in on a pile of boxes, peeking through a slot between a row of crates down to where the ship was docking. I turned my attention to her as she was tied up at her berth and a couple of men muscled her gangplank into position. A handful of sailors were the first to disembark, followed by a short, round, bearded man wearing a disheveled-looking Russian uniform. He went directly to the bobbies clustered at one side of the gangway.

"Must be the captain."

"He doesn't look much like a captain," I said.

"It's a cargo vessel, not a passenger ship. That chap has little need for epaulets, uniform whites, or reflective shoes. He'd have a hell of a time trying to convince any seasoned crew to follow him with that kind of artifice. His crew is far more akin to pirates than our naval lads. Need I remind you why we're here?"

I gave him a pointed look before answering, "He looks exactly like the kind of scoundrel who'd kidnap girls for sale."

"I have to agree. I'd say they were put aboard his vessel with both his knowledge and a sizeable payment, probably half at embarkation and half upon delivery. He won't be happy about missing that second bit. And his cargo delivery is going to be woefully late as well." He grinned. "This episode will end up costing him quite a sum."

"You think they'll arrest him?"

He shook his head and sighed. "For what? For being a selfless humanitarian who, at great personal expense, turned his ship around the moment he discovered those deceitful young girls stowed away?"

"You cannot be serious. . . ."

"Proof can be a pitiful burden," he muttered, and I noticed his brow suddenly furrow. "And look at this. Here comes our young charge now."

I turned and caught a glimpse of Michael heading around behind the small crowd gathered at the gangplank. He was moving slowly, not with the kind of enthusiasm that would be expected, seeming almost reticent, and it made me wonder if there'd been bad blood between him and his sister.

My curiosity was further piqued when he continued to saunter past the waiting queue of people, moving resolutely toward the front of the ship, not far from where we were concealed. Yet, given the number of police milling about, I determined that his hesitation in standing among them made sense, since there was a better than average chance that at least one of the bobbies had run into him at some point in his doggedness to provide for him and his sister by whatever means necessary. I began to feel foolish for not having had some modicum of faith in the boy, but felt better when Colin said, "I'd say the men in blue are keeping our boy from emptying any pockets."

I started to chuckle when a sudden commotion at the gangplank seized my attention. A tall, clearly overwrought woman in a massive sun hat was howling at the police even as the group of stowaway girls—the scrawniest, scruffiest-looking assemblage I had ever seen—made their first appearance at its top.

"What do you suppose she's going on about?" I asked as the woman flailed her arms wildly.

"One of those girls is probably her ill-used niece or ward and she's causing a great fuss in order to deflect the mountain of questions that are bound to come the moment she moves in to claim her. A show of outrage is much more likely to get her what she wants than not."

"So cynical."

He shrugged, his brow stitching itself again as I glanced over and saw Michael. He had managed to skirt the agitated knot of people congregated at the gangway, but was now standing almost directly across from us at the ship's bow. I watched as he slunk around the ship's moorings as though he knew something no one else did, and after a couple of minutes discovered that, in fact, he did.

The movement on the ship was minuscule, hardly noticeable until the first frail leg, smudged with dirt and filth, popped out and took hold of the forward anchor rope. The second leg quickly followed, allowing me to make out the figure of a young girl as she began to slither down the tether with unmistakable expertise. She was no more than a waif really, much less significant than a girl of almost thirteen should be. Her body was rail thin and she had limp, stringy hair dangling about her shoulders. I knew it was Angelyne, because even as she lowered herself to the dock, Michael never took his eyes from her.

"So you were right," Colin muttered.

"Well, I didn't think she was going to shimmy down the rope like vermin, but it would seem given her proficiency that she might have done this before."

"To be sure. She handles that rope like a gymnast. No wonder he told us not to come. It's a scam. Only this time something obviously went wrong. And will you look at this...." He gestured to Angelyne as she jumped free only to be swiftly seized by her brother. "Their happy reunion would seem to be little more than rebuke for having fouled things up. That little shit dragged us into this to make sure he'd get her back, always feeding us just enough information." He abruptly turned and glared at me. "You should've been more insistent."

"What?!" I nearly laughed in his face, but he grabbed me and propelled me farther back into the maze of cartons.

"The little tykes seem to be coming our way," he groused.

I peeked around the crates and saw that the two of them were indeed heading to almost the exact spot we'd been hiding, moving with great purpose. Michael had a firm grip on Angelyne's skinny arm, and though I could not hear them yet, it was clear they were in the midst of a row.

"Not a word," Colin warned needlessly. "Let us allow them to spill their conniving hearts."

As soon as they'd reached the relative safety of the first row of crates, Michael wheeled around on his sister with unbridled ferocity. "... Bleedin' idiot ... what in 'ell were ya thinkin'?!"

"Piss off," came the reply.

"Piss off? Piss off, eh?! Is that what ya woulda told them bloody Cossack bastards when they was tryin' to bugger ya?"

"I ain't without means."

Michael slapped her hard in an attack that would have sent her to the ground had he not still been holding her arm. "Yer jest a stupid pup. You ain't gonna be worth nothin' soon anyway. But if ya ever pull a ruddy stunt like that again—"

"Where are ya, ya blasted, sawed-off, half-breed little shite," a familiar female voice abruptly cut through Michael's diatribe, causing him and Angelyne to jerk around. "Yer damn lucky yer brother and I didn't leave ya on that blasted ship!" Mademoiselle Rendell continued to bellow as she stepped across my eyeline clutching an oversized sun hat.

"I thought that was her." Colin gave a crooked grin.

"You knew that was Mademoiselle Rendell causing that fuss?"

"I suspected *she* was involved. She was too willing to give up her Bulgarian attaché to make sure we got the information we needed to get that ship turned around. But I didn't realize about the little one."

"The little one?" I flicked my eyes back to the three of them. "Angelyne? What about her?"

He smirked, one eyebrow arching high. "Haven't you figured it out?" I looked from the scrawny girl to Colin and back again, without a single thought entering my vacant brain. "Angelyne is a boy," he finally said. "See the budding Adam's apple? It's a shell game. They sell him as a prepubescent girl with the intention that he'll sneak off the ship just as it's on the verge of leaving—before their deception is discovered. That's how it's *supposed* to work. They knew where he was the whole time. They just needed us to figure it out so we could get that ship to come back. They'd lost their golden goose. And they almost got away with it had you not been so suspicious." He grinned as he squeezed my arm and coaxed me forward. "But now it's time we put an end to this."

Mademoiselle Rendell had her back to us as we stepped out, but Michael and the other boy spotted us at once. "Oh shite," Michael said.

Mademoiselle Rendell spun around, and as her eyes landed

on us she sagged as though suddenly void of air. "Dammit to 'ell," she lamented. "I knew gettin' this pair were a mistake."

"A mistake?!" Colin said with mock offense. "I've been called many things in my life, but never a mistake."

"I'd be 'appy ta call ya worse."

"I'd rather hear from the little one." He turned his attentions to the long-haired boy cowering at Michael's side. "And what do they call you when you're not in a dress?"

"Drew, sir," he answered.

"Drew." Colin gave a tight smile. "I think it's time you let him go, Michael, or I'll separate your arm from your shoulder." Wisely, the older boy did so at once. "Come over here, Drew."

"I ought not, sir."

"It's all right. Your brother and . . ." He paused.

". . . Me mum, sir," the boy piped up, causing my heart to sink.

"Yes." Colin spoke slowly, his own distaste evident. "Your mum. They'll not harm you. You've nothing to fear from them anymore. This game has come to an end."

"It weren't so bad. . . ."

"Well, perhaps you'd prefer to be a boy. Go to school. Learn your disciplines."

Drew glanced from Michael to Mademoiselle Rendell before turning back to us. He nodded, but said nothing.

"Then you shall have that."

Drew winced as he stepped away from his brother, clearly expecting a blow that would not come. His scrawny limbs were streaked with the same filth caked on his bare feet, as black as the sludge between the cobbles in the street. I doubted he'd ever had a haircut since that was a part of his ruse, and could tell by the knots and tangles peppered throughout that some time had passed since a brush had been worked through it. The timid voice and abject politeness was a glaring dichotomy to what stood before us, yet to be saleable, he had to be controlled. This pair had done their job appallingly well.

Colin put his hands on the boy's shoulders and turned him back around to face his mother and brother. "You've done your damage to this child for the last time, as you'll find it impossible to do so from prison. By the time they let you out . . . ," he flicked his eyes to Mademoiselle Rendell, ". . . the only thing anyone will pay you for is to bugger off. And as for you . . ." He glared at Michael. "You'll likely end up rather like your little brother here, except that the blokes you'll be spending your time with won't pay you for your favors."

"Ya can't threaten us," Mademoiselle Rendell spat back, pulling herself to her full height.

"It is not a threat," Colin answered. "I give you my word."

"Yer word. What da you know? Livin' in yer fancy flat with yer lady waitin' on ya and ridin' round in carriages passin' judgment. You ain't got no idea. No idea at all."

"You don't own hard luck *or* bad choices," I sallied back at her. "But your failure to rise above them belongs to you."

"Ah . . . piss off," she spat, and before I knew it she launched herself at me, gripping me by the hair. I stumbled backwards with the sudden force of her weight and landed on my backside, her coiled fists flailing at my head with such determination that all I could do was try to ward off her blows until, just as quickly as it had begun, her siege ended.

She let out a pitiful shriek as she was unceremoniously wrenched off me, seeming to levitate into the air by her armpits, her legs and arms batting uselessly as they failed to make contact with anything. I peered up and saw Colin behind her, solid, impermeable, and formidable. He heaved her to the side like a sack of grain into a crumpled heap with nary a grunt, turning to face her with his hands stabbed against his hips. "Next time," he growled, "I will remove you by the throat!"

"You mustn't, sir," Drew spoke up. "She's just me mum."

"And I could scarcely be sorrier for that," he answered. "You tried to play us for fools," he turned on Michael with a sneer, "acting the part of the loving brother when all along you were nothing more than the snake Mr. Pruitt kept insisting you were. Fifteen years old and without a shred of decency. How proud you must be."

The young man scowled with the ferocity of the feral thing he was. "You got nothin' ta say ta me!" he growled back. "All full a yerself when you thought you was helpin' out the little urchin boy. I think you're just pissed 'cause I almost got one over on ya." He snickered. "If that's your decency then you can shove it up your arse."

I sucked in an infuriated breath to blast the pompous smirk off his face when I felt Colin's hand grip my arm and heard him say, "Don't. Just go fetch us a couple of bobbies." I did as he suggested, knowing he was right; there was nothing I could say that was going to make a whit of difference to Michael and my protestations were only likely to confirm his point.

In the blink of an eye I returned with a cluster of policemen. We gave a hasty report, based more on Colin's name than any real substance, but promised a trip to the Yard for a more formal debriefing later. Colin was adamant that we couldn't go with them just then as he was about to solve the Arnifour murders. The bobbies stared at him with a mixture of skepticism and alarm, but not one of them called him on it.

As we made our way off the pier I felt relieved to be getting away from there. It was a pitiful case, but even so, I could not bring myself to turn back for one last look as the officers led Mademoiselle Rendell, Michael, and little Drew away.

CHAPTER 32

Just over an hour later we were climbing down from a hansom cab onto the cobbled driveway at the Arnifour estate.

As with every visit before, Mrs. O'Keefe only grudgingly allowed us entry, making no effort to hide her disdain at our continual insistence on showing up with neither an appointment nor an invitation nor, as was now the case, even a reason for being there. I glanced at her more closely than I'd meant to as I slid past her, wondering if Kaylin might truly be her daughter and what it would be like to keep such a secret the whole of one's life. My thoughts earned me nothing more than a ferocious glower from her. Nevertheless, her rabid anger suddenly made some sense and I couldn't help the trifling pity that gnawed at me as she took us to the same study as always before curtly announcing that we'd be joined by Lady Arnifour at her leisure. It left me wondering if that meant within the hour, the day, or the week.

We settled in to wait the indeterminate time and just as Mrs. O'Keefe was about to take her leave Colin asked whether Victor might be available to join us for a few minutes. She appeared to ruminate on the idea quite thoroughly before finally consenting to let him know we were there. Even so, she slammed the doors with a great deal more bravado than necessary as she left us on our own.

I turned back to Colin to seek his thoughts on Mrs. O'Keefe and what Eldon had told us only to find a deep furrow creasing his brow. "Are you all right?" I asked quietly. "You're going to need to be on your best behavior if we're to have any success here. After all, we're not working for them any longer. . . ."

Inexplicably, the furrow in his brow deepened. "I know that," he said. "You needn't worry. I'll behave."

I pretended to chuckle but still feared that his impatience would get the best of him and bring our impromptu visit to a frustrating and permanent conclusion. I was on the verge of pressing the point against my better judgment when Victor Heffernan suddenly presented himself, barreling into the room with his usual good cheer. "It's good ta see ya both," he said with genuine appreciation.

"And you as well." Colin smiled and shook his hand. "It's kind of you to meet with us despite our appalling lack of notice."

"I think ya know I'm not one ta stand on ceremony." He sat down by the fireplace looking more fragile than ever. "I'm hopin' you've come to straighten things out for Nathaniel. He keeps threatenin' to stow away to America. I don't know what I'd do without him. That boy's been the best part of my whole life." He pinned his gaze on the dancing flames in the fireplace and yet I could see his eyes were glassy. It looked like he hadn't slept in days and I suspected that was more than likely true.

"I have every intention of proving your son's innocence," Colin said, sitting down opposite Victor, "even though he hasn't made that easy. His unwillingness to trust me has hampered my investigation considerably."

"I know. He's as stubborn as his mother was—"

Colin held a hand up, giving Victor a sly smile. "Nathaniel may have slowed me, but he will not stop me. Justice is a belle I *like* to court. And as I've said repeatedly, I believe Nathaniel is innocent. I'll stake my reputation on it."

"Then do share." Lady Arnifour stood just inside the doorway, her face rigid with displeasure. "Just who is it you've come to wield your peerless reputation against?"

"Who indeed?" He smiled easily as he stood up. "Would you think any less of me if I demurred my answer for a moment?"

"Don't be tiresome, Mr. Pendragon. I believe your business with us was concluded on your last visit."

"And so it was." He held his smile. "But this visit is solely on me. Please . . . ," he gestured to a chair, ". . . indulge me."

I thought her on the verge of expelling us, but after she threw a quick glance at Victor's glum face she heaved a heavy sigh and perched herself on the edge of the proffered seat. "I must insist you keep this exercise brief."

"Exercise?" His smile wavered as he cast a quick glance at me. "What an unorthodox way to describe the solving of two murders."

"Do get on with it," she sniffed.

"As you wish . . ." He slowly ambled around behind Lady Arnifour's chair. "So what I'd like to know is if you ever told Elsbeth about Desiree Helgman?"

Lady Arnifour turned her head so quickly that it sent her great stout wig in a slightly discordant direction. "*I have no idea what you're talking about!*" She bolted up, affecting a look of deep offense even as she sent Victor a withering sideways glance.

"Come now. . . ." Colin moved behind her again, forcing her to twist around. "There's no need to be coy any longer," he whispered before abruptly heading to the fireplace. "Very few secrets are able to be kept forever."

Lady Arnifour held herself steady, glaring at Colin without the slightest feint, and for a moment I thought she might storm from the room, but after a minute more she slumped back into her chair and heaved a grave sigh. Her fingers shot up to her temples and rubbed at them as though a searing pain had suddenly settled there, and I imagined it had. As I continued to watch her, I realized that she had become just as frail as Victor, that their mutual unraveling was as preordained as their lives together had been. "I have known a lifetime of betrayal, Mr. Pendragon." She spoke in a voice that quivered with brittleness. "I am sure you are aware of that."

"I meant no offense," he answered. "I am only seeking the truth, even if it is a truth you are eager to conceal."

She did not look up, but remained as she was: hunched over, her fingertips pressing at her temples. "The marriage I endured with my husband . . . ," she said in a voice that was both flat and void of inflection, ". . . was happy for the span of about two years. Of course that was so long ago I may yet be remembering it with more charity than it deserves. The period after Eldon was born was . . . wonderful. A pristine, young family. And yet I'm sure my husband's wandering eye had already gotten the best of him. I really don't recall. Not until Kaylin. Samuel gave up all attempts at discretion while I was burdened with our second child. I never imagined such a complete and utter end to his interest in me, but that is exactly where I found myself, Mr. Pendragon: with two small children and a husband who came around only when he needed money."

"You mustn't go on." Victor leaned forward and touched her elbow tenderly.

"It doesn't matter." She offered him a game smile, but otherwise made no move to shy away from his intimacy. "You've been my salvation," she said. "You are a man of inestimable kindness. You see, Mr. Pendragon, Victor only responded to the plaintive tears of a young wife and mother all those years ago. He saved me, not once, but twice."

"No, no, it was you who saved *me*," he rushed to correct.

"Hush now," she scolded with affection. "I'm telling the story." She looked at us for the first time since withering in her seat and I recognized a liberation in her gaze I had never seen before. "Victor listened to me. He *cared* for me. And some time thereafter, when I realized I'd fallen in love with him, not only did he accept it, but he returned that gift a thousandfold. And I was certain we would be fine. I thought we would be permitted our indiscretion given the depth of my husband's forays, but I was again deceiving myself. Little more than a year and a half after Kaylin was born I discovered I was once more with child. I knew the baby didn't belong to my husband and, of course, so did he. My husband was many things, but he was not a fool.

"We agreed I had to go away, so I created a story about a sister who'd been in a terrible carriage accident while with child, and then left my own small children. I moved into a flat in the city under that name: Desiree Helgman. It was a freeing time though it was also unbearably hard. I couldn't see my children until after Elsbeth was born, not once. I had to placate myself by sending them letters regularly, making up stories of what I was doing and telling them how much I missed them, knowing their nanny would read the letters aloud. . . ." The thinnest smile tugged at one corner of her mouth. "But there was also joy in those months. Victor came to see me often and brought me food, and took care of me, and made me feel like a new wife on the brink of a new family all over again. That was wonderful. Me and Victor in that tiny apartment waiting for that child conceived in love to make her presence known . . . ," she caught her breath, ". . . it was—" But her voice cracked and she dropped her eyes to her hands, which were fidgeting with the twinned ends of her tasseled belt, back and forth, as though they were attempting to weave something.

"But I undid myself when she was born because I could not bear to let the midwife hasten that tiny baby away without taking one peek at her. I'd girded myself to give her up, but I still wanted to see her, to hold her, just once." She took a deep breath and then pushed on. "I cradled her in my arms and smelled her sweet, soft skin, and stroked the fuzz dusting the top of her head." She chuckled. "Her perfect, little fingers curled around my own..." Her smile dropped and her eyes clouded. "...I couldn't let her go. That baby, that child, that perfect little girl..." She sagged back into her chair and closed her eyes. Her face was still, but it held a calmness that looked too long removed.

"Shall I finish?" Victor asked softly.

"No." She gave him a gentle smile. "You've covered for me for long enough."

She looked back at Colin and me. "I bundled that baby up and brought her home with me to this house, *my* house, the ancestral home of four generations of Langhems, and told everyone my sister had died during the birth. I said there'd been no husband, so I'd done the only charitable thing I knew; I'd brought her home to raise as my own.

"Samuel was outraged." She glanced at her hands again and I finally understood where her story would inevitably end. "My husband told me that I would either pay him a handsome monthly stipend or he would ruin me. Simple. And that was when my antipathy for him became hatred. What was worst of all was that I had handed him the tool of my destruction myself. That baby... that innocent who had made me fall in love with her..." She shook her head. "Samuel knew just how to strike at me, how to make my life even more miserable than it had already become. And to tell you the truth, Mr. Pendragon...," she lifted her eyes and glared at him, ". . . if there was ever a time I wished my husband dead, it was then."

"Don't . . . ," Victor hushed her.

"Why not? It's the truth."

"Mother?" Kaylin was standing in the door. "Are you all right?"

"Don't come in." Lady Arnifour buried her head in her hands. "These are such tawdry proceedings."

"Then by all means . . ." Eldon shoved past his sister. "If the Arnifours are to be flung into the mire I think we should all wallow together. And tell me, Mr. Pendragon, is it true that you've seen my father's club burned to the ground and Mr. Vandemier laid up in the hospital?" He moved to the bar and poured himself a drink. "Can't say I give a bloody piss about the latter, but the former has me sick. You know what that'll cost me? Do you have any idea what that little parcel was worth?"

"How dare you. People lost their lives!" Lady Arnifour snapped.

"One of them could have been me," he sneered. "I'd every intention of going there last night to have a word with that tosspot Vandemier—"

"No doubt you were unconscious long before you could make good on that threat," she shot back.

"And there you have it." He set his glass down. "A mother's love."

"And you have become a despicable man."

"I am what you made me," he said before turning back to Colin. "And there you have it, Mr. Pendragon, proof that rats aren't the only mammals who devour their young."

"That's enough, Eldon," Kaylin spoke up. "Purge your demons somewhere else."

He scowled at her but kept quiet as she went and sat next to her mother. "They aren't blaming you for this, are they?"

"I deserve a little more credit than that," Colin said, still hovering in front of the fireplace. "I'm not so incompetent as to believe a woman of a certain age could have the stamina to ride out into the evening, strike two people down from the back of a horse, set a barn ablaze, and ride back without arousing suspicion."

"That is a relief." Kaylin gave a tight smile as she pulled a lace handkerchief from the sleeve of her dress and began tugging it between her fingers. "Everyone here, including that inspector from Scotland Yard, believes that Nathaniel Heffernan is—"

"Please don't," Lady Arnifour said. "You mustn't speak of what you know nothing about."

"Do my ears deceive me?" Eldon moved across the room, his voice tight and accusing. "Is that some sort of veiled confession?"

"And I was wondering . . . ," she sallied right back, ". . . if it isn't *you* who might have something to confess."

His face went rigid. "So that's it, then? My own mother accuses me of murder?"

"Excuse me . . . ," Colin said, flicking his eyes around the room until he had everyone's attention. "While I am sure this is serving some purpose, it is not serving mine, and I do have a few things I should like to have clarified so that we can put an end to all of this for good."

"Well, I've had enough." Victor pushed himself to his feet. "I'm tired of hearing my boy's name tossed up. You've already said he's innocent, Mr. Pendragon, so I'll have no more part in this."

"It's too late for that." Lady Arnifour gave him a pained smile. "You inhabit every part of this."

"Yes . . . ," Colin started to slowly circle the room, ending up by the doors, which he quietly pulled shut, "I'm afraid that you do, Victor."

"Then it's settled." Kaylin made to rise from her seat. "I'll have Mrs. O'Keefe send for the inspector and we'll finish with this horrible business."

"I'm afraid it won't be quite so easily done." Colin remained at the doors. "And we'd best all be of the same mind before our dubious inspector is summoned."

I glanced at the faces around me: Lady Arnifour, veiled and grim; Kaylin, flushed with emotion; Eldon, locked behind his bottomless tumbler; and Victor, who looked worn to the bottom of his very soul. While they each harbored their own set of resentments, I couldn't tell who was capable of so heinous a crime: a crime against two of their own.

"First, let me state for the *last* time that Nathaniel Heffernan is innocent of these murders," Colin said. "Nathaniel probably cared more for Elsbeth than anyone else in this room. He alone understood the binds of family. Certainly more than you, Victor. Your determination to keep the truth from ever being borne out prevented you from showing so much as a hint of affection to her, a profoundly regrettable decision on your part. Or you, Lady Arnifour, as you unwittingly found yourself encumbered by a child who came to represent the worst mistake of your life. You would have done yourself and the child far better to have followed your first instinct and given her away."

"What are you talking about?" Eldon asked, looking around at the assembled faces for an answer that would not be forthcoming.

"Hush!" Lady Arnifour finally snapped. "That you insist on sitting here is reprehensible enough, but I do not owe you any explanations."

"Which does bring us to you, Eldon," Colin quickly spoke up. "You have clearly chosen to climb into the bottom of a cask rather than face the ambivalence of your parents, wearing the wounds of your childhood like a badge of honor. Very different from your sister, Kaylin. My dear, you've allowed your mother to shroud you in a veil of fragility even as you extol the increasing howl of suffrage—"

"Really, Mr. Pendragon," she interrupted. "What horrible things you're saying." She twisted around to get a clear view of her mother. "And whatever does he mean about a child you should have given away?"

Lady Arnifour stared across the room at Victor, her pallor ghostly white. "I'm afraid I've made some terrible mistakes, little one. I can only hope you will forgive me. . . ." Her eyes held Kaylin's even as her face remained inscrutable. "Elsbeth was not your cousin. She was born to me. She was your half sister."

"What?!" Kaylin pulled back from her mother. "That can't be—"

"It's true."

She looked about to swoon as she glanced from her mother to Victor, who had dropped his eyes and sagged forward in his chair. Nothing more needed to be said. The truth had been there all along.

Lady Arnifour slowly began to speak again, telling the same story to her children that she'd already confessed to us. And once again there seemed to be something freeing in her words, and I understood that to be true. But while Lady Arnifour seemed to gain strength from the imparting of her story, neither of her children looked to be likewise affected. Eldon's expression grew increasingly aghast while Kaylin started to cry softly into her handkerchief.

"Mr. Pendragon is right," Lady Arnifour finished with the assurance of hindsight. "I should have set her free from the start."

Several seconds crept past before Eldon turned and stumbled back to the bar. "Is there any bloody wonder I drink so much?" he mumbled to no one.

"Why didn't you tell us?" Kaylin said in a pitifully small voice. "How could you have let us think . . ."

"I know. . . . I was wrong. . . . I should have . . . I just . . ." Her words trailed off in the absence of any reasonable explanation.

"Did Elsbeth know?"

"I don't think so. . . . She never spoke to me about it." She glanced over at Victor, but he kept his head down. "I suppose I can't be certain. I have no way of knowing what your father may have told her."

"No wonder Father hated you," Eldon said as he took a deep drink.

"*Eldon!* . . ." Kaylin howled.

"Let him say what he wants," Lady Arnifour said. "What does he understand of love? The only thing he's ever loved is a bottle."

"Whiskey is that only thing that makes living with you tolerable. It should have been *you* in that field that night—"

"*How dare you!*" Victor leapt to his feet.

"Enough!" Colin moved to the center of the room and for once I was glad to see him chastising this herd of cats. "Since I am no longer working for a fee I don't feel the least obliged to subject myself to a moment more of this twaddle. *I* shall ask the questions and each of you will answer, and only after I've finished and left this house behind may you choose to continue this discourse. Failure to follow this directive will bring a rash of blue-suited bobbies and Yarders down upon your heads so quickly that you'll each be explaining yourselves from now until the turn of the century. Are we clear?"

No one answered.

"Very good. Then I should like to know about the relationship between the Earl and Elsbeth; does anyone deny that they were having an affair?"

The stoic faces that countered his question confirmed what we already knew.

"Fine." He allowed a tight smile. "I also know one of you had a row with Elsbeth about that affair the night she and the Earl were attacked. Would anyone like to confess? . . . Or shall I do it for you?"

"There's no need," Victor spoke up. "We both know it's me you're talkin' about. But I've got nothin' to hide. And you're right, Mr. Pendragon, I was no kind of father to Elsbeth and will have the rest a my life to think on it. But at least I tried to help her that one time. I knew she was goin' out to that barn to meet the Earl. I also knew he was usin' her 'cause he knew how much it was hurtin' his wife. It was unforgivable—"

"And this from the man who cuckolded him," Eldon sneered.

"Not another bloody word!" Colin snapped. "Go on, Victor."

"I confronted her that night after her argument with Nathaniel. Told her she was bein' played a fool." He shook his head. "She didn't care what I had to say. Even denied it right to my face, but after a few minutes I could see she was takin' some joy in it. I think she was proud of herself. Thought she had it all figured out." He rubbed his forehead. "Then she just started hollering that I had no right to say anything to her. And she was right. I was just the help to her. I never earned the right to say anything." He slumped back in his chair and looked drained. "I was no one to her."

"Victor . . . ," Lady Arnifour muttered.

"And what about you, Eldon?" Colin said as he turned to the young man. "Did you ever argue with your father over his affair with Elsbeth?"

"Me?! Now why the hell would I give a ruddy toss about what *he* was doing?"

"Because he was ruining the estate," Colin answered. "Your inheritance. But then he was holding you off with a threat of a different sort, wasn't he? While you worried that someday you'd be left with nothing more than a mountain of debt and a house crumbling about your feet, your father was keeping you at bay by refusing to share in the profits from his lucrative clubs unless you did his bidding."

"*Clubs?!*" Lady Arnifour stammered.

"Yes, I'm afraid Warren Vandemier's been holding out on you." A tight smile teased Colin's lips. "But you know that already, don't you, Eldon?"

I was mystified as I turned to look at Colin, wondering if he was inventing things just to elicit a reaction from Eldon, until I saw Eldon flush in the span of an instant.

"I assume Abby Roynton let that slip . . . ?" Eldon said as he struggled to regain his composure.

Colin's eyes flashed as a corner of his mouth curled up, making it clear that he had indeed garnered much more information from the seductive widow than he'd admitted to me.

"That woman . . . ," Lady Arnifour hissed.

"What I want to know, Eldon . . . ," Colin spoke over her, ". . . is what the argument was about between you and your father the night *before* the attack? At the Whitechapel club. The one a lovely young woman who worked there was only too eager to report to me."

"You would take the word of an addict?" Lady Arnifour reproached.

"An addict can be far more honest than someone with something to hide. Am I wrong, Eldon?"

"No," he said with defiance. "She wasn't lying. I was there that night. And we had a hell of a go of it. I'm just glad I got a chance to tell him what I thought before someone made the laudable choice to snuff him."

"*Eldon!*"

"Then tell me . . . ," Colin continued over Lady Arnifour's outburst. ". . . Tell us all what you said."

His face clouded. "My father was vile and loathsome, and he cheated or used everyone in his life to get whatever he wanted. And I include in his notable list of dupes Abigail Roynton, as remarkable and vivacious a woman as there's ever been." He smirked at his mother. "So it was my pleasure to carry on my father's questionable carnal finesse when it became clear that he'd tired of the extraordinary widow. I will admit, at first I only seduced her to raise the old sod's ire, but I quickly realized that she was a font of information about him, and a willing one at that. I knew I'd be able to use what she confided in me if only to protect my *own* best interests. And I was right.

"Abby told me he'd not only founded half a dozen clubs in town, but that he'd also invested in that many more in China. Most of his employees were smuggled in on cargo ships from Shanghai. They'd arrive as indentured slaves and my dear father would seal their fates by making them addicts." He finished another shot of whiskey and took the time to pour a refill before continuing. "The only thing I couldn't figure out, the only thing even Abby didn't know, was where the hell he'd gotten the capital. I knew it had to be coming from somewhere unsavory, but I never dreamed he was bilking it from his own wife." He shook his head. "And to think it was over her bastard child. How repulsive we've all become—"

"You have no right!" Kaylin howled.

"*Please!*" Colin bellowed. "Will you go on. . . ."

Eldon tilted back another quick sip. "I decided to have it out with the old swindler. I told him he could either cut me in on his other businesses or I would confess to my mother everything I'd found out." His eyes seethed with anger. "You can just imagine my astonishment when he only laughed at me. Now I know why. How pathetic I must have looked, threatening to turn him over to the very person who was bankrolling him. Consistent right up to the end, aren't I!" he growled.

"And what about you, Kaylin?" Colin turned to her, looking smaller than ever from her perch on the couch next to her mother. "What did you make of your father's character and livelihood?"

"There have already been too many ugly revelations here, Mr. Pendragon," she said quietly. "I haven't the heart for any more."

"Ah, but you mustn't refuse. We are finally getting somewhere."

"You will mind yourself, Mr. Pendragon," Lady Arnifour warned. "I've had about enough of this."

"Of course you have. We can summon Scotland Yard if you'd prefer. I'd be perfectly content to continue with the inspector and a stream of bobbies in attendance. But let me assure you, this *will* be done. You were saying, Kaylin?"

"What is it you want from me, Mr. Pendragon?"

"The truth. Were you aware of your father's dealings?"

"Absolutely not." She glanced over at her mother with what looked to be both pity and regret. "He left me alone. I have nothing to say against him."

"Did you ever visit him at his club in Whitechapel?"

"And why would I do that? Those places represent everything I despise."

"How so?"

"They prey on weak-minded people, Mr. Pendragon, and foster addiction in the name of business." Her voice was tight. "Women are treated like baubles, dangled in front of eager clients with no greater expectation than to entice them to ruin their lives. And haven't you been listening to my brother? Those same women are enslaved, their loyalty assured by virtue of the dependence on opium they're forced to cultivate. Isn't that reason enough?"

"My apologies." He nodded his head slightly.

She nodded back, but her glare was wintry cold.

"I can see you've given this a great deal of thought. It's commendable that you're able to be as compassionate of your father's memory as you are. I assume you've made your peace with him."

"I have."

"And Elsbeth?"

"Elsbeth?" She shook her head and dropped her gaze. "I had no quarrel with her," she said.

"Oh?" Colin furrowed his brow as he continued to scrutinize her. "Then I am confused. Elsbeth was a woman you thought to be your cousin and yet you've already admitted by your silence that she was also someone you understood to be having an affair with your father. I also recall you being most disparaging when discussing your father's trysts with Mrs. Roynton. So while you demurred to name Elsbeth as the new object of your father's affection, you made it clear that you neither condoned nor excused him or his mistress. All of which makes me believe that your coyness is decidedly unconvincing."

"And yet *we* are the ones being disparaged, Mr. Pendragon, as you persist in spinning a flimsy web of hunches around us. Surely my mother's payments to you have earned us more than that?"

Colin smiled, his dimples framing the edges of his mouth with significant pleasure. "Well spoken. And you are absolutely right. So now it is time for me to admit that I myself am guilty of a bit of coyness. I will ask you to indulge me by returning to the night before the attack. The night Eldon admits to finally purging his soul. What you have not admitted is that you followed Eldon there that night, didn't you?"

"That's enough." Lady Arnifour bolted to her feet. "I'll not have you accusing my daughter of dishonesty. You will remove yourself from this house at once or the inspector will most certainly be sent for."

Colin stood firm a moment before nodding as though in agreement. "Mrs. O'Keefe!" He pulled open the door and hollered out into the foyer, "*Mrs. O'Keefe!* Would you please be so kind as to fetch the inspector and a contingent of bobbies." He slammed the doors shut and turned back to us. "While we wait the hour it will take that rabble to make their way here, I shall finish my postulation."

"This is appalling," Lady Arnifour stammered, shifting her weight as though getting ready to leave the room, and yet she still did not. Perhaps she understood as I did that Colin would not let her. And in the space of that moment, Mrs. O'Keefe quietly slid the door open in response to having been summoned and hovered just inside.

"Appalling?" Colin rolled right along, having adopted an air of faux indignation. "I would say appalling was your decision to remove your daughter from the house in the aftermath of the murders for fear she might be found out. Appalling is your willingness to allow the son of a man you supposedly love to take the fall for a crime you *know* he did not commit. Appalling is trading one life for another because *you've* decided one is more valuable. Appalling is bearing a child whom you turn away from because she reminds you of your most profound mistake. . . ."

Lady Arnifour clutched at her chest and sank back onto the sofa, her face as ashen as spent cinders. Her eyes had lost their focus and she appeared to no longer be aware of anything around her.

"For the longest time," Colin spoke again, choosing his words deliberately as he too stared at Lady Arnifour, "I've been unable to figure out who you've been trying to protect. Have you been covering your own complicity? Or were you doing so for someone else? I see now that it was a bit of both."

No one spoke.

"Let me tell you what I know to be true, and then let me tell you what I *believe* to be true," he said after a moment. "Because of the affair Elsbeth and the Earl were having, she came to understand the truth of her parentage. Nathaniel made me realize that. I'd made the blunder of misconstruing his devotion toward Elsbeth as romantic passion, but I was wrong. It wasn't a lovers' quarrel overheard between the two of them the night of the attack, but rather a disapproving argument between siblings. Nathaniel was insisting she end the affair even as she warned him to stay out of her business.

"And do any of you comprehend what that conversation tells us about Nathaniel and Elsbeth?" He glanced at their faces but did not wait for a response. "It tells us how close they were. Which makes perfect sense when you remember that neither Elsbeth nor Nathaniel was an Arnifour. The two of them lived on the periphery of this willful and self-possessed family. Fortunate for them, I suppose, until Elsbeth learned the truth. Only then could she finally rid herself of her feelings of dissociation, for through her biological mother, she now belonged.

"It was their shared secret which allowed them to have the sort of confrontation they had on the night she was attacked. But Elsbeth was not to be so easily dissuaded from her perch at the Earl's side. For in spite of Nathaniel's words, she rode out to meet the Earl just as she'd been doing for months—whenever Kaylin wasn't along. And while all of you established that a walk was a customary part of the Earl's evening, only one of you knew that Elsbeth and the Earl went many nights to that barn. The two of them headed out in separate directions at differing times, but Elsbeth would double back and pick him up, riding down with him for their indiscretions.

"Only Kaylin had spied them from her promontory on the boulders across the field on nights she would go there on her own. She would watch the two of them ride up like young lovers, her father and her cousin, disappearing into that barn. . . ." Colin let his voice trail off as he held his gaze on Kaylin, finally perching on the ottoman by her feet. "Am I correct?" he asked. "Did they tarnish your perfect view?"

She exhaled deeply as her eyes flicked about. "I loved that place. It was so peaceful." She shook her head. "Then *they* started showing up."

"Did it make you angry? The scandal that was sure to denigrate your family's name if they were found out?"

"The Arnifour name has withstood graver injustices over the centuries than my father's infidelities against my mother," she said flatly. Lady Arnifour leaned over and seized her daughter's hand, squeezing it firmly.

Colin flashed a quick smile before standing and turning his gaze back to Eldon. "And what do you say? Do you agree with your sister?"

Eldon stared at her, his expression confounded. "I don't know," he mumbled.

"Are you quite finished, Mr. Pendragon?" Lady Arnifour turned on him, sounding for a moment like her normal self.

"You told your sister about your father's multiple business dealings after Mrs. Roynton divulged them to you, didn't you, Eldon?"

"She had a right to know," he answered with a bit of a stammer. "He was cheating us."

"And you suspected your sister would do something about it—"

"No!"

"How *dare* you!" Lady Arnifour pushed herself to her feet.

"Sit down!" Colin barked. "We will finish this *now*." He wheeled on Eldon. "You set your sister up. You told her everything you knew and then led her down to the club the night before your father was killed. The only thing you earned for your efforts was your father's scorn, but your sister caused quite a stir." He turned back to Kaylin. "You made a veritable spectacle of yourself, swinging an oil lamp around and threatening to burn the club to the ground until your father and his security blokes finally managed to hustle you out. You were memorable, Kaylin. In spite of their altered states, you left everyone shaken, which is exactly what Eldon had intended.

"About the only one you failed to ruffle was your father. He had no idea how much you already knew, or the ways in which your brother was manipulating you: telling you stories of the family's impending doom, the squandering of your mother's fortune, the repugnant trade he was in.

"Which brings us to the night of the attack. I'll bet tensions at the dinner table were exceedingly high that night, Eldon and Kaylin infuriated by what they viewed as their father's treachery, and Elsbeth feeling mistakenly emboldened by her secret knowledge. And then there was the Earl. He would have still been convinced that only *he* had all the pieces in this game. But that's where he was wrong.

"Kaylin excused herself from the table partway through the meal with complaints of a headache. Everyone else finished and went their usual disparate ways, the Earl setting off on his nightly jaunt, Elsbeth to the stable to get her horse for her rendezvous, Nathaniel to finish up in the stable, Victor to his garden, Mrs. O'Keefe to clean up her kitchen, and Eldon to the nearest bottle.

"Unfortunately for Nathaniel, this was the night he decided to confront his beloved half sister about what she was doing. He wanted better for her. But Elsbeth disagreed. They argued intensely, unwittingly providing a motive for the imminent attack. A happenstance all of you, with the sole exception of Victor, have been too happy to hide behind.

"The Earl and Elsbeth met at their usual spot," he moved to the fireplace, "a well-trampled patch of grass not more than a third of the way to the barn, and rode the rest of the way together as was their custom. I suppose they thought they were being clever, though they were hardly discreet, yet neither of them knew that someone had already arrived there ahead of them. Someone who had taken a horse while Elsbeth and

Nathaniel were fighting and was now waiting just inside the edge of the trees by that barn.

"When they arrived that night there would have been no sign that this evening was any different from any other. I suspect they were probably so caught up with their passions that they didn't realize something was amiss until the barn was set ablaze. And from there, everything unfolded with lightning speed.

"They would've fled outside where they were immediately set upon, their hunter waiting for them. The Earl was run down first. He received several blows to the back of his head from a large knot of wood the killer had found among the trees. Once the Earl had been felled, the killer turned back to go after Elsbeth. She had not gotten very far, mistakenly choosing to turn and hold her ground, thinking, perhaps, that she might be able to convince her attacker not to hurt her. But she was wrong. This attack was as much about her as it was the Earl. Though the blows she suffered lacked the ferocity of those that had been wielded against the Earl, it was only because the killer was already fatigued. Isn't that right, Kaylin?" He turned to her. "So tell me, what did Elsbeth say when she came to your room that night to, as you said, check on you? It certainly wasn't to ask you to go riding, was it?"

No one spoke for a moment as everyone turned to Kaylin.

"Don't say a word," Lady Arnifour suddenly blurted in a voice that sounded as detached as it was hollow. "He's got nothing but a cluster of speculation."

"That's all you've got to say?!" Eldon sputtered.

"Not one more word from you. You don't know a thing."

"At least I'm not being accused of murdering anyone—"

"Stop!" Kaylin bellowed, stabbing at her temples. "Isn't it enough already? Isn't it?!" She turned on her brother. "*You did this.* You took me to the club that night after telling me how Father owned a dozen of them, addicting patrons and enslaving women. You let me go in there and threaten him, threaten the whole bloody place, and when we went home that night you told me it was the last vestiges of our inheritance. All we would be left with were those vile clubs and this crumbling house—"

"Don't—," Lady Arnifour pleaded.

"It's too late!" Kaylin snapped, casting her gaze to Colin. "It was an outrage, Mr. Pendragon, the mockery my father made of all of us. I wasn't about to become a spinster with an ownership in opium clubs! Oh . . . I despised him for what he was doing to me, but unlike my pathetic brother, I decided I would do something about it."

"You mustn't. . . ." Lady Arnifour started to sob as she seized her daughter's arm, but Kaylin only shook her off and stood up.

"I decided I would go out that night when he went for his walk and have it out with him, one way or another. I wasn't going to sit idly by and watch him annihilate everything around us." She shook her head and moved over by the windows, wrapping her arms around herself as though she were suddenly cold. "You were right; dinner was awful that night. The room was intolerable and when I couldn't take it anymore, I complained of a migraine and left.

"I went upstairs and changed into my riding things and that's when Elsbeth came up to see me." Her face clouded and her lips pursed. "She came up to ridicule me. My father had told her that Eldon and I had come to the club the night before, and she laughed at me for thinking I could have any effect on what he was doing. It made me mad . . . it made me outraged . . . to think she presumed that whoring around with my father gave her the right to say such things to me! I hated her. . . ."

"Oh, Kaylin." Lady Arnifour shrank back on the couch, weeping piteously.

"I knew they would meet up that night. The two of them so proud of themselves. So while Elsbeth was arguing with

Nathaniel, I took one of the horses without a saddle or bridle or reins and rode down to the barn and waited for them. And I didn't have to wait long. They came trotting across the field on one of the bays, one of my favorites, and they'd barely dismounted before he was pawing all over her, her laughing and letting him do whatever he pleased. It was sickening. And never once did they bother to look around and see if anyone might be there, might catch them, never in all the times I'd seen them. They didn't care. The two of them, they were deplorable.

"So as soon as they disappeared into the barn I crept forward and set it ablaze. Let them have their fire with their passion. . . ." She gave a hollow chuckle that died in her throat. "My father came out first; he spotted me and started hollering at me, said I was bloody starkers. Can you imagine? I rode him down, Mr. Pendragon, just as you said, and I struck him with a knot of burl I'd found in the woods. It felt good; watching him blubber like the pathetic creature he was, it only made me angrier. And she . . . she was no better than him. I should've known she was born of my flesh. We are a contemptible lot, but at least I kept them from destroying everything. . . ." Her voice trailed off and I wondered if she yet had any real understanding of what she had done.

"I'll need you to come with us," Colin said softly.

"I'll not fight you," she answered. She went over to him as I got up, planting herself before him with defiance as Eldon sagged against the bar and Lady Arnifour's wrenching sobs filled the silence. I glanced over toward the door and noticed that Mrs. O'Keefe was gone, though she had left it ajar in her evident haste to leave. And it made me wonder if perhaps Lady Arnifour was grieving for a daughter who was not her own after all.

CHAPTER 33

The deepest part of the night is the time I find myself most able to collect my thoughts. It's also one of the few times I can watch Colin without self-consciousness lest the eyes of anyone else should take disapproving note. Some nights I will reach for him; other nights I am content to leave him be and simply marvel at the wonder of it all.

This night found me quite lost to my thoughts. In the space of a single day we had rent two very disparate families, although it could be said that they had severed themselves long before we had been called upon. It made me wonder, this business of family. The stricture of its definition seems careless and arbitrary given the aberrations that can be found within its framework. How well I know that. Twenty-six years after the tragedy that took my life without ending it I still choose to believe that my mother did the best that she could given the phantoms blighting her mind. I will never know for sure. In truth, I hardly even remember her. She has morphed into a cautionary figure of what to be vigilant against. What makes it worse is that I remember even less of my father. So it is my life with

Colin that represents the pinnacle of the promise of that word: "family." And, of course, Mrs. Behmoth, though I'm not as certain how I feel about that.

Colin reached out with a yawn, peering at me through heavily lidded eyes. "Can't sleep?"

"I guess not."

He curled up next to me, his arm stretching across my belly. "What's keeping you awake?"

"I was thinking about Kaylin. What's going to happen to her?"

"That's easy." He exhaled deeply. "Her mother will purchase the best defense and she will be sentenced to a spell in a sanitarium somewhere out in the country. They'll ascribe her behavior to female hysterics and it will likely run until she's long into her middle years."

"When you say 'her mother,' do you mean Lady Arnifour or Mrs. O'Keefe?"

"In this instance I am referring to Lady Arnifour, but it really doesn't matter who gave birth to her. I suppose they both loved her in their own way, and it didn't seem to make the slightest bit of difference to her life. It's just a travesty that nature doesn't see fit to make some people barren."

"What a thing to say," I muttered halfheartedly, knowing that I would never have been born had such a natural selection been in place.

"Come now, you know I'm right. And I mean to include Mademoiselle Rendell in that too. None of them was fit to procreate."

"At least now Drew will have a chance in a decent home," I said with genuine cheer, determined to relegate my maudlin thoughts back to where they belong: where I can abide them. "Do you think your father will get him placed quickly?"

"That boy will be living like royalty within the month. And in India he'll be safe from both his mother and brother."

"Which is good, since Michael's not likely to remain in the workhouse for more than a couple of years."

"I'm sure you're right. And then he'll be back on the streets: ill equipped, angry, and even more conniving than ever. At least their mother will be spending the better part of the next decade paying for her complicity. Nevertheless, it does seem rather a small price to pay given the destruction she's wrought on those boys."

"She has to live with that for the rest of her life."

"Not everyone has a conscience, you know."

"They do. Some just learn how to ignore it . . . or anesthetize it."

He yawned again. "That is the unfortunate truth. But let me ask you a question: Where do you suppose Li Shen disappeared off to?"

"She'll go to another club somewhere else in the city where they don't know who she is. It's what she knows and she is an addict."

"It's a shame."

"It is." And for a moment a chill tore up my spine as I recognized that could have been me. "Do you think there's any chance Inspector Varcoe will stop by tomorrow to thank you for keeping him from arresting the wrong person?" I chuckled.

He snickered. "Only if Mrs. Behmoth discovers she's the long-lost sister of our Victoria."

"Unlikely then, I suppose," I drolled, but I could tell by the way his breath was already beginning to even out that he was succumbing to sleep. Lost to my own thoughts once again, I didn't sleep much more that night, but it was gratitude, not fear, that held my mind enthralled.

CHAPTER 34

"It seems ta me ya oughta be celebratin'," Mrs. Behmoth said as she set the tray of tea and scones by the fireplace. "I didn't like a single one a them uppity Arnifours and I'm glad ya found 'em all guilty."

I rolled my eyes.

"I didn't find them all guilty . . . ," Colin started to say.

"Ach." She waved a hand at him. "They were all guilty a somethin'."

"I suppose." He shrugged, one eyebrow arching up as he fussed over our tea. "But it's hard to feel satisfaction given the cost to their family."

"Family . . ." Mrs. Behmoth snorted. "They were a regular rogues' gallery. Ya best appreciate what ya got," she scoffed.

A sudden and savage pounding on our door brought her to her feet. "We expectin' someone?" she asked as she ambled for the stairs.

"Not that I'm aware of," Colin said as he poured a touch of milk into his tea.

Another harsh pounding reverberated from downstairs as

Mrs. Behmoth hollered, "Ya better 'ave a good reason for makin' such a racket!"

Colin laughed as he passed me my tea and then snatched up his own. "I heard a carriage clattering up and was rather hoping it might be coming here."

I couldn't help smiling. "I'm sure you were."

The sound of a slight scuffle came from downstairs, followed by the hurried pounding of feet barreling up. It was clearly not Mrs. Behmoth, and the trailing fury of her voice only confirmed it. "Ya got no ruddy manners. I don't care if ya *are* wearin' the old bird's crest."

Before I could guess who Mrs. Behmoth was referring to, a sour-faced young man, somewhere shy of the quarter-century mark, appeared on our landing. He was dressed in the scarlet tunic and black-panted uniform of Her Majesty's Guard. He held a steel helmet in the crux of one arm atop of which sprayed a white plume like the tail of a prideful show horse. "I apologize for the intrusion . . . ," he said in a tone that did not support his contention, ". . . but I've been sent on the most urgent and sensitive business."

"So I would presume." Colin smiled thinly as he stood up. "And by whose command do you come in such a manner?"

The young man sent a sideways glance in my direction as he let his pause lengthen.

"You will speak to both of us or neither of us," Colin said. "I really don't care which."

To his credit, the guard appeared to carefully consider his options before turning back to Colin with a bit more acid. "All right then."

No one said anything for a moment as Colin slid out a crown and quietly began weaving it through his fingers. It took another full minute before Colin finally spoke up, keeping his eyes fixed on the young officer as he said, "I'm waiting, Sergeant."

"Sir?"

"I asked who sent you here."

He reddened and pulled himself straighter. "Isn't that obvious, sir?" he said with noticeable disdain.

Colin strode over to the windows, the coin continuing to slide smoothly between his fingers as he glanced outside. "The only obvious thing, Sergeant, is that you wish me to believe you are on Her Majesty's business. Arriving thunderously in one of her lesser carriages and parading about in the garments of one of her Life Guards. Yet we all know our matriarch has a multitude of both coaches and staff, and were you actually to be on *her* business, I would expect a far less ostentatious entrance. What's your name?"

"My name?"

"Come now." Colin turned from the window and stared at the young man. "I haven't stumped you already, have I?"

The sergeant scowled and I struggled to suppress a smile. "Sergeant Dwight McReedy," he finally answered.

"Well done. And so, Sergeant McReedy, now that we know our Victoria has not sent you, can you tell us who has?"

The sergeant held his own, staring back at Colin with thinly veiled dislike. "While I may not be here at the personal request of Her Majesty, I *have* come at the behest of a senior member of her staff."

"A *senior* member of her staff?" Colin smirked. "Why, that could be anyone from a personal maid to my father. Has my father sent you?"

The man's face went taut. "Sir?"

Colin shook his head and returned to his seat. "I'll not ask my question a fourth time, Sergeant. You may take your leave. Good day."

The sergeant glanced at me in disbelief. Whereas before he'd considered me an intruder, I could now see he was hoping I might intercede on his behalf. I gave him a shrug.

"Sir . . . ," he began again with some measure of grit in his voice, "I've been ordered to escort you back to Buckingham Palace."

"And suppose we're not in the mood to go until sometime next week? Would you be obliged to spend the next days counting cobbles and praying against rain?"

The young man managed to hold himself steady. He was clearly a quick study. "You mustn't dismiss me, sir. I've been ordered by Major Dashell Hampstead of Her Majesty's Life Guard. It is on a matter of the utmost delicacy and urgency."

Colin looked up at him. "So it's the Guard itself who requires my assistance?"

Sergeant McReedy blinked. "I'm sure I don't know," he answered. "Collecting you was the extent of my orders."

"Well now, that makes me feel like an old alley cat."

"You must come with me, sir. I must insist on it."

"Insist?" Colin finally stopped flipping the coin as he looked over at the young man.

The sergeant cleared his throat and lowered his voice. "It's a most foul business. Major Hampstead would not trouble you otherwise."

"How foul?"

"Sir?"

Colin waved for him to get on with it.

"It's murder, sir," came the reluctant reply. "The most brutal sort."

Colin scowled as he stood up again. "Return to your carriage," he said.

"Sir?"

"We will be down shortly. Go on now. I don't need you watching us get ready."

The young man nodded curtly and took his leave, bolting back down the stairs with as much tumult as his arrival.

"Was it really necessary to set him through such paces?"

"Hmm." Colin shrugged as he pulled his vest on. "That lot can be so full of themselves. And him just a young toady."

"Nevertheless, it's not every week we're summoned by Her Majesty's Guard."

"Thankfully."

"It sounds like a nasty bit of business."

"Murder usually is."

I could not help the sigh that escaped my lips. "We've only just completed two cases. Shattered two families. I'd rather hoped we might have a spot of time off."

"Those families imploded long before we were sent for." He stopped and looked at me. "Makes me appreciate what we have all over again. You and me. That's all I need." And I could see by the warmth in his eyes that he meant it.

"And Mrs. Behmoth?" I teased.

"But of course." He laughed. "Where would we be without our dear Mrs. Behmoth?" And I knew he meant that too.

ACKNOWLEDGMENTS

While writing is a solitary sport, a published book is the culmination of hard work by many people. In my case, Diane Salzberg, Karen Clemens, and Melissa Gelineau read innumerable drafts and offered insightful notes with nary a rolled eye or shrug of *"this again?!"*. John Paine gave me an early vote of confidence and helped focus the story into something I could show around. I would be nowhere if Kathy Green and her son hadn't read the book. Especially since her son convinced her to take me on! The folks at Kensington have been amazing, keeping me honest and making me wonder how I ever passed an English class. Particular kudos to John Scognamiglio for his support, direction, and friendship. Special thanks to my parents and sisters for their love and support through all and everything. And there has been a lot! The very same to Tresa Hoffman. Lastly, a second bow to Lovey, without whom I would never have made it this far. A heartfelt *cheers!* to all of you.

Please turn the page for an exciting sneak peek of
Gregory Harris's next Colin Pendragon Mystery

THE BELLINGHAM BLOODBATH

coming in September 2014!

CHAPTER 1

One of Her Majesty's coaches was waiting to whisk us off to Buckingham Palace. We had only just been told about the killing of a captain in Her Majesty's Life Guard and his wife, and were being summoned, presumably, to solve their murders. The sergeant sent for us had made it sound like an ugly business indeed.

I stared across the room with a mixture of dread and morbid curiosity as I watched Colin continue to fiddle with one of his derringers. Surely he meant for us to leave . . . yet there he sat, painstakingly wiping every centimeter of the little gun until I could finally stand it no longer: "What the bloody hell are you doing?"

He looked up at me with an inconceivably guileless expression. "What?"

"Buckingham?!" I blurted as though speaking to someone quite undone. "The sergeant who came to fetch us is waiting outside. . . ."

"I know," he answered simply.

"Well, are we going?"

"The sergeant's a pompous little twit. He can wait."

"He's an officer of Her Majesty's Life Guard—"

"I don't care if he's having it off with the old girl herself; let him wait. Be good to teach him some manners."

"So we're back in school then?" I parried just as a loud and insistent pounding burst up from the door downstairs.

"See what I mean," Colin grumbled.

"I'm sure he's only trying to follow orders. He wasn't sent here to polish the cobbles pacing."

A second pounding, even more determined, brought Colin to his feet. "If he does that again I shall go down there and shove my boot up his orders."

"No doubt Mrs. Behmoth will beat you to it," I said as the sound of her lumbering from the kitchen to the front door drifted up among her curses. I was certain she would roundly upbraid the young sergeant the moment she got the door open, but no such diatribe ensued. Instead I heard the voice of our elderly neighbor curl up the stairs. "It's Mrs. Menlo," I said with little enthusiasm.

"And what is she complaining about now?" He shook his head as he set his derringer onto the mantel. "Is the soldier out front giving her vapors?"

"I should think she's trying to wheedle information out of Mrs. Behmoth. You know how she despises not knowing our business."

"Yes. . . ." He snatched up his dumbbells and began curling them over his head. "Though I'm sure we could cause her a good deal of apoplexy with some of the things we get up to." He snickered. "For the moment, however, I believe it's time we learned something about this poor captain and his wife. We mustn't show up at the major's office completely unawares."

I stared at the stack of unread newspapers beside the hearth as he continued to train the already taut muscles of his arms. "Fine," I exhaled. "Let me see what I can find of it."

"Excellent," he muttered, dropping to the floor and busting out a set of push-ups on his dumbbells.

Turning my attentions back to the pile of papers, I was relieved when my search proved brief. Stretched across the morning edition of yesterday's paper was a banner that cried: QUEEN'S CAPTAIN AND WIFE BUTCHERED IN BLOODBATH. I read the article aloud while Colin continued his fevered push-ups, and it was only after I finished that he finally sat up, ran a sleeve across his sweating forehead, and asked me to read it again. This time he listened:

"*Sometime during the night of Sunday last, Captain Trevor Bellingham, 32, of the Queen's Life Guard, and his wife, Gwendolyn, 29, were brutally murdered in the Finchley Road flat they shared with their young son. Miraculously, the young boy, just past his fifth birthday, was found unharmed in his bedroom. Police had to break the boy's door down as it had been wedged tight, almost certainly by the murderer, though one source close to the investigation suggested that one of the parents may have secured the door in order to save their son.*

"*Mrs. Bellingham was reported to have been shot and killed in her bedroom, but Scotland Yard has yet to release the cause of death for Captain Bellingham, stating that the matter was still under investigation.*" I glanced over to where Colin remained sitting on the floor. "I wonder why the secrecy?"

"We shall have to find out."

"*Police did state that there did not appear to be any signs of forced entry, pointing to the possibility that the killer may have been known to Captain and Mrs. Bellingham. Scotland Yard's Inspector Emmett Varcoe . . . ,*" I read his name, enunciating it with mock esteem, "*. . . assures that everything possible is being done to solve this terrible crime against one of the Queen's own men and his young wife. However, the* Times *would like to remind its readership that Inspector Varcoe is the same investiga-*

*tor who remains befuddled by the identity of the vicious killer
known only as Jack the Ripper.*"

"It all sounds rather odd," Colin muttered as he stood up
and hurried off toward our bedroom, "though a spot-on sum-
mation of Varcoe. He should have retired a decade ago."

"That he should . . . ," I agreed as Colin returned with his
straw-colored hair slicked back and our coats over his arms.

"Shall we?"

Twenty minutes later the hansom cab he had flagged down
swung us around the drive of Buckingham Palace, and once
again I was struck by how austere and remote it looks. Partially
colonnaded in the Federalist style, it appears like neither a true
palace nor a home. Sprawling behind its massive bronze and
iron fencing with a contingency of guards precisely stationed
across its front, it seems very much to be holding itself with the
same reserve as our Queen.

I took note of the lone Union Jack on the roof and knew
Victoria was not in residence. Her colors would be flying atop
Sandringham this time of year, though even if she had been here
I knew it would have made little difference. One does not hap-
pen upon Her Majesty in the hallways. Nevertheless, it would
have been the closest I had ever come to royalty.

The coachman brought us alongside the gates and slowed almost to a stop as they began to swing inward at the behest of
our escort, Sergeant McReedy. We were ushered through and
driven across the parade grounds to the far side of the building
under the watchful eyes of a throng of spectators.

"They must think we're special." I chuckled.

"We are," he murmured as he surreptitiously squeezed my
hand.

"Perhaps so, but they'll still be disappointed when we
climb out."

He laughed as I turned to watch the stiff-postured guards

we were clattering past with their blazing red jackets and high bearskin hats. They ignored us as we went by, none so much as moving his eyes to follow our progress. "You can always count on this lot to put us in our place," Colin said.

Before I could answer we came to an abrupt stop and both doors were immediately swept open. Sergeant McReedy dismounted and led us through a side portico and down a hallway of unremarkable design that I decided no royal had ever passed along. Tiny offices lined both sides, providing the only contrast in the otherwise stark space. It was hardly what I had expected until I reminded myself that these were the niches of those who kept the palace functioning; what use did they have for moldings, ormolu, filigree, or even art?

The sergeant stopped at an office near the end of the corridor and barked out, "Colin Pendragon and Ethan Pruitt!"

An alabaster-skinned young man who looked too young to be in the service sat behind a small desk in the anteroom to a much larger office. "Oh . . . ," he said with notable surprise as Colin and I walked in. "Oh . . . ," he repeated as his eyes fell on me before quickly shifting back to Colin. "It's a pleasure to meet you, Mr. Pendragon," he said, holding out his hand. "I'm Major Hampstead's attaché, Corporal Bramwood." His gaze drifted in my direction again and I knew what was coming. "I am terribly sorry . . . ," he said coolly, ". . . but there seems to have been a misunderstanding." He looked back at Colin. "The summons from Major Hampstead was meant for you, Mr. Pendragon, and you alone."

"Ah . . . then there has indeed been a misunderstanding." Colin offered a smile. "I'm afraid I don't work alone, Corporal. You and your major will take us together or you will settle for my regrets."

Corporal Bramwood opened his mouth to say something, but nothing came out. I saw him glance behind me to where Sergeant McReedy remained in the doorway and then heard the sound of the sergeant moving off. This young man was apparently on his own.

"Have a seat . . . have a seat . . . ," he mumbled quickly. "I shall let Major Hampstead know you are *both* here." He gave an awkward nod before disappearing through the door behind his desk, making sure it latched firmly behind him.

"This lot seems to think they're all ordained by God," Colin muttered as he sat down.

I snickered. "I don't think that young corporal is used to having his major's orders countermanded."

"I was civil about it," he blithely protested.

Before I could say anything more the inner door burst open and Corporal Bramwood hurried out with an older man at his heels. "Mr. Pendragon . . . Mr. Pruitt . . . ," he sputtered. "This is Major Hampstead."

The major stepped forward, a tall man somewhere in his late fifties with a generous middle. He wore a thick, white mustache and sported huge sideburns that fanned out several inches along his jawline. His deportment suggested he had been a leader most of his life: ramrod straight with a swagger of marked self-assurance. "It is an honor to meet you, gentlemen," he said, and I knew he was also a diplomat.

"It's always a pleasure to meet one of Her Majesty's lifers." Colin smiled.

Major Hampstead snorted a laugh. "I should doubt the son of Her Majesty's emissary to India is so easily impressed. I would say your father has given nearly the whole of his life in service to her."

"He has." Colin flashed a tight grin. "But the life of a diplomat hardly compares to the work of a regimental guard. You mustn't give my father too much credit."

"I doubt that I am," he chortled. "Please come in, gentlemen. Tea, Corporal," he ordered before retreating back to his office and seating himself behind his massive desk.

Corporal Bramwood brought in a tray of tea and biscuits with a speed that conveyed just how much time he spent in that endeavor. The straining seams along the sides of the major's red tunic also attested to that fact. "I appreciate your willingness to come here without the slightest notice," the major said. "I'm afraid I have a very difficult matter to discuss. One that requires the utmost discretion."

"You are referring to the murder of that captain and his wife?"

The major winced. "I am. It's an awful business that has been made even more unseemly by the newspapers heralding it the way they've done."

"I'm afraid our countrymen are always keen for a scandal."

"Which is precisely my point." I could see him relax a bit at Colin's pronouncement. "The Queen's Guard simply *cannot* be party to any such scandal. It is inappropriate and unacceptable."

"That may be, but it would appear it is already done."

The major knit his brow. "I would venture otherwise, Mr. Pendragon. I have asked you here because I believe you can do a great deal to help us staunch this damage. You can impact the public record to not only cease the gossip concerning this very private, very regrettable event, but to allow *us* to deal with it ourselves, outside of the public's lecherous purview."

"Us?"

"The Guard, of course."

"I see," Colin said even as his own brow creased a notch. "You have summoned us here to divert the newsmen while you and your regiment, untrained in such things, attempt to solve these murders?"

"It is the Guard's business and should be handled as such."

"It is the murder of two British subjects, Major Hampstead, one of whom was in service to the Queen. I'm quite certain the public will remain very concerned about it until it is resolved.

The inference being, of course, that the very men proscribed with protecting Her Majesty cannot even protect themselves. Trying to steal this behind the public's eye will be quite impossible, Major. Unless, of course, you are trying to hide something?"

"Hide something?!" His face creased into a scowl. "I trust you are being facetious, Mr. Pendragon."

"I've been accused of worse," he muttered.

"Let me assure you that my request comes only out of concern for Her Majesty's Guard," the major said in a tone as filled with condescension as assurance. "The first lesson a man learns when he enlists is that it is not about the individual, but the regiment. Every man who serves under Victoria's banner understands that."

"While I'm sure that's true," Colin allowed with a tightening smile as he fished a crown out of his pocket and began effortlessly weaving it between the fingers of his right hand, "I don't see how it is relevant."

"Then you are missing my point," the major sniped. "The Queen's regiment has a prestige to uphold and cannot afford to be mired down in such things. This Bellingham situation is anathema to everything the Guard represents."

Colin instantly palmed the crown. "Do I understand you correctly, Major? Do you presume to speak for the Queen with such rhetoric?"

"Now Mr. Pendragon," he exhaled deeply before popping a biscuit into his mouth, "you misunderstand me. Captain Bellingham was one of my most trusted leaders and a man I considered a personal friend. No one in this company is more determined to bring the perpetrator of his murder to justice than me. And I had the utmost respect and adoration for his lovely wife. A kind and wonderful woman whose senseless killing demands all the resources at the Guard's disposal. Yet even so, decorum dictates that it *must* be done with discretion.

You said yourself that the public will have no faith in our Guard if they perceive that we cannot even fend for ourselves. I'm sure I don't need to remind you that Her Majesty's Life Guard represents the finest of our country's protectorate and as such cannot bear so much as a *whiff* of scandal. This matter *will* be solved by this regiment, but we shall do it *outside* of the gaze of the common masses."

"The common masses?" One of Colin's eyebrows arched up. "Does Victoria encourage her Guard to look down on the very people God has granted her the authority to rule?"

"Mr. Pendragon . . . ," he started to say, only to fall silent. The ticking of the small clock on the major's credenza was the only sound to be heard for several seconds until Colin began to coax the coin between his fingers again. I started to wonder if we weren't about to be dismissed, but I had miscalculated the major. Quite suddenly, without the slightest hint that it was coming, he abruptly let out a bellowing laugh. "You are toying with me, Mr. Pendragon. You mean to prod me into a rise and you almost succeeded. But I shall not be so easily dissuaded." He leaned forward. "I'd bet you would like to see the Bellingham flat for yourself. There is much the newspapers have not reported. Much they do not know."

A cool smirk overtook Colin's face. "And now you are toying with me."

"So I am." He leaned back in his chair with a satisfied smile. "You must understand my position, Mr. Pendragon. Anything concerning the Queen's Guard inevitably implicates our sovereign as well. And I'm sure I needn't remind you that Her Majesty is seventy-seven and in failing health."

"That woman is as delicate as a plow horse," he shot back. "And I find it hard to believe she has any but the most passing familiarity concerning the murder of one of her guardsmen with whom she probably never once spoke. I believe you are trying to hide behind her skirts, Major."

"Do you presume to be privy to what goes on in Her Majesty's household?"

"My father transferred John Brown from Victoria's stable to her personal duty after Albert's death, so I would say I know a bit more about Her Majesty's household than you think. What I don't understand is why you want to bring me here to feed nonsense to the press? I don't control those men."

"You underestimate yourself, Mr. Pendragon. They hang on your words like they are spun from gold." A cloying smile clung to his lips. "If you were to release a statement that you had conducted an investigation and determined the case to be closed, say a burglary gone bad, or a case of mistaken identity, why, they would be only too happy to embrace your conclusion and return their attentions to the horses at Ascot and which lady is wearing what. Everyone would be satisfied, which would allow me and my men to handle this case with the delicacy Captain Bellingham and his wife deserve."

"And the perpetrator?"

"I will personally see to it that their murderer receives the full wrath of the law."

Colin sat up and neatly tipped the crown back into his vest pocket. "And what makes you think these murders will be so easily dispatched? Murder is a complex business in the simplest of cases. . . ."

"I said I will take care of it," the major restated with noticeably greater force. "And I could use your help with Scotland Yard. I've got them circling like schoolyard boys, on top of which the *Times* is calling the Guard's reputation into question, and the public is terrified for their safety. Until we can release a conclusive statement, Mr. Pendragon, this discord will be relentless."

Colin stood up. "I'm sorry, Major. You seem to have gotten the notion that my integrity can be bargained for. If I have earned the respect of the press it is because I do not spin fables and, in spite of your desire for discretion, cannot see why I should start now. If you would like to hire me to solve this case I will gladly do so, but until you come to your senses I will bid you good day." He turned for the door.

"Mr. Pendragon!" The major sounded perplexed as I got up to follow. "*Mr. Pendragon!*" he howled as we reached the door. "With all due respect to your esteemed integrity, the public wants immediate answers to their fears. They want the world to return to the status quo. They will not tolerate remaining under a veil of anxiety. You can blame the unsolved Ripper murders for that. And *that's* why there are men like you and me. To ensure that our republic gets what it needs. Now I am beseeching you, Mr. Pendragon, to offer the public a reasoned solution to a horrible crime so that they can get on with the mundanity of their lives. Where is the harm in that?"

"If that's what you're after, Major, then I would suggest you get the Yard to be your mouthpiece. Inspector Varcoe is always good for hot air."

"Nobody wants to hear from that blasted lout. You *will* do this for me, Mr. Pendragon. You are the only man with the reputation for it and I *will* insist."

"Insist?" Colin chuckled. "Are you proposing sticking a hand up my bum to move my lips?"

"You will be handsomely compensated. Now how can I convince you to perform this service for the Crown?"

Colin pursed his lips and I could tell he had already thought of something. "There is one way I can conceive . . . ," he said casually, ". . . and it is the *only* way I would consider it. . . ." He let a moment pass to emphasize his determination. "You must announce to the press that you have retained my services to solve the murders of the captain and his wife. . . ."

"Yes?"

"And then give me the next three days to do so. During those three days you must ensure I have the full cooperation of this regiment as well as access to whomever I want."

"Not Her Majesty or her family."

"I should hardly think that will be necessary."

"And at the end of the three days?"

"I will deliver the truth of the case to you."

"And if you cannot?"

"I will." He smiled harshly, even as my stomach clutched at the very idea. I couldn't fathom how he had come up with the notion of three days.

Major Hampstead frowned. "Absolute proof, Mr. Pendragon. You must bring me absolute proof of whatever supposition you're championing or I shall have your word that you will face that mob of newsmen and sell them whatever I deem appropriate."

He gave no more than an ambivalent nod.

"Three days then." The major glanced back at his clock. "That would be twelve o'clock on Friday." He turned back to us. "I shall give you until seventeen hundred. Plenty of time for the newsmen to make their Saturday morning edition."

"Most generous," Colin muttered.

"*Corporal Bramwood!*"

"Sir?" The young man opened the door so quickly I knew he had to have been hovering nearby.

"Alert the newspapermen that Her Majesty's Life Guard has retained the services of Colin Pendragon to bring a swift and just conclusion to the tragic murders of Captain and Mrs. Bellingham. And let them know that Mr. Pendragon will have an announcement to make at seventeen hundred hours this very Friday."

"This Friday, sir?"

"Yes, Corporal. *This* Friday."

And with that the young man was gone, though I did notice he left the door ajar.

"I will solve this crime, Major Hampstead," Colin said with the simplicity of one discussing the weather. "I shall bring you the resolution Friday and we will see what gets delivered to the press."

"I admire a man of confidence," the major replied with a tense grin. "But listen very carefully, Mr. Pendragon, because if, at the end of your three days, you should find yourself stymied by this case, then I *alone* will decide what is told to those newsmen. You will say what I decide and you will walk away. Are we clear?"

Colin flashed an equally rigid smile. "You have been most clear, Major. And now I should indeed like an escort to the Bellingham flat so I may get started. Someone from Captain Bellingham's regiment would be my preference."

"Sergeant McReedy will take you. He reported to the captain." Major Hampstead's smile relaxed and I couldn't help but feel it was with the arrogance that comes when one perceives imminent success.

GREAT BOOKS, GREAT SAVINGS!

When You Visit Our Website:
www.kensingtonbooks.com
You Can Save Money Off The Retail Price
Of Any Book You Purchase!

- **All Your Favorite Kensington Authors**
- **New Releases & Timeless Classics**
- **Overnight Shipping Available**
- **eBooks Available For Many Titles**
- **All Major Credit Cards Accepted**

Visit Us Today To Start Saving!
www.kensingtonbooks.com

All Orders Are Subject To Availability.
Shipping and Handling Charges Apply.
Offers and Prices Subject To Change Without Notice.